Gilbert Cope

Genealogy of the Dutton Family

Anatiposi

Gilbert Cope

Genealogy of the Dutton Family

Reprint of the original, first published in 1871.

1st Edition 2023 | ISBN: 978-3-38212-682-7

Anatiposi Verlag is an imprint of Outlook Verlagsgesellschaft mbH.

Verlag (Publisher): Outlook Verlag GmbH, Zeilweg 44, 60439 Frankfurt, Deutschland
Vertretungsberechtigt (Authorized to represent): E. Roepke, Zeilweg 44, 60439 Frankfurt, Deutschland
Druck (Print): Books on Demand GmbH, In de Tarpen 42, 22848 Norderstedt, Deutschland

GENEALOGY

OF THE

DUTTON FAMILY

OF PENNSYLVANIA,

PRECEDED BY A HISTORY OF THE FAMILY IN ENGLAND FROM THE
TIME OF WILLIAM THE CONQUEROR TO THE YEAR 1669;
WITH AN APPENDIX CONTAINING A SHORT ACCOUNT
OF THE DUTTONS OF CONN.

COMPILED BY

GILBERT COPE.

WEST CHESTER, PA.:
PRINTED FOR THE AUTHOR, BY F. S. HICKMAN, PRINTER.
1871.

(

PREFACE.

The publication of this work has been delayed longer than anticipated, but this has not been to its disadvantage. More care and labor
might have been expended in its preparation, but for the potent argu-
ment, *it will not pay.* The fault finding critic may ask himself how
much more *gratuitous* attention he would have bestowed upon the
work. To the practical genealogist no apology is necessary for its
incompleteness, while to the general reader it may be remarked, that
it is difficult to ascertain the whereabouts of the different branches
of a family, and when found one half will probably treat letters of
inquiry with silent indifference. Some who appear interested in the
subject have but a vague idea of the scope of Genealogy, or the kind
of information wanted; and a few manifest a silly weakness in re-
gard to dates, as though the public estimate of character were based
on age. There are doubtless errors in this work, and the writer
earnestly desires that those who can, will forward any additions or
corrections within their knowledge, and these will be entered in a
copy of the book to be deposited in the library of the Historical Society of Pennsylvania, in Philadelphia, Pa., for the benefit of future
investigators. This Society is now making a specialty of collecting
genealogical or family records, and as a member thereof, the writer
requests copies of such records to be forwarded, either to himself, or
to the Society in Philadelphia.

The coat of arms given on page 12, is printed from a cut made by
the writer with a carpenter's chisel, and is but too correct a copy of
the rough original.

G. C.

Highland Home, June 24, 1871.

GENERAL INDEX.

INDEX TO CHRISTIAN NAMES

Of the Duttons of Penn., including all who have borne the name —those who have received the name by marriage being in *italics*, while the numbers given refer to individuals, and not to the pages.

Aaron L., 388.
Abigail, 119.
Adelaide V., 1007.
Albert, 829, 1142.
Alcinda, 237.
Alexander, 635, 1020.
Alfred B., 791.
Alice, 163, 503.
Alice, 271.
Almira, 490.
Alonzo, 983.
Alvin J., 552.
Amor, 168.
Amy, 16, 837.
Amy, 147,
Angerett, 288.
Ann, 30, 134, 366,
Ann, 6, 116, 135, 161, 313, 387.
Anna, 984.
Anna, 119, 364, 770.
Anna L., 838.
Anna M., 641.
Anna S., 1065.
Anne, 141.
Anne, 10, 335, 388.
Annie G., 755.
Arabella, 827.
Arthur P., 1146.
Asa, 124.
Augustus P., 636.
Benjamin, 86, 86, 140.
Benjamin B., 881.
Benjamin F., 506.
Benjamin V., 307.
B. Franklin, 1139.
Bessie, 823.
Beulah, 383, 779.
Blanch, 555.
Caleb, 142.
Caroline, 825, 1187.
Caroline, 769, 776.
Catharine, 125, 311.
Catharine M., 209, 637.

Catharine T., 1008.
Charles, 391.
Charles L., 848.
Charles R., 677.
Charles S., 678, 1074.
Clara, 833, 1132.
Clarence B., 830.
Cora M., 533.
Cynthia, 240.
David, 23, 49, 68, 112, 223, 232, 517.
David H., 386.
David D., 273.
Deborah, 222.
Edith H., 1006.
Edmund 332, 697.
Edward, 4, 782.
Edwin, 492.
Effinety A.. 285.
Elisha, 113, 215.
Eliza, 219, 837.
Eliza, 589,
Eliza June, 237.
Elizabeth, 2, 32, 56, 62, 65, 78, 87, 127, 133, 360, 758.
Elizabeth, 3, 12, 18, 37, 137, 331, 492, 766.
Elizabeth B., 293.
Elizabeth J., 372.
Elizabeth L., 535.
Elizabeth M., 683.
Elizabeth R., 549.
Elizabeth R., 385.
Elizabeth W., 847.
Ella, 497.
Elmer E., 531.
Elmira, 137.
Emeline, 494.
Emily, 390, 824.
Emily L., 389.
Emma, 500, 613, 772, 785.
Emma F., 680.·

Enoch G., 594.
Esrey P., 1136.
Esther P., 362.
Ethan G., 283.
Eugene, 764.
Ezra, 241.
Fanny, 568
Flora, 979.
Florence E., 596.
Francis, 48, 114, 125.
Frank, 497.
Franklin, 249, 263.
George, 136, 145, 292, 564, 639, 681, 1143.
George F., 996.
George G., 757.
George S., 699.
Guliema, 381.
Gwin, 4.
Hannah, 8, 55, 59, 70, 122, 148, 216, 235, 242, 268, 308 369, 327, 679.
Hannah, 11, 14, 48, 49, 69, 140, 310, 335.
Hannah B., 826.
Hannah E., 675, 845.
Hannah E., 331.
Hannah H., 380.
Hannah H., 391.
Hannah J., 251.
Harriet, 270, 631.
Harriet, 288, 756.
Harry, 557.
Helen, 675.
Henry, 38, 973.
Henry B., 830.
Henry H., 759.
Henry L., 794.
Henrietta, 761.
Hicklen G., 287.
Horace H., 821.
Howard, 832, 1145.
Howard J., 846.
Huldah, 232.

INDEX TO SURNAMES

Of families intermarried with the Duttons of Penn., which will
be found under the numbers of the individuals to whom married.

viii INDEX TO SURNAMES.

EARLY HISTORY

OF

THE DUTTON FAMILY.

In several works, the early history of this family is treated of to a greater or less extent, but unfortunately they do not agree in all points, while some of them are so evidently deficient as to be unworthy of notice. The fullest account met with, is contained in a volume, entitled "Leycester's Historical Antiquities," published in 1673, by Peter Leycester, baronet,* in which the author treats of the history of Cheshire, England, and more particularly, of all the principal families and estates in that division of the county called Bucklow Hundred. As both he and his wife were descended from the Duttons, and the genealogy appears to have been carefully compiled from authentic histories, deeds, wills and ancient records of the family, it is probably nearly correct. It will be given as the text of the following pages.

---

* A copy of this work may be seen in the Mercantile Library, of Philadelphia, Pa. I am indebted to William John Potts, of Camden, N. J., for a transcript of the Dutton pedigree.

DUTTON.

I find this town of Dutton,* thrice named in Doomsday-book, as held then in the Conqueror's time by three persons. One Part Odard held immediately of the Earl of Chester, as it were *in Capite:* Another Part was held by William Fitz-Nigell, Baron of Halton, of the Earl, in like manner: Another Part did Osberue Son of Tezzon, Ancestor to the Boydells of Dodleston, hold also of the Earl of Chester.

Odard's Part seems to be the greatest Part, which one Ravene held before at the coming in of the Normans. The Baron of Halton's Part, and Osbern's Part, one Edward held before, and did then likewise hold Osbern's Part under the said Osbern. But both Osbern's Part, and the Baron of Halton's Part, at last came to the Posterity of Odard: For Osbern's Part was sold by his heir, Sir William Boydell, who released all his Seignory unto Thomas, son of Hugh Dutton of Dutton, in all the lands which the said Thomas held of him in Dutton, 15 Edw. 8, 1341.

As to the Baron of Halton's Part, John, Constable of Cheshire, Baron of Halton, gave to Adam de Dutton, (younger son of Hugh Dutton of Dutton, and Ancestor to Warburton of Arley,) those four Oxgangs of Land in Dutton, which Walter Heron held: This was about the end of the Reign of Henry the Second: And Sir Geffrey de Warburton releaseth all his Right unto Thomas, son of Hugh de Dutton aforesaid, in all those Lands in Dutton, which the said Thomas held by Lease, from the said Sir Geffrey: Dated at Dutton, 28 Edw. 3, 1354. So that Thomas de Dutton was now invested in the whole Town of Dutton entirely.

This Township, in the ancient record of Doomsday-book, is written *Duntune:* Dun, in the old Saxon language, signifies A Hill, for which we now use the word Down: So that Duntune signifies as much as A Town upon a Hill or Down; now contracted to Dutton.

From this Town did the ancient Family of the Duttons assume their Sir-name: For Odard being seated here in the Conqueror's time, his Posterity were sir-named de Dutton, from the place of their residence; where they have continued ever since to this present 1666, about 600 years: A family of great worth and antiquity, and

---

* The Township of Dutton lies about five miles East of Frodsham, on the river Wever, in Cheshire.

as it were almost a constant succession of Knights; but now, alas!
ready to change its name, being devolved by a daughter and heir
unto the Lord Gerard of Gerards-Bromley in Staffordshire.

The Mannor-house of Dutton is well seated, and hath great store of
mendowing by the River side belonging to the Demain, which is ac-
counted the largest and best Demain within our County, compre-
hending 1400 Statute Acres by Survey. This House standeth upon a
pleasant Prospect to the opposite Hills of the Forest; and hath in it
an ancient Chappel, built first by Sir Thomas Dutton towards the end
of Henry the Third's Reign; unto whom Roger de Lincoln then
Prior of Norton, and the Convent there, did grant *liberam Cantariam
in Capellis suis de Dutton & Weston infra Limites Parochiarum nos-'
trarum de Budworth & de Runcorne; id est,* Free liberty of Reading
Divine Service, or Singing the same; so as the Mother-Churches re-
ceive no detriment either in their greater or lesser Tythes. That of
Weston is long since vanished; but this Chappel at Dutton yet remains, and is now a Domestick Chappel within the Mannor-House of
Dutton, unto which Sir Piers Dutton, of Hatton, after he was adjudged next Heir Male to the Lands of Dutton by the Award of Henry
the Eighth, did annex his new Buildings at Dutton, Anno Domini
1539, as appears by the Inscription round about the Hall of Dutton
yet extant, adjoining those unto the Chappel, and so making it as one
continued Building; before which time the old House stood a little
distance from the Chappel aforesaid.

In the Demain of Dutton is also another Chappel of Ease, called
Poosey-Chappel, within the Parish of Runcorne; but is now ruinate
and in decay. It is seated between the River and the Park-Pool within the Demain of Dutton, but not in the Township of Dutton; for all
the town of Dutton is within Budworth Parish. It was called Pooseye
from its situation, [Ey] in our old English-Saxon Tongue signifies
a River or Brook; and because it stood close by the River and the Pool
also, it was called Poos-ey Chappel, as it were, The Chappel by
the River and the Pool. In our old Norman writing, and French
way, I find it in Old Deeds written Pul-sey; but in our common
Language anciently, as the Country People at this day, did call a
Pool a Poo; and thence it was denominated Poo's-ey-Chappel. It
was built in the Reign of Henry the Third; and the Prior and Convent of Norton, granted to Hugh, Son of Hugh de Dutton, that they
would find a Chaplain to officiate at Poos-ey forever; and a lamp
burning at the time of Divine Service, about 1236, 20 Hen. 3, which
Chappel was constantly frequented by the neighborhood, until Robert, Lord Kilmorey, and Dame Ellinour his wife, came to live at Dutton, even in our days; who beautified the Domestick Chappel at Dutton with handsome Pews, and kept a Chaplain in his house constantly, whereunto all the Neighborhood resorted every Sunday: Then
began Poos-ey Chappel to be neglected, and is now totally in decay,
some part of the Structure yet remaining, 1666.

Now followeth the Pedegree of the Duttons of Dutton, faithfully collected from the Evidences of that Family, and other good Records and Deeds:

I. **Odard**, or **Udard**,sometimes also written Hodard and Hudard, came into England with William the Conqueror, and seated himself at Dutton; a good part whereof Hugh Lupus, Earl of Chester, gave unto him as before you have heard out of Doomsday-book. The ancient Roll of the Barons of Halton saith that with Hugh, Earl of Chester, came one Nigell, a nobleman; and with Nigell came five brethren, to wit: Hudard, Edard, Wolmere, Horswyne,and Wolfaith, a Priest, to whom Nigell gave the Church of Runcorne; and unto Hudard, the same Nigell gave Weston and Great Aston, (now divided

Quarterly, Argent & Gules, in the second and third Quarters a Fret Or.

into two Townships, Aston Grange and Aston juxta Sutton,) *pro uno Feodo Militis;* and from this Hudard came all the Duttons. And in the Record of Doomsday, Odard held Aston under William Fitz-Nigell, Baron of Halton; and also Odard and Brictric held Weston under the said William, Anno Domini 1086. Whether those five Brethren aforenamed, were Brethren to Nigell, is a doubt; for then methinks he should have said *Quinque Fratres sui:* whereas he says onely, *cum isto Nigello Venerunt quinque Fratres,* and so names them.*

---

* The Warburtons claim consanguinity with the ancient blood-royal of England, being descended from Rollo, the first Duke of Normandy, through William, Earl of Eu, who married a niece of William the Conqueror.

Richard, Duke of Normandy, (grand-son of Rollo) sur-named SANS-PEUR, had issue (besides his son Richard who succeeded him, his daughter Emma, Queen of England, and other children) two younger sons, Godfrey and William. To Godfrey, his father gave the earldoms of Eu and Brion. On his decease the latter earldom became the héritage of his posterity, branching out into the now extinct houses of the Earls of Clare and Pembroke, while William, the younger brother, succeeded him in the earldom of Eu. He had (besides others) his successor, Robert, father of William, who married a sister of Hugh Lupus, Earl of Avranches, (afterwards Earl of Chester) named Jeanne, and niece of William the Conqueror.

There was issue of this marriage (besides William's successor in the earldom of Eu and another child) six sons, named Nigel, Geffry, Odard or Huddard, Edard, Horswin and Wlofaith.

These six brothers accompanied their uncle, Hugh Lupus, into England, in the train of William the Conqueror, their great-uncle; and on the establishment of the Norman power had various estates and honors conferred upon them. Nigel was created Baron of Halton and constable of Cheshire; Geffry was Lord of Stopfort; Odard, Lord of Dutton; Edard, Lord of Haselwell; Horswin, Lord of Shrigley; and Wlofaith, Lord of Halton. Odard, the third son, was the ancestor

This Hudard's, or Odard's Sword, is at this day, 1665, in the Custody of the Lady Elinour Vicountess Kilmorey, sole Daughter and Heir of Thomas Dutton, late of Dutton, Esquire, deceased; which Sword hath for many ages past been preserved, and passed from Heir to Heir as an Heir-loom, by the name of Hudard's Sword; and so at this day it is by Tradition received and called.

II. **Hugh**, Son of Hodard, had those Lands which he held in Capite, or immediately of the Earl of Chester, confirmed unto him by Randle the Second, air-named de Gernoniis, Earl of Chester, about the latter end of Henry the First. These Lands, I conceive, were those which he held in Dutton.

III. **Hugh de Dutton**, Son of Hugh, Son of Hodard, had the Lands which his father Hugh held of the Baron of Halton, confirmed unto him by William, son of Nigell, Constable to Randle the Second, and by William his son, on that day when the said William the Father, and William the son, did visit Hugh, the son of Hodard on his Death-bed at Kekwick; at which time Hugh, the son of Hodard, gave unto William the Father his Coat of Mail and his Charging-Horse; and Hugh, the son of that Hugh, gave unto William the son, a Palfrey and a Sparrow-hawk. This was about the end of the Reign of King Henry the First. The Lands here confirmed, I conceive to be Weston and Kekwick, and perhaps some others.

This Hugh de Dutton had issue, Hugh Dutton, son and Heir; Adam de Dutton,† another son, from whom the Warburtons of Arley

of the Duttons, now extinct in the male line; the Barons of Chedill, also extinct, and the Warburtons.—BURKE'S LANDED GENTRY, p. 1508.

Odard, son of Yvron, viscount of Constantine, (whose name is written in most records of later date, Hodard or Hudard) was the immediate ancestor of the ancient and numerous family of Dutton of Dutton.—LYSONS' MAGNA BRITANNIA, VOL. II.

Leycester mentions the fact that William, Earl of Eu, married a sister to Hugh Lupus, and gives the paternal ancestry of the latter, but says nothing of their relationship to either William the Conqueror, or the six brothers above named. He says elsewhere that Sir George Warburton denied him the perusal of the Warburton papers, which may account for the lack of information on this point.

†Adam de Dutton, by his marriage with Agnes Fitzalured, (dau. and heir of Roger Fitzalured,) became proprietor of the manor of Warburton, as mesne Lord, in the time of Henry II. One half he gave to the canons of Warburton, for the soul of his son John, (who was buried there,) among other reasons. The other half he gave to the Knights Hospitallers, who re-granted the same in 1187. Adam had issue: I. Geoffry, his eldest son and successor; II. John, buried at Warburton; III. Agatha. The elder son, Sir Geoffry Dutton, resided principally at Sutton. He obtained Aston, near Budworth, in which Arley lies. The name of the lady he married does not appear, but Lysons suggests that Alice, the dau. of John Lacy, constable of Chester, Baron of Halton, may have been his wife; which said Alice, many heralds have given as a wife to Adam, his father. This conjecture receives a strong confirmation from a family Deed, by which John Lacy gives the manor of Clifton to Geoffry Dutton, with the expression, SCILICET DE UXORE DESPONSATA. Adam de Dutton, as well as his cousin, the Baron of Halton, had emulated each other in donations to religious establishments, and in this generation the representatives of both families, John de Lacy and Geof.

are descended; Geffrey de Dutton,‡ another son, from whom the
Duttons of Chedill in this county were propagated, who assumed the
sir-name of Chedill, and continued to the Reign of Edward the Third,
till Sir Roger de Chedill, (the last of that family,) dying 1 Edw. 3,
1327, left his Inheritance to be shared by his two daughters and heirs,
Clemence and Agnes; and out of that family de Chedill, branched
Hamon Dutton under Edward the First, younger son to Sir Geffrey
Dutton of Chedill, to whom his father gave Ashley, (13, Ed. 1, 1285,)
which he purchased for him. The posterity of this Hamon assumed
the sir-name of Ashley from the place of their residence, as was the
manner of those ages; which Family of the Ashley's of Ashley continued to the end of Henry the Eighth; about which time Thomasin,
daughter and heir of George Ashley of Ashley, Esquire, brought that
Inheritance to Richard Brereton of Lea-Hall, not far from Middle-
wich, by marriage, who was a younger son of Sir William Brereton
of Brereton in this county; in which name of Brereton of Ashley it

ry Dutton, followed up the zeal of their fathers and raised the banner of the
Cross. Sir Geoffry before his departure, consigned by deed, a portion of his estates to his friend Herbert de Orseby. The crest of Warburton is born to com-
memorate an exploit performed by this Geoffry. In the Harleian MSS. 139, p. 68,
is a transcript from an ancient family record, taken by Lawrence Bostoke, in 1572,
in which this exploit is thus alluded to: THIS GALFRID LIVED 1214; HE WAS SER-
VYNGE HIS PRYNCK AND VANQUYSHED A SARRAZIN IN COMBATE, THEN BROYN-
KYNGE TO SEALE WITH THE SARRAZIN'S HEAD,

Sir Geoffry had a son and heir, Sir Geoffry Dutton, Knt., (Generally styled,
D'NUS GALFRIDUS FILIUS GALFRIDI DE DUTTON,) to whom the premonstratensian
canons re-granted the other half of Warburton, in 1271. He also obtained the
mediety of Lymme from the Boydells, by grant. To one of his Deeds there is
this seal, viz: a man's arm in a manche or loose sleeve, with a fleur-de-lis in his
hand; written about, SIGILLUM GALFRIDI DE DUTTON, in a roundlet, not in an
escocheon. His second wife was Isabella. Sir Geoffry had issue I. Peter, his
heir; II. Thomas, to whom he granted Thelwall, in 1238-59; and, III. Margaret,
wife first of Robert de Denbigh, and secondly, of Nicholas de Leycester.—BURKE'S
LANDED GENTRY, p. 1508.

This Geoffrey Dutton, son of Adam, lived at this Town of Budworth: for in
the Deed of the purchase of Claterwigge, a Hamlet in Little Legh, by Sir Thomas
Dutton, of Dutton, one of the witnesses subscribed was,—SIR GEFFREY, OF BUD-
WORTH, SON OF ADAM DE DUTTON. And I have seen him styled Geffrey de Budworth, in many other Deeds; and so was Geffrey, his son, often so styled, who
lived there also. But Peter Dutton, son of the later Geffrey, removing his habi-
tation unto Warburton, towards the end of Edward the First, his son Peter was
styled de Warburton, according to the manner of those Ages, under Edward the
Second; from which time downwards, his posterity hath wholly retained the
Sir-name of Warburton, even to this day. But his succeeding Heirs, afterwards,
disliking the seat at Warburton, either for the inundation of the water, or for
some other cause, removed their seat to Arley, in Aston, near to this Budworth,
about the beginning of Henry the Seventh's Reign; which house of Arley was
built by Peter Warburton, Esquire, who died Anno Domini 1495; where they
have ever since continued, to this day, as their Chief Mansion House.—LEYCES-
TER's HIST. ANTIQ., p. 226.

‡ Burke says that Geffrey Dutton, brother of Adam, married a daughter of Hamon Massy. Leycester says that Hamon Massy the Third, had issue by Agatha,
his wife, (amongst others) a daughter Agnes, with whom her Father gave half of
Bollinton in Free-Marriage to Geffrey Dutton, of Chedill, son of Geffrey Dutton.

continued but four descents, and was divided among the three sisters
of Thomas Brereton, (the last Brereton of Ashley,) and their heirs,
Anno Domini 1601. See more hereof above in Ashley.

IV. **Hugh Dutton** of Dutton, son of Hugh, married ————
daughter of Hamon Massy, Baron of Dunham-Massy, *regnante Hen-
rico Secundo;* with whom her father gave in free marriage, Lands
in Suttersby, in Lindsey in Lincolnshire; and had issue,† Hugh
Dutton, eldest son, Thomas Dutton, John Dutton, Adam Dutton.
He purchased Little Moldesworth for fifty Marks, from Robert, son
of Mathew de Moldesworth, about 1250. Also Alice, wife of William
Boydell of Dodleston.

†V. I do conceive here was another Hugh Dutton, son and heir of this Hugh;
who married Muriel, daughter of Thomas le Dispenser, and he had issue, Hugh,
Thomas, John and Adam, as there followeth. And if so, some of these Acts
may belong to that Hugh, which are ascribed to this Hugh.

This Hugh Dutton bought Preston nigh Dutton, of Henry de
Nuers and Julian his wife, *reddendo octo Solidos annuatim, ad Festum Sancti Martini;* which Randle Blundevill, Earl of Chester, confirmed, about the Reign of King John. He purchased also the Town
of Little Legh, in Fee-Farm, from Simon, son of Osberne, rendring
the yearly rent of two Marks of silver at the feast of St. Martin ;
which rent is yet paid by his heirs to the Earl of Derby, as of his
Mannor of Harden, Anno Domini 1666. And Roger Lacy, Constable of Cheshire, and Baron of Halton, acquitted this Hugh Dutton
de Judice de Leyha, that is, of finding a Judger to serve at Halton
for Little Legh yearly, about the Reign of Richard the First, or
beginning of King John's Reign.

He purchased also, the Moiety of Barnton, from William, son of
Henry, son of Serlo, which Robert de Mesnilwarin held.

He had also the Magistracy, or rule and authority, over all the
Letchers and Whores of all Cheshire, granted unto him and his heirs,
by John, Constable of Cheshire, and Baron of Halton, as freely as
the said John held the same of the Earl of Chester; saving the
Right of the said John to him and his heirs: Which are the very
words of the Deed, onely rendred by me in English. So that he holds
it, as it were, under the Baron of Halton, who reserves his own
Right by a Special Reservation.

This privilege over such loose persons, was granted first unto Roger
Lacy, Constable of Cheshire, under Richard the First, by Randle,
sir-named Blundevill, Earl of Chester, in memory of his good service
done to the Earl in raising the Siege of the Welsh-men, who had
beset the Earl in his Castle of Rothelent in Flintshire; for the Constable having got a promiscuous rabble of such like persons together,
and marching towards the said Castle, the Welsh, (supposing a great
army to be coming,) raised their Siege and fled: So saith the ancient
Roll of the Barons of Halton. This Roll saith, that rabble consisted
of Players, Fidlers and Shoe-makers. The Deed here toucheth
Letchers and Whores. The privilege and custom used at this day

by the Heirs of Dutton, is over the Minstrelsie and common Fidlers ;
none being suffered to play in this County, without the Licence of
the Lord of Dutton, who keeps a Court at Chester yearly, on Mid-
somer-day, for the same, where all the licenced Minstrels of Cheshire
do appear, and renew their licences ; So that the custom seems to have
been altered to the Fidlers, as necessary attendants on revellers in
Bawdy-houses and Taverns. And it is to be observed, that those
Minstrels which are licenced by the heirs of Dutton of Dutton, within
the County Palatine of Chester, or the County of the City of Chester,
according to their ancient custom, are exempted out of the Statute of
Rogues, 39 Eliz., cap. 4.

VI. **Hugh Dutton**, of Dutton, Son and Heir of Hugh, lived
1234, 18 Hen. 3. He purchased from Richard de Aston, son of Gilbert de Aston, Six Bovates of Land in Aston juxta Dutton, in the
beginning of the Reign of Henry the Third ; which land belongs to
Dutton-Demain at this day, 1666. He also built Poosey Chappel
about 20 Hen. 3, 1236, of which I have spoken before ; which undoubt-
edly stood upon part of that land bought from Aston, for that Chappel is in Runcorne Parish.

This Hugh gave to John, his brother, the third part of all the Town
of Bolliiton in Maxfield Hundred, which Thomas le Dispenser gave
in Free-marriage *Hugoni Putri meo cum Muriela Matre mea* ; which
Deed was made about the Year of Christ, 1234.

This Hugh de Dutton died without issue, and Thomas, his brother,
succeeded Heir.

VII. **Sir Thomas Dutton**, of Dutton, Brother and Heir to
Hugh, lived Anno Domini 1249, 33, Hen. 3, and 1268, 53, Hen. 3. He
purchased Clatterwigge, a Hamlet in Little Legh juxta Barterton,
from Hugh de Clatterwigge, about 1244, 29, Hen. 3. He built the
Chappel at the Manor-house of Dutton, towards the end of Henry the
Third's Reign.

He married Philippa, Daughter and Heir of Vivian de Sandon, or
Standon, by whom he had lands in Staffordshire ; and had issue,
Hugh Dutton, Son and Heir ; Thomas, another son, to whom his
father gave Great Rownall and Little Rownall, in Staffordshire, by
the consent of Philippa, his wife. But I conceive this younger son
Thomas died without issue, because I find Philippa in her Widow-
hood granting these two Mannors of Rownall to Sir Robert Dutton,
her other son, and to Agnes, his wife, daughter of William de Mere,
in Staffordshire : Margaret, a daughter, married William Venables,
son and heir of Roger Venables, of Kinderton, 38 Hen. 3, 1253. And
Katharine married John, son of Vrian de Sancto Petro. So I find it
in an old Pedegree.

This Sir Thomas was Sheriff of Cheshire 1268, 53 Hen. 3. He died
in the beginning of the Reign of Edward the First.

Philippa was living a widow 1290 and 1294.

VIII. **Sir Hugh Dutton,** of Dutton Knight, Son and. Heir of Sir Thomas, bound himself to the Abbot of Vale-Royal, to make a Foot-Bridge at Acton, and to find a Boat and Ferry-man at Acton Ford, about 1286. The same is now made a County Bridge.

He also was bound to William Gerard his Squire *in una Roba Armigerorum annuatim ad totam vitam suam ad Festum Natalis Domini*, 13 Edw. I. 1285.

He purchased Barterton, and married Joan, daughter of Sir Vrian de Sancto Petro, vulgo Sampier; I have no authority for this but an old Pedegree; and had Issue Hugh Dutton, son and heir; and William Dutton, who married Maud, daughter and co-heir to Sir Richard Stockport, of Stockport, 1305; which William, with others, was Indicted 35 Edw. I, for taking away the said Maud by force from Dunham-Massy, being then in the custody of Hamon Massy; whom they took out of her chamber into the court, stripping her of all her clothes, save her smock, saith the Record: Robert Dutton, Parson of Eccleston, 1320. Also Margaret, a daughter. This Sir Hugh died 22 Edw. I, 1294. Joan his Lady survived; she was living 1298.

IX. **Sir Hugh Dutton,** of Dutton Knight, son and heir of Sir Hugh, born the eighth day of December, 5 Edw. I, 1276, at Dutton; and Baptized at Great Budworth the day following. He sued the Prior of Norton, before Adam Burum and Nicolas Gruchundelee, Commissaries of the Bishop of Lichfield and Coventry, at the Visitation of the Arch-Deanery of Chester, Anno Domini 1315, for not finding a Chaplain and Lamp at Poosey Chappel, according to the original Grant, which he there produced; And John Olton, then Prior, confessed the same, and was ordered to find them. This Priory was of the Order of St. Augustine.

He married Joan, daughter of Sir Robert Holland, of Holland in Lancashire, and had Issue Thomas Dutton, son and heir; William, Parson of Thornton, 22 Edw. 3; Geffrey Dutton, another son; Robert Dutton, another son. This Sir Hugh was made Steward of Halton, 24 Decembris, 20 Edw. 2, and died I Edw. 3, 1326, at the age of fifty years.*

Joan, his widow, afterwards married Edmund Talbot, of Bashall; and after, to Sir John Ratcliff, of Urdeshall, in Lancashire, living 11 Edw. 3, & 20 Edw. 3. .

X. **Sir Thomas Dutton,** of Dutton, Knight, Son and Heir of Sir Hugh and Joan, was fifteen years old on Whitsunday, 1329. 3 Edw. 3. He purchased those lands in Dutton, which formerly belonged to Halton-Fee; and also those lands in Dutton, which formerly

---

* Hancock, a younger son of Sir Hugh Dutton, who died in 1326, settled in Denbighshire. Edward Dutton, Alderman of Chester in 1613, proved his descent from the said Hancock.

Richard, his son, was also alderman of Chester, and had a son of his own name, but we have not been able to trace their posterity to the present time.—LYSONS' MAGNA BRITANNIA, VOL. II.

belonged to Boydell of Dodleston; and so made the Township of
Dutton entirely his own; as I have more particularly shewed before.

This Thomas, was made Seneschal, Governor, and Receiver of the
Castle and Honour of Halton, in Cheshire, by William Clinton, Earl
of Huntington; and also of all his Lands and Mannors in Cheshire
and Lancashire, *quamdiu bene se gesserit* which the Earl farmed
unto him for 440 marks yearly; Dated at Maxstock, 19 Edw. 3.

It seems he was indicted, for that he and others came with armed
power, (when King Edward the Third, was out of England,) within
the verge of the lodging of Lionell the King's son, Protector of England, and assaulted the Mannor of Geaumes, nigh Reading in Wiltshire, and there slew Michael Poynings, the uncle, and Thomas le
Clerke of Shipton, and others, and committed a rape on Margery the
wife of one Nicolas de la Beche, for which the King pardoned him;
and he found Sir Bernard Brocas, Sir Hugh Berewyk, Philip Dur-
danyt, and John Haydoke, his sureties in the Chancery for his good
abearing, 26 Edw. 3, 1352.

He was by several Commissions, employed for the apprehending
of certain Malefactors, Robbers and Disturbers of the Peace in this
County. One is directed unto him by the name of Thomas Dutton,
Equitator in Foresta de Mara, and to Richard Done, Forester of the
same Forest, 14 Edw. 3. Anno Domini 1379, 3 Rich. 2. William
Eltonhed, Prior of the Hermit-Fryars of the Order of St. Augustine
at Warrington in Lancashire, and the Convent there, grant to Sir
Thomas Dutton, Knight, a perpetual Chantry; to wit, That a sufficient Fryar of the Convent of Warrington, shall be especially
elected to pray for the salvation of Sir Thomas, his children, and of
Philippa his wife, and her parents; and for the soul of Dame Ellen,
late wife of the said Sir Thomas, their children and parents when
they shall die, at the Great Altar of their Church yearly for ever;
and that their names be written down in their Martyrology: Whereunto the Prior and Convent were bound under a penalty of 3s. 4d.,
to be levied by the Provincial Prior upon omission of such Form
of Service; and if for a week or a fortnight it were omitted, then
must they double the time omitted in manner aforesaid: if neglected for six Months, then upon pain of suspension: if for a year, then
upon excommunication, until the time omitted be made up: Whereunto are witnesses, Thomas, Abbot of St. Werburge of Chester,
Stephen, Abbot of Vale-Royal, Richard, Prior of Norton, and Roger,
Prior of Berkenhed.

This was confirmed by Henry de Towesdale, Provincial Prior of
the Hermit-Fryars of the Order of St. Augustine in England, with
a special Injunction, That the said persons be yearly twice commemo-
rated before the whole Convent; once at the first entrance of the
Prior of Warrington into the Convocation-house yearly; the other
time, on the election-day of a Fellow-Prior for a Provincial Convoca-
tion. Dated at Warrington on Sunday next after the Feast of St.
Martin, *Anno Supradicto.*

This Sir Thomas sealed usually with his Coat of Arms and Crest, to wit, Quarterly, a Fret in the second and third; over which, upon the Dexter-Angle of the Escocheon, a Helmet, and thereon a Plume of Feathers.

Anno Domini 1844, Robert Monning of Tatenhale, grants to Thomas de Dutton and his heirs, all the Magistracy of the Minstrels, *cum omnibus pertinentiis, prout in Charta Originali plenius continetur*. I conceive he was but a Feoffee.

This Thomas was Sheriff of Cheshire, 30 & 33 Edw. 3, and was a Knight, 35 Edw. 3. He married two Wifes: The first was Ellen, one of the Daughters and Heirs of Sir Peter Thornton of Thornton, the eldest Daughter, by whom he had Issue Sir Peter Dutton, who died without Issue 35 Edw. 3. Thomas Dutton, another Son, died also without Issue: Lawrence Dutton succeeded Heir to his Father: Edmund Dutton, another Son: Henry Dutton, fifth Son: and William Dutton, another Son.

His second wife was Philippa the widow of Sir Peter Thornton; she was (as I conceive) a later wife to Sir Peter Thornton, not mother of the Co-heirs.

This Sir Thomas Dutton died 4. Rich. 2. 1381. aged Sixty-six years: Philippa his widow died 13 Rich. 2. 1389.

Edmund Dutton, younger Son of Sir Thomas, married Joan Daughter and Heir of Henry Minshull de Church-Minshull, by whom he had the Mannors of Church-Minshull and Aston-Mondrum; and had Issue Sir Peter Dutton, who became Heir to his Uncle Sir Lawrence Dutton of Dutton: Hugh Dutton, second Son of whom the Duttons of Hatton nigh Warton in Cheshire, whose Posterity afterwards, in process of time, became Heirs of Dutton-Lands under Henry the Eighth: Lawrence Dutton another Son; and Thomas Dutton, another Son: Agnes de Dutton, a Daughter, married William Leycester of Nether-Tabley, 1398. 22 Rich. 2; and Ellen, another Daughter.

This Edmund died before his Brother Sir Lawrence; and Joan his widow afterwards married William de Hooton, and had Issue by him. Joan died 11 Rich. 2. 1387, at which time Peter Dutton, her Son and Heir was twenty Years old.

XI. **Sir Lawrence Dutton** of Dutton Knight, son and Heir to Sir Thomas, had two wifes, Alice and Margaret; but who was father to either of them, I find not. He had no Issue by either, leaving his Inheritance to descend to Peter Dutton, eldest son of Edmund Dutton his younger Brother.

Sir Lawrence was a Knight 44 Edw. 3, and Sheriff of Cheshire 44, 45, 46 Edw. 3, and also 1. Rich. 2.

He had four parts of the seven of Thornton's Estate. One part he had as Son and Heir to Ellen, eldest Daughter and co-heir of Sir Peter de Thornton: He purchased the part of Elizabeth, late wife of Roger Venables, of Golborne, (Daughter and Heir of Margaret, wife of William de Golborne, which Margaret was another of the Daughters and Heirs of Sir Peter de Thornton,) 12 Rich. 2. Another part he purchased from Matthew de Weverham, Son and Heir of Hugh de Weverham, and Emme his wife, another of the Daughters and Heirs of Sir Peter de Thornton, 14 Rich. 2 1391. The part of Katharine, who was out-lawed for Felony, Thomas Dutton, his father, had formerly bought of the Prince. Mary, another Daughter and co-heir, had the Mannor of Helsby; she died without Issue. Maud, another Daughter and co-heir, married Henry Beeston, of Beeston. Elizabeth, another Daughter and co-heir, married Hamon Fitton, of Bollin, and had Issue Joan, Daughter and Heir, mother of William Venables, of Bollin.

Sir Lawrence had Licence from the Earl of Chester, to carry away the Chappel of Kingsley, formerly belonging to Sir Peter de Thornton, being within the boundary of the Forest; 45 Edw. 3.

He sealed constantly with his Escocheon of arms, *Quarterly, a Fret in the second and third Quarters;* inscribed about the seal,— SIGIL. LAURENTII DE DUTTON MILITIS. Which very seal was extant 1665, in possession of the Lady Kilmorey.

He made his will at Dutton, on Sunday, being the day after the conversion of St. Paul, or 26 *Januarii,* Anno Domini 1392. 16, Rich. 2, wherein he bequeaths his body to be buried at Norton, and gives his black horse before his body to the Convent of Norton for a Heriot; also sixteen torches, and five tapers, about his body on the burial-day, with sixteen poor men in Gowns to carry the lights; also ten Marks to the poor, and thirty pound to sufficient Chaplains to celebrate for his soul the next year, two in the Parish Church of Budworth, and four others in the Chappel of Dutton:—Also to Agnes and Ellen, daughters of Edmund Dutton, forty pounds for their marriages;—and makes Margaret his wife, and his Cosin Hugh Dutton, his Executors, and the Abbot of Chester Overseer of his Will.

This will was proved the tenth day of February following before William Neuhagh then Archdeacon of Chester.

So that Sir Lawrence died 1392. 16 Rich. 2, aged fifty-three years. Margaret his widow married afterwards Sir William Brereton of Brereton, 21 Rich. 2.

XII. **Sir Peter Dutton** of Dutton Knight, Son and Heir of Edmund Dutton, which Edmund was younger brother and next Heir to Sir Lawrence Dutton of Dutton. This Sir Peter married Elizabeth, daughter of Sir William Butler of Beusy, Lord of Warrington; and had issue, Sir Thomas de Dutton, who married Alice, daughter of Sir John Stanley, but died without issue about 9 Hen. 6, in the life-time of his father: Alice, his widow, after married John Wolton, 11 Hen. 6, *ut per inquisitionem post mortem Johannis de Dutton,* 24 Hen. 6. John Dutton, second son, who succeeded Heir to his father; Richard Dutton, another son, living 1440, & 1451, which Richard had issue, Lawrence Dutton, senior, 10 Hen. 7, who died without issue; Parnell, daughter of Sir Peter, married Hugh Venables, Baron of Kinderton; after to Richard Booth, 29 Hen. 6, 1451. Elizabeth, another daughter, married John Done, Son and Heir of John Done of Utkinton the elder, 12, Hen. 4, 1410. Ellen, another daughter, married Griffith Hanmere, Son and Heir of John Hanmere, Esquire, 3 Hen. 6, 1424. And Sibill, another daughter, married Geffrey Starky, Son of Randle Starky of Stretton in Cheshire.

Sir Peter Dutton was a Knight, 7, Hen. 4, and also 5, Hen. 4. The King granted him a pardon for taking part with Henry Percy the Son, sir-named Hotspur; dated at Cirencester, 3 *Novembris*, 5 Hen. 4, 1403. He was made Lieutenant or Deputy in the office of the Seneschalcy of the County of Chester, by Elizabeth, Countess of Salisbury, while they both should live, and to be of Council with her; for which service she gave him two marks Annual Rent, which he ought to pay her for his Lands of Little Legh, held of her Castle of Harden, during the term aforesaid; 1403, 10 Hen. 4.

Great Contention fell between this Sir Peter Dutton, and Sir William Athurton of Athurton in Lancashire; insomuch that they made Inroads and Invasions one upon the other; And the said Sir Piers Dutton, and his Adherents; to wit, Sir Rafe Bostock of Bostock, Richard Warburton of Budworth, Thomas Warburton of Halton, John Done of Utkinton Junior, John Manley of Manley, Hugh Dutton of Hatton the elder, William Leycester of Nether-Tabley, Sir Peter Legh of Clifton, (ancestor to Legh of Lyme), and John Carington of Carington, were all sued by Sir William Athurton, for taking away forty of his Oxen and forty Cows, out of his Closes at Athurton, and for beating of his Servants. But this Variance was composed between them by the Award of John, Duke of Bedford, Earl of Richmond and Kendall, Constable of England, and Regent of the Kingdom in the absence of Henry the Fifth; Dated 9 Aprilis, 7 Hen. 5. 1419. Restitution being awarded on both sides: The Horses and Saddles taken by Sir William Athurton, to be restored to Sir Piers Dutton; and the Cattel taken by Sir Piers, to be restored to the said Sir William. Sir Peter de Dutton was made *Parcarius de Northwood*, or Governor of Northwood Park in Over Whitley, during his Life, with all the Fees thereof, 1 Hen. 6. 1423: Out of which he had Orders from William Harrington, Chief Steward of Halton under Henry, Archbishop of Canterbury, and other Feoffees of King Henry the Fifth, to deliver one Oak for the Repair of Witton Bridge, then in decay; and another for the Repair of Farnworth Chappel; Dated 9 Hen. 6.

Sir Peter died 12 Hen. 6. 1433. aged Sixty-six years.

XIII. **John Dutton** of Dutton Esquire, Son and Heir of Sir Peter, married Margaret Daughter of Sir John Savage of Clifton, 6. Hen. 5. 1418, and had Issue Thomas Dutton, Son and Heir; Roger Dutton, another Son, afterwards Lord of Dutton; John Dutton, slain with his Brother Sir Thomas Dutton at Blore-Heath, 1459. *Stow.*

Robert Dutton, another Son, died without Issue; Margaret married Hugh, Son and Heir of Raufe Egerton, 21 Hen. 6. 1443. Maud married Sir William Booth of Dunham-Massy, 21 Hen. 6. 1443. Agnes married Richard Wynnington, of Wynnington nigh Northwich, (Son and Heir of Robert Wynnington, Son and Heir of Sir Richard Wynnington) 25 Hen. 6. 1446. Ellen married Edward Son and Heir of Richard Longford of Lancashire Esq: 28 Hen. 6. 1450. Elizabeth married John Merbury Son and Heir of James Merbury, of Merbury nigh Comberbach, Esquire, 1458.

This John Dutton of Dutton died 24 Hen. 6. 1445. aged forty two Years: Margaret his Wife survived and was living 1450.

XIV. Sir Thomas Dutton of Dutton Knight, Son and Heir of John and Margaret, married Anne Daughter of James Lord Audley, and had Issue Peter eldest Son, slain with his father at the Battel of Blore-Heath, as Tradition hath it: John Dutton, second Son, who succeeded Heir to his Father: Anne married Sir Thomas Molineaux of Sefton in Lancashire: Isabel married Sir Christopher Sothworth of Sotheworth in Lancashire: Elizabeth married Raufe Bostock of Bostock in Davenham Parish in Cheshire, Esq. by whom he had Issue Anne Daughter and Heir, married to Sir John Savage of Clifton in Cheshire, juxta Halton; which Elizabeth, after the death of Raufe Bostock, married Thomas Scriven of Frodsley in Shropshire, and she died Anno Domini 1510, 5 *die Februarii,* 8 Hen. 8, Margaret, another Daughter of Sir Thomas Dutton, married Thomas Aston of Aston juxta Sutton, Esquire, 7 Edw. 4. 1467. Afterwards she married Raufe Vernon of Haslington in Cheshire, Esquire; and Elinour, another Daughter, married Richard Cholmondley of Cholmondley in Broxton Hundred, Esq.

This Sir Thomas was slain at the Battel of Blore-Heath in Staffordshire, September 23, 38 Hen. 6, 1459, *Stow in his Annals;* and in the thirty-eighth year of his age. Anne, his widow, afterwards married Hugh Done of Olton in Cheshire; and she died 19 Hen. 7, 1503.

XV. John Dutton, of Dutton, Esquire, Son and Heir of Sir Thomas and Anne, was made Steward to the Prior of Norton for his Life, of all the Lands and Tenements belonging to that Priory, Robert Leftwich being then Abbot of Norton; and for which the said John Dutton had three Pound yearly for his Fee: Dated at Norton, in September, 38 Hen. 6. 1459.

He married Margaret, Daughter of Richard, and Sister to Sir Thomas Molineaux of Sefton in Lancashire; but died without Issue 13 Edw. 4, 1473, leaving Roger Dutton his Uncle to succeed in his Estate; Margaret his widow, married William Buckley of Eaton, junior, 15 Edw. 4.

XVI. Roger Dutton of Dutton Esquire (younger Brother to Sir Thomas, and Heir to his Nephew John Dutton) married Joan Daughter of Sir Richard Aston of Aston juxta Sutton, and had Issue Lawrence Dutton Son and Heir.

This Roger died 14 Hen. 7. 1499. Joan his widow afterwards married Sir Richard Strangewales.

XVII. **Lawrence Dutton** of Dutton Esquire, 14. Hen. 7, Son and Heir of Roger and Joan, married Joan Daughter of Robert Duckenfield of Duckenfield in Cheshire Esq.; but died without any Lawful Issue, Anno Domini 1526, aged fifty Years.

He had a Bastard-Son called John Dutton, to whom he gave the Messuage in Preston nigh Daresbery, called the New Mannor, for his Life; 1526. He had also two Bastard-Daughters, Isabel and Joan.

Upon the failing of Issue Male of this Line of Dutton, there fell great Controversie and suits of Law concerning this fair Inheritance of Dutton, between Sir Piers Dutton of Hatton in Broxton Hundred, as next Heir Male, on the one part; and the Daughters and Co-heirs of Sir Thomas Dutton of Dutton, and their Heirs, on the other part. At last it was composed and ended by the Award of King Henry the Eighth, Dated the sixteenth day of May, 26 Hen. 8. 1534, and Confirmed by Act of Parliament 27 Hen. 8, after seven Years Suit, and above.

The Lands allotted to the Co-heirs were the Lordships of Church-Minshull, Aston in Mondrum, and Kekwick; and all the lands which the Ancestors of Dutton held in Kingsley, Norley, Chorleton, Codynton, Pulton-Lancelyn, Bradley, Budworth in le Frith, Milneton, Barnton, Over-Whitley, Aston nigh Moldesworth, Hellesby, Frodsham, and in the City of Chester.

The Lands allotted to Sir Piers Dutton of Hatton, and now adjudged the next Heir Male, were, the Mannor of Dutton, the Advowry of the Minstrels in Cheshire, the Advowson of Poosey Chappel, the Lordships of Weston, Preston, Barterton, Little Legh, Nesse in Wirrall, Little Moldesworth, Acton, and Harpesford; and all the Lands which the Ancestors of Dutton held in Weston, Clifton, Preston, Barterton, Legh, Nesse, Little Moldesworth, Acton, Harpesford, Stony Dunham, Michbarrow, Stoke, Picton, Arrowe, North-wich, Halton, Theiwall, Oneston, Middle-wich, Stanthorne, and Over-Runcorne.

And now before we proceed to the next Lord of Dutton, we must look back to the first Ancestor of this Sir Piers Dutton of Hatton, which branched out of the family of Dutton of Dutton, and bring that line to this Sir Piers Dutton, and then proceed.

So then we find Hugh Dutton, the first Dutton of Hatton, in Right of Petronill* his wife, Daughter and Heir of Peter de Hatton juxta Warton, branching out under Richard the Second. This Hugh was a younger son of Edmund Dutton, which Edmund was a younger son of Sir Thomas Dutton of Dutton. [X.]

---

* Burke says this Hugh Dutton married Petronella, daughter of Ralph Vernon of Hatton in Cheshire, Esq.

1. This **Hugh** had Issue John Dutton, Son and Heir; Lawrence Dutton, another Son; Randle, Rector of Christleton nigh Chester; also Hugh, another Son. Elizabeth, a Daughter, married Richard Manley·of Manley. Hugh Dutton of Hatton was Sheriff of Cheshire 10 Hen. 5. 1422, and had a second wife, namely, Emme the widow of Hugh Venables of Golborne, and Daughter of Nicholas Warren of Pointon, 16 Hen. 6.—*John Booth of Twamlow's Book of his own Collections.*

2. **John Dutton** of Hatton, 19 Hen. 6, Son and Heir of Hugh and Parnell, was Mayor of Chester 30 Hen. 6, and married Margaret Daughter of William Atburton of Atburton in Lancashire, and had Issue Peter, Son and Heir; Richard* another Son; Geffrey, another Son: Cicely married John Byrd of Broxton: Ellen married one Gillbrand.

3. **Peter Dutton** of Hatton Esquire, Son and heir of John, married Elizabeth eldest daughter and one of the Heirs of Robert

* Richard Dutton, 2nd son of John Dutton of Hatton, had issue Ralph Dutton, who had two sons William and Richard. This Richard, who was an alderman and J. P. of the city of Chester, was removed by parliament for having been in arms against the commonwealth.

William Dutton, eldest son and heir of Richard Dutton, lived at Chester and had issue by his wife Agnes, daughter of John Conway of Flintshire, several children, whereof the 2nd son Thomas purchased the Manor of Sherborne in Gloucestershire. This Thomas was the father of William Dutton, Esq, who was sheriff of Gloucestershire. John Dutton, Esq., of Sherborne, son of William, was one of the Knights for that county to sit in parliament, 1640, but being frightened thence by the tumults that came up to the parliament doors, as other royalists were, he conveyed himself privately to Oxford and sate there. He was a learned and prudent man, and as one of the richest, so one of the meekest men in England. He was active in making the defence and drawing up the articles of Oxon when the garrison was to be surrendered to the parliament; for which and his steady loyalty he was forced to pay a round sum in Goldsmith's Hall, London. He left two daughters. Elizabeth and Lucy, but no son, and his estate passed to a nephew. Lucy married Thomas Pope, Earl of Downe, and their only daughter Elizabeth married Sir Francis Henry Lee of Ditchley.

Sir Ralph Dutton, brother of John of Sherborne, was gentleman extraordinary to King Charles I, and high sheriff of Gloucestershire in 1630. His estate was sequestered during the great rebellion and he was obliged to fly the country. He sailed for France but was driven back by storms and died on Burnt Island in 1640. He left several sons, the eldest of which, William, succeeded after the rebellion to the estate of his uncle John Dutton, and several of the other sons left the country. The family, however, was continued in England by William Dutton, Esq., and after him came his brother Sir Ralph Dutton who was created a baronet 22 June, 1678, and who was succeeded by his eldest son Sir John Dutton. Sir Ralph's daughter Anne married James Naper, Esq., and their son James Lenox Naper inherited the estate of his uncle John Dutton, (who died in 1743 without issue,) and assumed the name of Dutton. This James dying in 1776 left issue James Dutton, M. P. for Gloucestershire, who was elevated to the peerage 20 May 1784, by the title of Baron Sherborne. He died in 1820 and was succeeded by his eldest son John Dutton who now wears the title.—BURKE'S LANDED GENTRY &c.

Lysons states that the Duttons of Sherborne, as also the Duttons of Claughton in the East Riding of Yorkshire, who are supposed to have been long extinct, were descended from Richard Dutton, uncle of Sir Piers Dutton of Hatton. He should probably have said great uncle.

Grosvenour of Houlme in Allostock, Esquire, 1464, and had Issue Peter Dutton junior, Rafe, Richard, and Randle.

4. **Peter Dutton** of Hatton Esquire, Son and Heir of Peter, married Elizabeth Daughter of Sir Robert Fouleshurst of Crew in Cheshire, and had Issue Sir Piers Dutton, who was adjudged next Heir Male to all Dutton Lands, 26 Hen. 8. Elizabeth married Sir George Calveley of Lea nigh Eaton-boat: Elinour married Randle Brereton of Malpas: Jane married George Leech of Carden.

This Peter died about 20 Hen. 7, for Elizabeth his widow married Thomas Leycester of Tabley Esquire, 22 Hen. 7. 1506, and she was the third wife of the said Thomas Leycester.

XVIII. **Sir Piers Dutton** of Hatton and Dutton both, Son and Heir of Peter Dutton of Hatton Esquire, was a Knight 19 Hen. 8, and adjudged next Heir Male to Lawrence Dutton Esquire, [xvii.] 26 Hen. 8, 1534. He is the eighteenth Lord of Dutton since the Conquest, and the fifteenth Person in Lineal Descent from Odard. He built the Hall and New Buildings of Dutton-House, which he joyned to the Chappel, Anno 1539, before which time the House stood a little more remote from the Chappel.* He had two Wifes. Elinour Daughter of Thomas Legh of Adlington was his first Wife, by whom he had Issue Peter Dutton, eldest Son, who died without Issue; Hugh Dutton, second Son; Rafe Dutton, third Son, to whom his Father gave all Hatton Lands, from whom the Duttons of Hatton† yet in being, 1666, are propagated; Katharine, a Daughter, married Sir Roger Pilston of Emrads: afterwards she married Richard Grosvenour, younger Son of the Grosvenours of Eaton-boat: Elizabeth married William Manley of Manley; afterwards she married

---

* The remains of Dutton-Hall, once the splendid mansion of the ancient family of Dutton, are now converted into a farm house; the hall appears to have been spacious and handsome with an enriched wooden roof; it is now converted into several rooms and divided into two or three floors. Over the principal door are the arms of Dutton quartering Hatton, and this inscription in text hand:

𝔖𝔦𝔯 𝔓𝔢𝔶𝔯𝔰 𝔇𝔲𝔱𝔱𝔬𝔫 𝔜𝔫𝔤𝔤𝔥𝔱 𝔛𝔬𝔯𝔡𝔢 𝔬𝔣 𝔇𝔲𝔱𝔱𝔬𝔫, 𝔞𝔫𝔡 𝔪𝔶
𝔜𝔞𝔡𝔶 𝔇𝔞𝔪𝔢 𝔍𝔲𝔩𝔦𝔞𝔫 𝔥𝔦𝔰 𝔴𝔦𝔣𝔢 𝔪𝔞𝔡𝔢 𝔱𝔥𝔦𝔰 𝔥𝔞𝔩𝔩 𝔞𝔫𝔡 𝔟𝔲𝔶𝔩𝔡𝔦𝔫𝔤
𝔦𝔫 𝔱𝔥𝔢 𝔶𝔢𝔯𝔢 𝔬𝔣 𝔬𝔲𝔯 𝔛𝔬𝔯𝔡 𝔊𝔬𝔡 𝔞 𝔐.ℭ ℭ ℭ ℭ ℭ 𝔛 𝔍 𝔍 𝔍
𝔴𝔥𝔬 𝔱𝔥𝔞𝔫𝔨𝔢𝔱𝔥 𝔊𝔬𝔡 𝔬𝔣 𝔞𝔩𝔩.

LYSONS' MAGNA BRITANNIA, Vol. II, p. 457.
The date here given is incorrect.

† Ralph Dutton, a younger son of Sir Piers Dutton above mentioned, continued the male line of Dutton of Hatton, extinct by the death of Peter Dutton, Esq., in 1690. IBID. p. 361.

We have been informed that the Rev. Edward Dutton, curate of Harthill, who died in 1773, was of a younger branch of the Duttons of Hatton and that he supposed himself to be the last male heir of that family. IBID. p. 535.

4

Thomas Brown of Nether-Lee: Anne married to Hamnet Massy of
Sale in Cheshire; after to Edward Barlow of Barlow in Lancashire:
Margery married John Booth, younger Son of Sir William Booth of
Dunham-Massy; Margaret married Raufe Sherman; Mary married
Mathew Ellis of Overly; Alice died unmarried.   See the *Inquisition
post mortem prædicti Petri Dutton Militis*, 37 Hen. 8, which names
the Daughters; but their Husbands I had out of the Herald's Books.

Sir Piers married to his second Wife Julian Daughter of William
Poyns of Worthokiton in Essex, Esquire; who with her husband
built the Hall of Dutton, and the new Chambers there, 1539, as appears by the Inscription round about the Hall of Dutton, within the
Hall.

He was Sheriff of Cheshire 34 Hen. 8, and died 37 Hen. 8, 1546, and
had a Bastard-Son called John Dutton, and a Bastard-Daughter,
called Elizabeth, as appears by the Office taken after his death.

Hugh Dutton, Second Son and Heir to Sir Piers, married Jane
Daughter of Sir William Booth of Dunham-Massy, 12 Hen. 8, and
had Issue John Dutton, Son and Heir; and Anne, married to Cris-
topher Son and Heir of Thomas Holford of Holford nigh Nether-
Tabley in Cheshire, Esquire.   This Hugh died in the Life-time of
Sir Piers his Father, and Jane his widow married Thomas Holford
aforesaid.

XIX. **John Dutton** of Dutton Esquire, Son and heir of Hugh,
and Grandson to Sir Piers, married Elinour Daughter of Sir Hugh
Calveley of Lea nigh Eaton-boat, and had Issue Peter, eldest Son,
who married Elizabeth Daughter and Heir of Richard Massy of
Aldford in Cheshire, 27 Eliz. 1585, and died the thirtieth day of May,
35 Eliz. 1593, without Issue Male of his Body then living, in the Life-
time of his Father: See John Dutton's Office, 7 *Jacobi*.   Also John
Dutton, second Son; and Hugh, third Son; both died without Issue:
Thomas, fourth Son, succeeded Heir to his Father: Lawrence,
Raufe, Adam, Geffrey, and George, all five died without Issue: Jane
died unmarried: Anne married one Hersey; and Elinour died unmarried.

This John had also John Dutton Bastard-Son, who was after Gar-
diner at Dutton, and died 1604.   And Elizabeth, a Bastard-Daughter,
married Mr. Marshall, Chaplain to the Lord Gerard of Gerards-
Bromley in Staffordshire, Mother to the two famous Women-Actors
now at London, called The two Marshals.

The same John sued Raufe Dutton of Hatton, his Uncle, for all
Hatton Lands, as Heir at Law: But this Suit was composed by the
award of Robert Earl of Leycester, the fifth day of July, 14 Eliz.
1572, wherein he gave to John Dutton the Lands of Claverton, and
in Honbridge in the City of Chester, and in Littleton in Cheshire,
and the Lands in Harden and Mancote in Flintshire, and also 500
Marks to be paid by Raufe Dutton to the said John: And all the
rest of Hatton Lands he continued and gave to Raufe Dutton.

John Dutton of Dutton died the thirtieth day of January, 6 *Jacobi*, 1608, at Dutton, aged seventy Years. See the Office taken, 7 *Jacobi*.

XX. **Thomas Dutton** of Dutton Esquire, Son and heir of John, married Thomasin Daughter of Roger Anderton, younger Brother of Anderton of Anderton in Lancashire, and widow to John Singleton of Stany in Lancashire; by whom he had Issue John Dutton, who married Elizabeth eldest Daughter and Co-heir of Sir Thomas Egerton, late Son of Sir Thomas Egerton Lord Chancellor of England 3 *Jacobi*, 1605. But this John died without Issue the ninth day of February, 6 *Jacobi*, 1608. at Tarvin in the Life-time of Thomas his father : Also Elinour, a Daughter, who became sole Heir to her Father.

This Thomas Dutton of Dutton was Sheriff of Cheshire 1611. 9 *Jacobi*, and died 1614. 12 *Jacobi*; aged forty-six Years : Elinour his Heir being then aged eighteen Years.

Thomasin his widow afterwards married Sir Anthony St. John, elder Brother to the Earl of Bolingbroke; but had no Issue by him. She was second Wife to Sir Anthony, and he was third Husband to her.

XXI. **Elinour,** sole Daughter and Heir of Thomas Dutton, married Gilbert Gerard, Son and Heir of Thomas Gerard, Lord Gerard of Gerards-Bromley in Staffordshire, 7 *Jacobi*, 1609, she being then but thirteeen Years old: Gilbert was afterwards Sir Gilbert Gerard Knight of the Bath, 30 *Maii* 1610. at the Creation of Henry, eldest Son of King James, into the Title of Prince of Wales and Earl of Chester: And after the death of Thomas Lord Gerard his Father, he was then Gilbert Lord Gerard 1618. and had Issue Dutton Lord Gerard; and Thomas who died in his Infancy : * Also Alice, eldest Daughter, born in Chester 12 *Junii*, and Baptized 18 *Junii*, 1615. She married Roger Owen, Son and Heir of Sir William Owen of Cundor in Shopshire, who died 1660, and Alice his Wife after married Henry Heylyn of Oxfordshire, 1663. nephew to Dr. Peter Heylyn. Frances, second Daughter, married Robert Nedham, Son and Heir of Robert Viscount Kilmorey, by whom he had only one child, called Elinor, which died young, 1643. Frances, was Buried at Great Budworth, 25 *Maii* 1636. She died in Child-bed : And Elizabeth, third Daughter, born at Gerards-Bromley in Staffordshire, *Anno Christi* 1620. married Peter Leycester of Nether-Tabley in Cheshire, Esquire, 6 *Novembris*, 1642. afterwards Sir Peter Leycester Baronet 1660. the Author of this Book.

* James Duke of Hamilton having married Elizabeth only daughter and heir of Digby the last Lord Gerard, descended from Gilbert Lord Gerard, who married Elinor daughter and sole heir of Thomas Dutton of Dutton, was in 1711 created Baron Dutton of Dutton in Cheshire which title has descended to the present Duke, whose son the Marquis of Douglas was in 1806 called by summons to the house of Peers in right of his father's barony of Dutton.—LYSONS' MAGNA BRITANNIA, vol. II. p. 852.

After the Death of Gilbert Lord Gerard who died 1622. Elinour his
Lady married Robert Nedham of Shenton in Shropshire, Viscount
Kilmorey in Ireland : She was second Wife of Robert, and had
Issue by him Charles Nedham, afterwards Lord Kilmorey, who died
at London 1660. George, second Son, died at Chester without Issue
1644. Thomas Nedham third Son, now living 1669. Arthur, another
Son, died an infant, over-laid by his nurse : Anne died in her Infancy:
Elinour first married Peter Warburton, Heir to Arley Estate, 1638.
She was then but eleven years old : But Peter dying without Issue,
and under Age, of the Small Pox, at Oxford, Anno 1641. she married
afterwards John Lord Byron of Newstede in Nottinghamshire, Anno
1644. then Governor of Chester, who died in France, without any
Issue by her, Anno, 1652. This Elinour (a Person of such comely
Carriage and Presence, Handsomness, sweet Disposition, Honour,
and general Repute in the World, that she hath scarce left her Equal
behind) died at Chester the twenty sixth day of January, 1663. about
the Age of thirty six Years, and was Buried in Trinity Church in
that City. Susan, third Daughter, married Richard Scriven of Frodsley in Shropshire, Esquire, 1652. She died in August 1667. at Frodsley. Katharine, the fourth Daughter, died unmarried at Dutton, 11
Martii, being Sunday, 1665. Mary, fifth Daughter, now living, and
unmarried 1669. Penelope, sixth Daughter, married Randall Egerton of Betley in Staffordshire, Esquire, 1653. Dorothy seventh
Daughter, died unmarried at London in June, 1669. And Elizabeth,
youngest Daughter, now living, and unmarried, 1669.

Robert Viscount Kilmorey, died at Dutton 12 *Septembris*, 1653.
So that the Lady Elinour Kilmorey survived both her Husbands;
in whose Custody Hudard's Sword, as Tradition hath it, now remains,
whereof I made mention in the beginning. This Lady Elinour died
at Dutton the twelfth day of March, 1665.. aged sixty-nine Years;
and her Daughter Katharine also dying at Dutton the day before,
were both Interred at Great Budworth together on the Fryday following, being the sixteenth day of March, 1665.

So ended the Family of Dutton of Dutton.

The foregoing account of the Duttons of Dutton, in Cheshire,
England, is taken from " Leycester's Historical Antiquities," pp.
248-260. The quaint spelling in the original has been preserved, but
the author's many references to other authorities have been omitted.
It may be noticed that he gives the names of Rafe and Raufe for
Ralph, and Piers for Peter; while the spelling of many other names
varies from the more modern style.

THE DUTTONS OF PENN.

While nothing is at present known respecting the ancestry of John Dutton, the settler in Pennsylvania, it would be idle to assert that he belonged to this or that branch of the family; yet it is safe to assume that he was descended from the great Odard of more than 600 years before. At a moderate computation the descendants of one person, at the end of such a period, would exceed the total population of England; but as John came from Cheshire, the ancient home of the Duttons, we do not need the full benefit of this calculation. He was probably descended from one of the younger branches which possessed neither titles nor great estates, and it is possible that even he was ignorant of his relationship to those who were so possessed.

It appears that he had identified himself with the Quakers in his native land, and thus became exposed to the persecutions which an intolerant populace, with more zeal than humanity, heaped upon this quiet and peaceable sect. Several of his neighbors who had suffered persecution came also to Pennsylvania, and as some of them became the ancestors, maternally, of some of the Duttons, the following recital of their sufferings may be of interest to their descendants.

From Besse's "Sufferings of the Quakers," we learn that Robert Taylor of Clutterwick in Cheshire, and twenty eight others, were indicted "for unlawfully assembling together at the house of John Dove in Coddington, within the County aforesaid, the 19th Day of November last past, [1662,] upon Pretence of joining together in religious Worship of God;" and for this offence were imprisoned.

In 1674 or 1675 Thomas Brassey, for preaching at Willison, had goods taken from him worth £28. "About the same time, by warrants from Justice Manwaring, Cattle and Goods worth about £100 were taken from sundry persons in and about Namptwich. The chief Informer was one John Widowbury of Hanklow Esq., who being indebted £40 upon Bond to Thomas Brassey,a Member of that Meeting; upon his Demand of Payment was incensed against him, and thus vented his Wrath upon his Friends. He also got an old Excommunication revived against the said Thomas Brassey and sent him to prison, and swore that he would send his wife thither also."

1678. "John Simcock, fined for Preaching, had taken from him eight Cows and eleven Heifers, worth £90.

1679. "The same John Simcock, for speaking some Words of Exhortation at a Funeral, had his goods taken away to the value of £100.

Anno 1681. "John Simcock of Stoak, by the Statute of 23 Eliz., made against Popish Recusants, had Goods taken from him worth £40."

"In the same year Distresses were made on the Goods and Chattels of many Persons in this County, for Fines laid on them for their Absence from the National Worship, to the Amount of £17 and upwards. And such as had no Goods, which through frequent seizures was the case of some, were sent to Prison; of whom were Thomas Frier of Kingsley, Thomas Stretch of Overton, and John Cotton of Frodsham. From one JOHN DUTTON of Overton the Prosecutors extorted a Demand of 7s. by forcibly haling him out of his House when his family were in Bed, carrying him to an Alehouse, and threatning instantly to send him to Goal: by which they so affrighted a Kinswoman of his that she paid them." *Vol. I. p.* 108.

1683. On the 31st of the Month called January, Thomas Needham and Philip Egerton, Justices, came to a Meeting at Newton, and finding a Person at Prayer, Justice Needham fell upon him, bent him on the head and punched him on the breast with his cane, pulled his Neckcloth in pieces and threw him down and kicked him. He also struck several others so that their Heads were swelled with the Blows. The other Justices desired him to forbear, saying, let us prosecute the Law upon them but not abuse them. Thus checked he forbore striking but continued railing; telling them they were Dogs, and no Men; no more Christians than their Horses, &c. Then they took their names, fined them, and granted Warrants for Distress, by which was taken

	£.	s.	d.
From John' Williamson of Creewood-hall a mare worth -	8:	0:	0.
John Clark of Frodsham, Cloth worth - - -	5:	0:	0.
Elizabeth Sarrat of Woodhouse, Goods worth - - -	2:	0:	0.
Peter Hatton, James Hatton and Richard Sarrat, - -	0:	15:	0.

" Thomas Roland of Acton was also fined 5 s, which a neighbour paid to keep him from Prison, he having no goods left; for all his personal Estate had been lately seized by an Exchequer Process for 20l per month, for absence from his Parish Church."

" In 1670, several Inhabitants of Edlestone, Stoake, and adjacent places, suffered for their religious meetings, Distress of Goods to the value of 86 l, 17 s. It was observed that when Thomas Badcock a man active in making Distress on the Goods of John Simcock, one of the sufferers, was soon after visited with sickness, he complained that his having an hand in that persecution did grievously burden his conscience; wherefore he sent to the said John Simcock who visited him in a tender Christian spirit, freely forgiving the Injury done to himself, and also prayed to the Lord to forgive him."

Such was the spirit with which the early Friends were persecuted, and such the spirit in which that persecution was received. These are comparatively mild examples of persecution, but we may readily suppose that the sufferers felt it desirable to exchange their situation, for one in which they might enjoy their religious opinions without restraint; even though this freedom were obtained at the expense of the hardships and privations incident to a new settlement. Such an asylum was now to be established. In 1681 William Penn, a wealthy Quaker, obtained from King Charles II, a Charter for a large province in America, to which he wished to give the name of *Sylvania*, but the King ordered the prefix Penn to be added in honor of Admiral Penn the father of the grantee. William Penn immediately offered his lands for sale at forty shillings per hundred acres, and within the same year found purchasers for a large amount, which was to be surveyed and laid out thereafter in Pennsylvania. Among these purchasers were John Simcock, Robert Taylor, Thomas Brassey and Thomas Rowland, whose names have already been mentioned. The last obtained one thousand acres by deeds of lease and release, dated 2nd and 3rd of March 1681-2; and by an Indenture dated 22nd of May 1682, in which he is styled "of the County Palatine of Chester, yeoman,"conveyed one half thereof to"John Dutton of Overton* in the said County, yeoman,and Mary his wife"; "for divers good causes but especially in consideration of the sum of ten pounds." There is a tradition that Thomas Rowland was an uncle to Mary Dutton and it is probable there was some connection between the families. Whether the ties of relationship were among those "divers good causes," or not, it appears the money paid was no less in amount than the price at which William Penn was then selling land.

As witnesses to the last mentioned conveyance were Robert Taylor and Thomas Brassie who came over to Pennsylvania soon after, and it was doubtless on account of their prospective emigration that it was considered desirable to have their signatures to the writing. Thomas Brassie arrived here the same year and it is likely that Robert Taylor came about the same time, though his wife and most of his children did not arrive until the 29th of 7th month 1683. It is even not improbable that Thomas Brassie,Robert Taylor and John Dutton all came together. The first settled in Chester township, the second† in Springfield, and the last in Aston township, (now) Delaware County.

The Surveyor General directed the following order to his deputy in Chester County :

"By order and Directions from the Governor for setting out Lands to the Purchasers in Pensilvania, &c : I hereby Authorize thee to survey or lay out to Tho : Rowland's assign four hundred and eighty acres on the western side of Upland Creek, next to Nathaniel Evans ; and next lay out to John Warel two hundred and forty acres ; and next lay out to John Neild two hundred and forty acres ; and next

* The township of Over lies about five miles nearly south of the ancient family seat of Dutton.

† Robert Taylor was styled of "Little Leigh" in the old Deeds, while his wife and children were said to have come from Clatterwitch, which latter place was a hamlet in Little Leigh and formerly owned by the Duttons, as may be seen on page 16. J. Bayard Taylor of Chester County, the widely known traveler and author, is descended from Robert Taylor by the following line : Robert,—Isaac,—Josiah,—Abraham,—John,—Joseph,—J. Bayard Taylor.

John Edge, one hundred and twenty ; and return to me a true Dupli-
cate of the fileld work and Protracted fligures which are to remain
in my office.

Dated the 10th of ye 7 mo., 1682.   THO: HOLME, Surv'r.

To Charles Ashcome, Surveyor."

To which the following return was made :

"October the 8th 1682. Laid out for John Dutton 500 of Land on
the west side of Upland creek, beginning at Nathaniel Evans' corner tree," &c. The courses run were W. S. W. "into the woods,"
565 perches to a red oak : N. W. 150 perches to a white oak : E. N.
E. 598 perches to a red oak by the creek, and down the same to the
beginning.

The return was signed by   CHARLES ASHCOM.

250 acres were laid out to John Neild Dec 10th 1682, next to John
Duttons land, on the north.

. The Dutton tract was about half a mile in width, and a little more
than a mile and three-quarters in length; extending from Upland
(now Chester) Creek W. S. W. across the present township of Aston; .
the northern line just touching the western branch of the creek. By
a re-survey twenty years later it was found to contain five hundred .
and ninety acres. Tradition says that John Dutton settled on this
land and built a house in the meadow near the creek, but being dis- ·
turbed by floods, he removed a few rods further back and erected ǀ
his dwelling on a large rock near a small rivulet. A portion of this ǀ
rock may still be seen near the road from Rockdale to Village Green; ǀ
the remainder having been removed for building purposes some ǀ
years ago. There are the usual traditions of bears and other wild
animals being plentiful in the woods ; of shad and other fish in the
creek ; of hardships and privations in which they were assisted by
the Indians who presented them with venison, &c.

The time of John Dutton's death is unknown, but his widow was
married again, as early as 1694, to John Neild, who was also one of
the first settlers ·in Aston. He was not a Quaker and the marriage
gave occasion for the following minute of Chester Monthly Meeting
of women Friends, held the 1st of the 5th month, 1695.

"The meeting orders Lydia Carter and Ann Brown to speak to ·
Mary Neeld, to see if she be willing to condemn her taking of John ·
Neeld to be her husband, he not being in the profession of the truth."

The following somewhat quaint entries from the Court Records
are here presented. The full meaning of the second is not obvious.

·12th Dec. 1693, " John Neales exhibited a petition to this Court for
·the custom of the country,—This being the second Court ; he having
served his time faithfully, and his Indentures being brought in Court
and expresses the custom of the country to be paid him. The Court's
order is that his master Robert Taylor shall pay him the said custom ; (his master Robert Taylor being called and asked where he had

paid anything to him, said no, nor would not.) Only Justice Hayes does not give his consent to it, but all the rest does order it."
At a Court held at Chester the 12th of September, 1694.

"George Stroud in behalf of himself and Thomas Green, and John Green and Richard Moore Past off unto John Neale articles of agreement for the consideration of the sum of thirteen pounds thirteen shillings and eight pence; and six pounds three shillings and four pence unto the said John Neale's wife, during both the natural lives of the said John Neales and his now wife; to be paid at four equal payments yearly; that's to say, at the four festival days; that's to say, the first payment to begin on the 22nd day of December next, and to be paid in silver money at some house within three miles of the town of Chester, in the Province of Pennsylvania; and so the next at the 25th of March, and the next at the 24th of June; the next the 29th of September; and so to continue during the natural lives of the said John Neales and his wife. And the forenamed George Stroud delivered a Bond in behalf of the forenamed Thomas Green and himself, and John Green and Richard Moore, for the performance of the aforesaid payments. The Bond was for two hundred and fifty pounds, bearing date the twentieth day of August, 1694."

At Orphans' Court, 5th of March, 1694–5. "William Brown and John Baldwin was called and appeared to answer the complaint of John Dutton, Edward Dutton and Thomas Dutton. The Court allowed that John Neeld & Mary his wife, at the request of the orphans, be guardians for the above named complainants, and do also allow Thomas Cartwright and Joel Baily as security for John Neald and Mary his wife, to the value of two hundred and fifty Pounds. And it is also ordered that the old Guardians' accounts be paid and cleared before us at the Court by the new ones."

No Will or Letters of Administration on the estate of John Dutton senior have been found, and it is not very clear what property rightfully belonged to his sons. The land purchased before leaving England was conveyed to both John and Mary Dutton, and as the survivor she became sole owner. Samuel Hall of Aston, who holds a part of the original tract, as well as the old deeds, thinks he formerly had among his papers a document of the nature of a marriage settlement between John Neild and Mary Dutton, but cannot find it now. It is probable there was some arrangement for securing to her children the joint estate of their parents, but whether this was the case or not, it would appear from the Grand Jury's return of a road laid out 17th of 2 mo., 1699, that three of her sons were in possession of or occupied the 500 acres of land, under some recognized division thereof. The road was laid out for the inhabitants of Concord, Bethell, Burmingham and Thornbury, on lands of Margaret Green, Thomas Green, Edward Penick, Edward Dutton, Robert Dutton, John Dutton, John Baldwin, John Bayles, and William Browne,

to Joseph Coebourn's mill. The land of Edward Dutton was of his
own purchasing, while the road did not touch on the share of his
brother Thomas. About the year 1702 or 1703, the township of Aston
was resurveyed and a draft made showing some of the subdivisions,
and from this it appears that Thomas, John and Robert Dutton then
held their father's land. It was subsequently confirmed to them by
deeds, as will be mentioned hereafter.   •
    John Neeld (Neild or Neal,) doubtless came from Cheshire, and
perhaps with Robert Taylor, under contract to work for him, as sug-
gested by his petition to Court "for the custom of the country ;"
which was probably a new suit of clothes at end of service. He
bought land of Penn in England, 250 acres, which was laid out in
Aston on the north side of and adjoining the Dutton tract. He also
owned various other tracts in that neighborhood at a later date. His
name is quite frequently mentioned in the Court records in connection with property, and there may have been more than one of the
name but I have seen no proof of it. From the expression, "his now
wife," it seems likely he was a widower when he married Mary Dutton, but this is only supposition.
    Job and Mary Darlington of Darnhall in Cheshire, Eng., had sons,
of whom John and Abraham came to Pennsylvania as early as 1711,
and several of the letters written to them by their parents are still
preserved. In one bearing date March 28th, 1713, they say, "Good
Abraham and John pray present both our dear loves to our brother
John Neild, and his wife our dear sister,—their sons unknown to us,
—and all his family ; hoping that he will take a fatherly care of you
in our stead now you are so far off us." From this the inference is
strong that Mary Neild was a sister of Job Darlington. Another let-
ter dated May 2nd, 1717, mentions an expectation of Robert Dutton
coming to Cheshire to look after brother Neild's concerns, he having
left property there which was rented. Jan. 30th, 1718-9, Job Darlington writes, "Good children remember my kind love and· my
wife's to brother Neild and his wife, unknown ;" from which it appears that John Neild had married again. I do not find that he had
any children by the widow of John Dutton.
    John Neild of Aston died intestate, and letters of administration on
his estate, were granted to his widow, Elizabeth, May 18th, 1724. She
was married again in that year to William Jefferis, and it appears
that she was the daughter of Nathaniel Ring.
    Abraham Darlington petitioned the Court representing that John
Neild, "a near Relation of this petitioner," died intestate, leaving a
wife and four children, and a considerable estate. The children were
Elizabeth, John, Jane and Elias,—all minors and the two younger
ones born after 1720. It is likely the last wife was much younger
than her husband and she survived him many years. Some of
her grandchildren by the second marriage are yet living. Jane
Neild married John Hannum of Concord, and was the mother of
Col. John Hannum of Revolutionary fame.

Those Friends who settled in Aston township, belonged at first to Chester Monthly Meeting; but Chichester meeting being more convenient to many of them, they at length made application to be joined to the Monthly Meeting of Chichester and Concord, then embracing these two particular meetings, and now known as Concord Monthly Meeting. The meetings of business were then held at private houses in rotation, and at one of these held 6 mo. 10th, 1690, at the house of John Kingsman in Chichester, "Robert Pyle reports to this meeting concerning Aston friends to be joyned to Chechester & Concord, that Chester meeting friends have bin Confered with by sum friends of Chechester, and they desired to consider of it till their next monthly meeting. This meeting continues Robert Pyle, with some women friends, to attend ye next monthly meeting of Chester friends to consumate ye Bussiness."

At the next monthly meeting held 7 mo. 14th, 1696, at Jacob Chandler's residence, called *Jacob's well*, "Robert Pyle Reports to this meeting that the Bussiness of Joyning Aston friends to the monthly meeting of Chechester & Concord is Efected by Joynt Consent of Chester friends."

Among those whose rights of membership were thus transferred to Chichester meeting were the Duttons, whose descendants in some of the branches have continued to be members of the same meeting to the present day. From the records of Concord Monthly Meeting, of which Chichester meeting is a branch, considerable information has been obtained respecting the movements of the early members of the family, which will be noted in the following pages.

SECOND GENERATION.

Children of John (No. 1,) and Mary Dutton.

2. **Elizabeth,** b. in England; d. in Penna. 10, 23, 1682; as recorded by Chester Monthly Meeting.

3. **John,** supposed to have been born in England about 1675. The Court records show that a servant girl, named Isabella Dugles, was indentured to him for five years from the 14th Dec. 1697, yet being unmarried it is a question whether he was keeping house at that time. He was one of the grand jury in the 10th Month 1699, as also in Nov. 1703, Aug. 1704, and Aug. 1705:—appointed supervisor of Aston, Nov. 28, 1710. At a Court held Nov. 1702, "William Brown and John Dutton is appointed fence viewers for ye township of Astown."

At a monthly meeting held at Henry Oborn's in Concord 7 mo. 11th, 1704, John Dutton and Elizabeth Kingsman declared their intentions of marriage with each other. James Brown and Joel Baily

were appointed to inquire into his clearness from others. At the
next meeting, held 9 mo. 18th, at Elizabeth Newlin's in Concord,
they appeared and declared their intentions of marriage the second
time, and no obstruction appearing they were given liberty to proceed. Joel Baily was appointed to see that the marriage was orderly
accomplished, of which he made report at the next meeting, held 10
mo. 11th, 1704.

Elizabeth Kingsman, daughter of John and Hannah Kingsman,
was born 9 mo. 6th, 1685, and was consequently but little over 19
years old at her marriage. Her mother was the daughter of John
Simcock of Ridley township, some of whose sufferings in England
on account of his religion have been noticed. Her father's mother
was Alice Kingsman, of Marlborough in Wiltshire, as appears by
letters to her children in this country.

March 15th, 1708, John Neeld of Aston, yeoman, and Mary Neeld
his now wife convey to her son John Dutton 200 acres in Aston,—it
being the middle part of the original tract,—for £90. This tract by
survey contained 230 acres. John Dutton had previously purchased
from Thomas Cartwright two tracts in Aston, of 100 and 150 acres,
but sold the greater part of these in 1708 to William Rattew. In 1712
he bought 55 acres, or one half of his brother Robert's part of the
original tract, and in the same year obtained 625 acres in Marlborough
township, Chester County, which had belonged to John Simcock.

John Kingsman resided in Chichester township, probably near the
line of Aston, where he owned 200 acres of land. This he devised to
his only surviving child, Elizabeth Dutton, during her life ; while
he gave to each of his grand-daughters, Hannah and Mary Dutton,
£10 and a silver cup. He died about the beginning of the year 1721,
and it is likely that John Dutton removed with his family to the
above land in Chichester not long after. He was living there in
1731, and in that year conveyed his lands in Aston to John Biard or
Bayard.

Both John Dutton and his wife were active members of the meeting and frequently appointed on committees. He was chosen overseer
for Chichester meeting in 1708, but was released from that station at
his own request in 1712. In 1728 he was appointed Elder in the room
of Robert Pyle, and continued in that station until his death. 11 mo.
5th, 1729, Francis Reynolds and John Dutton were appointed for
Chichester meeting to advise against the erection of tombstones, and
to procure the removal of such as had been placed at graves.

In his will dated 1 mo. (March,) 21st, 1735-6, he gives a small sum
of money to each of his children and the balance of property to his
wife Elizabeth. It appears from the probate, a month later, that
before the will could be prepared for signing he died ; so that his
death doubtless occurred on the above day.

5 mo. 7th, 1729, " Elizabeth Dutton is chosen overseer for Chichester meeting, Luce Dutton being removed by death." She was
living in 1745, but the time of her death is unknown,

4. **Edward**, it appears, purchased from Thomas England 107 acres in Bethel township, adjoining the Aston tract, by deed of 1 mo. 8th 1097–8. He settled on this land and there continued to reside until his death. In 1704 he appears at Court as constable for Bethel township.

At a monthly meeting held 4 mo. 9th, 1701, at Thomas King's in Concord, Edward Dutton and Gwin Williams declared their intentions of marriage with each other. John Kingsman and John Bales were appointed to inquire concerning his clearness from others. At a monthly meeting held 6 mo. 11th, 1701, at Nicholas Pyle's in Concord, they declared their intentions of marriage the second time, and were allowed to proceed. John Kingsman was appointed to oversee the wedding but his report of it is not recorded.

Robert Dutton having obtained 110 acres of his father's tract in Aston, sold one half thereof to his brother Edward, by deed of Sept. 29th, 1712, and the latter with his wife Gwin conveyed the same, together with 50 acres adjoining in Bethel, to their son John, Jan. 10th, 1729. The homestead with 100 acres, Edward devised to his wife during her life, to pass at her death to his son John. He also devised to his son William £20, and to his daughter Mary Davis £5. His will was dated 10 mo. (Dec.) 24th, 1731, and proven on the 14th of March following.

Edward Dutton took but little part in the affairs of the meeting. In 1735 and '36 a dispute between his widow Gwin Dutton and John Chads is mentioned on the records, from which it appears that she had assumed some of her son William's debts, but was not willing to abide by the decision of the committee appointed to inspect the difficulty. 3 mo. 7th, 1744, a complaint came from Concord meeting that Gwin Dutton, now Bennett, had been married by a Justice to one not in membership. After some months she made an acknowledgment for her offence, which was accepted. Her death probably occurred about 1753, as a final settlement of her first husband's estate was made at that time.

5. **Thomas**, b. in England 3 mo. (May,) 1st, 1679. There is a tradition that when the family went up by an Indian path from Chester, to settle on their land in Aston, Thomas carried the tongs as his share of the load. This seems unlikely if they settled there in 1682, for in that case he would need to be carried himself. He was constable for "Ashtown" in 1703.

"At a monthly meeting held at Robert Pyle, his house, the 10th of the 1st month, 1700–1."

"Thomas Dutton and Leusy Barnott laid their intention of marriage before this meeting, this being the first time; This meeting Appoynts John Bales and John Baldwin to inquire into his clearness, & Also into his Life and conversation, and make Report of the same to ye next monthly meeting."

"The 11th of ye 2d month, 1700. [1701?]"

"ffriends these are to satisfie you yt I have tould my mind to

John Baldwin and Leave it to your Consideration, wishing them well in their proscedure: This from John Neeld to friends of ye monthly meeting."

" At a monthly meeting held at John Kingsman, his house, the 14th of the second month, 1701.

" Thomas Dutton and Leusy Barnott Laid their intention of marring before this meeting, it being ye second time: friends finding things clear Left them to proseed in marring According to ye good order of Truth.

" John Kingsman is ordered to Attend ye marriag to se yt things are decently managed, and make Report thereof to the next monthly meeting."

The overseer's report is not recorded, but we may presume that the marriage was accomplished with due propriety within a week or two from the last date.

Lucy Barnard, b. 2 mo. 1681, was the daughter of Richard and Frances Barnard of Aston, who were among the earliest settlers, and said to have come from Sheffield, England. Her father died about the year 1698, and in 1702 her mother was again married to Thomas Bowater ; in reference to which marriage the following minute was made by Concord Monthly Meeting, held 29th of 5th month, 1702.

"Thomas Bolter and ffrances Barnet Appeared att this meeting and declared their Intentions of marriage with Each other, this being the first time: frances having severall children, being a widow, this meeting ordereth with the advice of the preparative meeting, to settle things in good order betwixt her and her children before the next monthly meeting."

John Neild of Aston, yeoman, and Mary his wife convey to her son Thomas Dutton, by Indenture dated 1st mo., (March,) 15th 1708, 200 acres in Aston for £90 ; it being the easterly part of the original tract, and by survey 250 acres. Thomas also purchased 50 acres adjoining this in Aston, and 50 more over the creek in Middletown township, in 1713. It is said he built a house of hewed logs of yellow poplar in 1704, nearly a mile west of the creek and on the original tract. This house remained standing and was occupied until 1850, when it was torn down by Mr. Huntingdon to make room for the Aston Ridge Seminary for young ladies.

Thomas Dutton was an active member of Chichester meeting, and very frequently appointed on committees and as a representative to the Quarterly Meeting. He was appointed overseer of Chichester meeting 12th mo. 9th 1707, in the room of James Whiticker, but was released 5 mo. 23, 1711, at his own request, and James Swaffer appointed in his stead. 10th mo. 14, 1713, he was again chosen overseer, James Swaffer having removed, but again released from the station by request 8 mo. 8, 1722, and Edward Robinson appointed in his place.

Lucy Dutton was also active in meeting affairs and occupied the

station of overseer in Chichester meeting at the time of her death.
She is said to have measured six feet without shoes, and some of her
descendants have been quite tall and stout. She died with measles in
the 10th month, 1728, in her 48th year. Thomas died with the small
pox in the 10th month, (Dec.) 1731, but a short time before his brother
Edward. His will here follows :

BE IT REMEMBERED that I, Thomas Dutton of Aston in ye County of
Chester and province of pennsylvania, being in perfect health of body, and of a
sound & disposing mind and memory, thanks be to god therefore, calling to mind
the uncertainty of time, it being appointed for all men once to die, do make and
ordain this my last will & Testament in manner & form following; that is to
say, IMP'S. it is my will & mind yt all my Just debts & funeral expenses be
paid as soon as convenient may be after my decease, by my executors hereinafter named. ITTM, I give & Devise & Bequeath unto my sone Richard
Dutton all yt my house & Tract of land on which I now live, with the ap-
purtenances thereunto belonging, situate in the township of Aston afores'd;
containing by Estimation two hundred acres, or thereabouts, be the same
more or less; to him, his heirs & Assigns forever; he yielding and paying
to my son John Dutton fifteen pounds current money of this province, when he
arrives at the age of twenty one years; and also paying to my daughters Lydia
Dutton, Mary Dutton, and Sarah Dutton, the sum of fifteen pounds each; to be
paid to each of them respectively as ye arrive at ye age of eighteen years: and
if any of my said children happen to die before such money becomes due or pay-
able, then such child or childrens' share to be equally divided amongst all of my
surviving children, Rich'd not excepted. ITT. I give devise and bequeath unto
my son David Dutton all yt my tract or parcel of land situate in the township of
Middletown, purchased late of Aron Coppock, formerly belonging to William
Johnson, Containing by Estimation fifty acres, to the propper use and behoof of
him the said David Dutton, his heirs and assigns forever. ITT. I give devise and
bequeath to my son Jonathan Dutton all that my tract or parcel of land situate
in the township of Aston, purchased late of Aron Coppock, formerly belonging
to John Neild, containing by estimation fifty acres, to the propper use and behoof of ye said Jonathan Dutton, his heirs and assigns forever, only reserving &
hereby giving to my sone Richard Dutton the benefits of such meadow land as is
cleared upon yt said Tract of fifty acres until my said sone Jonathan Dutton arrive at ye age of eighteen years. ITT'M. I give and bequeath unto my Daughter
Lydia Dutton a feather bed & bolster, bedding, bedsteads & furniture thereto belonging, standing or usually standing in the north corner of the room over the
house. ITT. It is my will and minde that all the residue and remaining part of
my personal estate be sold by my executors hereinafter named, and the money
arising by such sale to be disposed of as hereafter mentioned. IT. I give and bequeath unto my sone John Dutton thirty pound, to be paid by my executors
hereinafter named when he arrives to ye age of twenty one years. IT. I give
and bequeath unto my three Daughters Lyddia Dutton, Mary Dutton, and Sarah
Dutton, thirty pounds each, to be paid by my exr's hereinafter named to each
of them respectively as ye arrive at ye age of eighteen years. It is my will &
minde yt my sone Jonathan be put to a trade, and my daughter Sarah
placed out by my exr's hereinafter named, according to ye advise, and by the
direction of my Brother John Dutton & my sone Richard Dutton. IT. I give &
Bequeath to my children Rich'd Dutton, David Dutton, Jona. Dutton, Jno. Dut-
ton, Lyddia Dutton, Mary Dutton and Sarah Dutton, all ye residue & remaining
part of my estate, if any, whether real & personal of wt Nature or kind soever ye
same may be; to be equally divided amongst them after all my debts & Legacies
are paid; and Lastly I nominate constitute and appoint my Trusty friends
Thomas Barnet of Aston & William Pennell of Middletown, Husbandmen, to be
full & whole exec'rs of this my last will and Testament; hereby making void
& null all other wills & Testaments by me heretofore made ; Rattifying & Con-

firming this my last will & Testament: In witness whereof I have hereunto set
my hand & seal this ninth day of the tenth month, 1731.
                                                    THOMAS DUTTON, [seal.]
Signed, sealed, published, pronounced & Declared by the sd Thomas Dutton to be
his last will & Testament in the presence of us who have subscribed our names
as witnesses hereunto: Thos. Cummings, John Carter.

  Memorandum that I Thomas Dutton do by way of Codicil to this my last will
& Testament, add, that it is my will and minds, & I do hereby give to my sons
Richard Dutton the clock & case now standing in the house, to his own proper
use & behoof forever; as witness my hand & seal this tenth day of the the tenth
month Anno. 1731.   THOMAS DUTTON, [seal.]

  Sealed & Signed in ye presence of   Thomas Cummings, John Carter,

Proven Jan. 10, 1731-2, by the two witnesses on affirmation, coram Jo. Parker.

  6. **Robert,** was probably the youngest child of John and Mary
Dutton.

  In 1701 a project was started of settling a township on the Maryland line, and several persons of Chichester, Aston, and the neighboring parts, agreed to take shares in the enterprise; each share to be
one thousand acres. Among these were Robert Dutton and one Samuel Littler, who together took a share, or 500 acres each. A large
tract of 18,000 acres was laid out the next year and divided into small-
er parcels, for which the different purchasers drew lots. This large
tract was called Nottingham, but by the running of Mason and Dixon's line nearly all of the original township fell into Maryland. Robert Dutton and Samuel Littler obtained two lots, one on each side,
east and west, of the "Brick Meeting."

  William Brown a worthy Friend and member of Chichester meeting took 1000 acres in the new township, and settled there in 1704. A
meeting was established at his house the next year and held there
until 1709, when a meeting house was built. A majority of the settlers having belonged to Chichester and Concord Monthly Meeting,
the new meeting was considered a branch thereof, although forty
miles distant as then estimated, and the bounds of another monthly
meeting lay between.

  At a monthly meeting held at Philip Roman's in Chichester 7 mo.
8th 1707, Robert Dutton of Nottingham and Ann Brown of the same
township appeared and declared their intentions of marriage. Andrew Job of the same meeting and John Baldwin of Astowne were
appointed to inquire into his clearness from others.

  At a monthly meeting held at John Kingsman's in Chichester, 8 mo.
13th, 1707, they appeared the second time and were given permission to proceed in marriage. Andrew Job and John Churchman
were appointed as overseers, and they reported 12 mo. 9th 1707, that
the marriage was orderly accomplished at the house of William
Brown of Nottingham, on the 13th of the 9th month. She was the
daughter of William and Ann (Mercer) Brown, and was born 10 mo.
1st 1687.

  John Neeld of Aston and wife Mary, by deed of 6 mo. (Aug.) 15th

1712, convey to her son Robert Dutton "of Aston," 100 acres in Aston for £45. This was the west end of the original tract, and in reality 110 acres. Robert Dutton "of Nottingham," yeoman, and wife Ann convey to his brother Edward Dutton of Bethel, yeoman, 55 acres in Aston, Sept. 29, 1712, for £30. They also convey at same time and price 55 acres to his brother John Dutton of Aston; it being the remainder of the 110 acres.

At a monthly meeting held 1 mo. 13th, 1709-10, at Elizabeth Newlin's in Concord:—"Friends from Nottingham meeting Request to this meeting for John Bales [Beal] and Robert Dutton to be overseers in the room of William Brown and John Churchman: this meeting doth allow of it till further orders."

At a monthly meeting held 2 mo. 14th 1712, William Brown senior and James King were appointed overseers for Nottingham meeting, instead of John Bales and Robert Dutton, who desired to be released.

In 1715, Nottingham meeting was joined to Newark (now Kennett) Monthly Meeting, on account of being nearer, and on the establishment of Newgarden Monthly Meeting, in 1718, it became a branch of that. Nottingham Monthly Meeting was separated from Newgarden about 1730.

At Newgarden Monthly Meeting held 8 mo. 13th 1722:—" Robert Dutton has requested of this meeting a certificate in order to go to Antegoe or Jamaica about his occasion, in way of trading, therefore this meeting appoints John Churchman & James Wright to make inquiry concerning the settlement of his affairs, & of his conversation, & to give an account to next monthly meeting."

9 mo. 10th, 1722:—" The friends appointed to make inquiry concerning Robert Dutton have given an account that he has settled his affairs & hath consent of his wife: therefore the meeting granted him a certificate."

5 mo. 13th 1725:—" Robert Dutton having returned from Antegoa hath produced a certificate from thence to this meeting's satisfaction, & also returned the certificate he had from our monthly meeting." " Robert Dutton acquaints this meeting that he again desires to go to Antegoa, & in order thereto requests of us a Certificate: therefore this meeting appoints James Wright & James King to make inquiry into his conversation & circumstances, & prepare a certificate as they find things, & to make report to next monthly meeting."

Anne Dutton of Cecil Co. Md. was married 9 mo. 23, 1736, at the house of William Brown senior in Nottingham, to John Underhill of Cecil County. Those who were appointed by Nottingham Monthly Meeting to inspect her affairs before marriage, reported that her former husband's estate was settled by Law. Among the signers to her marriage certificate were Robert Dutton and Elizabeth Dutton, —doubtless her children. No further particulars have been obtained respecting her former husband or herself.

THIRD GENERATION.

Children of John (No. 8) and Elizabeth Dutton.

7. **John**, farmer, m. 8 mo. 4th, 1733, at Chichester meeting, to Prudence, dr. of Francis and Elizabeth (Acton) Reynolds of Chichester township. She was born 1 mo. 16, 1713. A complaint was made to the meeting 5 mo. 16, 1750 that John Dutton had been married by a priest, and for this he made an acknowledgment; but whether he was the above John, or his cousin, son of Thomas, is unknown. The above John became reduced in his circumstances, for it appears that the meeting paid for his board with his son-in-law Shelley in 1769.

8. **Hannah**, m. 8 mo. 29, 1730, at Chichester meeting, to Nathaniel Scarlet, farmer, son of Humphrey and Ann of Chichester. They removed to Newgarden township, Chester Co., the next year and became members of Londongrove meeting. Nathaniel died 11 mo. 2, 1784, in his 85th year. Hannah died 12, 31, 1782, in her 80th year it is said, but she could not have been so old.

Humphrey Scarlet of Chichester married Anne, widow of Anthony Weaver, and daughter of Joseph and Jane Richards of Aston. Their children were JOHN, m. Eleanor ———; SHADRACH, m. Phebe Bownter; NATHANIEL, (above); HUMPHREY; MARY, m. Thomas Hall; SUSANNA, m. Daniel Brown, 1721; ELIZABETH, m. Richard Cox, 1726; REBECCA, m. ——— Brown. The father died in 1746.

9. **Mary**, married Joseph Cobourn but nothing is known respecting her descendants. She was married "by a priest" prior to 4 mo. 1733, and refusing to make an acknowledgment, was disowned by the meeting.

10. **Kingsman**, carpenter, after the death of his mother became the owner of 200 acres of land in Chichester township, adjoining the south west corner of Aston. This was devised to him by his grandfather John Kingsman, doubtless on account of his name. The following extracts relate to his marriage, and will serve to show the manner of proceeding in such cases.

1 mo. 7th, 1736-7; "Chichester friends acquaints this meeting that Kingsman Dutton has gone to a priest and was married: this meeting appoints Joseph Pyle and Daniel Brown to spake with him and request him to come to our next monthly meeting."

2 mo. 4, 1737; "Those friends which were to spake to Kingsman Dutton reports they have spoke with him, but not appearing here this meeting appoints Joseph Pyle and Daniel Brown to acquaint him that if he do not come to the next meeting to give satisfaction, friends will be nesseated to give Testimony against him, and report to our next meeting.

4 mo. 6, 1737; " The friends appointed to spake to Kinsman Dutton reports that he utterly refuses to give any satisfaction for his marring by a priest, therefore this meeting appoints Joseph Pyle & Ralph Eavenson to draw up a Testimony against him and bring it to our next meeting."

5 mo. 4, 1737; " Whereas Kinsman Dutton having been Educated in religious profession with us the people called Quakers, but he not regarding the rules of our Religious Society, he was married by or before a Priest ; for which Errour of his he have several times been vissited in order to prevail with him to condemn the same, but those vissits not having the Desired Effect, therefore this meeting Declares him the said Kinsman Dutton to be no member of our religious society, until he from a sence of his Errour do Condemn the same, and do make such acknowledgment as shall be to the satisfaction of our said meeting ; the which we sincerely desire he may."—*Concord Monthly Meeting.*

The early Friends designated as "priests" all ministers of other denominations who officiated for wages.

Anne Dutton, wife of Kingsman Dutton, is believed to have been the daughter of Francis and Barbara Routh, and grand-daughter of Lawrence and Ann Routh, who came from Yorkshire, Eng., in 1683.

Kingsman erected a neat two-story brick house which is still standing, near the east branch of Chichester creek, about half a mile from the south-west corner of Aston township : now owned by Benjamin Elliott. In the east gable is a stone bearing the initials D., K. & A., and the date 1753. The ruins of a saw mill are near by.

Kingsman died about the year 1765, and his estate having become involved, was sold by the Sheriff in 1768. Anne became a member of meeting in 1748, and was living in 1774, but the time of her death is unknown.

11. **Jacob,** it appears, was disowned 11 mo. 4, 1741, for having gone out in his marriage with one who was not a member of the society. He resided in Upper Chichester, where he died intestate, and letters of administration on his estate were granted to his widow Hannah Dutton, Aug. 16th 1749. She subsequently married Charles Henszey or Henzley, and they filed accounts of their administration in 1752.

12. **Joseph,** millwright, m. 10 mo. 21, 1742, Elizabeth Smith, daughter of Thomas (and Elinor ?) of Birmingham township. This marriage was by a " priest," and he made an acknowledgment therefor to the meeting, 6 mo. 1st 1743. He continued a member during his life but took no part in church affairs, while his children do not appear to have been considered members at any time. He died 6 mo. 14, 1773, having survived his wife.

13. **Robert,** born prior to 1719, as he and the foregoing children of John and Elizabeth Dutton are mentioned in their grandfather

Kingsman's will of that date. He married out of the society, for which he made an acknowledgment to the meeting, 6 mo. 1st, 1743, but there is no further mention of him on the records. There is reason to suppose his wife was of the Crosby family.

14. **James.** At Concord Monthly Meeting held 10 mo. 8, 1753, Chichester meeting complained of James and Isaac Dutton for marriage by a priest, and William Peters and Joseph Gibbons were appointed to visit them. Their case was continued for several months, and 1st mo. 7th 1754 it was mentioned that "the said Duttons Lives at a considerable Distance·" 3 mo. 4th 1754, one of the friends appointed reports that he had an opportunity with James and Isaac Dutton, and they proposed to be at the meeting in the 5th month to make satisfaction, but being under an engagement to finish a piece or work could not come sooner. 9 mo. 2nd 1754, "Isaac nor James Dutton not appearing here in order to make friends satisfaction for their outgoing, notwithstanding friends several visits of Love, this meeting therefor appoints Benja. Reynolds and Wm. Clayton to draw a Testimony Separatly against them, and bring to next meeting."

It has not been ascertained what business the brothers were engaged in. James Dutton of Northern Liberties, Philadelphia county, died Aug. 1st, 1769, aged 45 ; and in his will dated six days prior to his death devised all his property to his wife Hannah during her life. She died Oct. 1st 1798, aged 65, and as they were both interred in the Coates family burying ground, now the S. E. corner of 3rd and Brown Streets, Philadelphia, it is likely that she was connected with that family.

15. **Isaac,** doubtless married about the same time as his brother James, and the two removed in company. His wife Mary was the daughter of John Coates of Philadelphia, brickmaker, who died about 1760. The will of Isaac Dutton of Kensington Phila. was dated Oct. 9, 1760, and proven Mar. 2, 1761; in which he gives all his estate to his wife during her life; and this included some lots on Delaware river, extending back to Queen Street. She, it appears, had been previously married to a Wright who left three children, George, Mary and Lydia. The will of Mary Dutton of Northern Liberties was dated Sept. 29, 1786, and proven May 20, 1791. She owned lots on Coates and Brown Streets which she devised to her daughters Mary Eyres, Lydia Eyres, and Sarah Brown, whom she appointed her executors.

16. **Amy.** At a meeting held 6 mo. 7, 1749, Chichester Friends informed that Emy Dutton, now Talley, had been married by a priest: and Elenor Peters and Esther Larkin were appointed to visit her. She declined to make any acknowledgment, but rather preferred to be disowned, which was accordingly done 11 mo. 1st 1749. Nothing further known respecting her.

Children of Edward (No. 4.) and Gwin Dutton.

17. **Mary,** m. 9 mo. 27, 1728, at Concord meeting, to Daniel Davis of Birmingham township, Chester County, son of John and Mary of Thornbury. Her descendants not ascertained.

18. **John.** To him his father gave two adjoining tracts of land,— the one of 50 acres in Bethel, and the other of 55 acres in Aston,— by deed of Jan. 10, 1729. By the will of his father, he was also to have the homestead in Bethel, after the death of his mother.

At Concord Monthly Meeting 12 mo. 7, 1736-7; "This meeting being informed that John Dutton, son of Edward Dutton, Deceased, was married by a Priest, and also hath joyned himself to the Prisbitarian Society : this meeting appoints Thomas Marshall and Joseph Cloud to treate with him in order to know the certainty of it, and report to our next meeting,"

1 mo. 7, 1736-7 ; The friends appointed reports that John Dutton "says that he thought it to be Deuty to Joyne himself to another society ; therefor this meeting do esteem ye said John Dutton to be no member of our Religious Society."

From the records of Christ Church, (Prot. Episcopal,) of Philadelphia, is obtained the marriage, "1735. Nov. 4. John Dutton & Elizabeth Dunlap."

John Dutton died intestate and letters of administration on his estate were granted to Elizabeth, his widow, and Richard Dutton, March 21, 1748-9. Hugh Lynn and Hugh Trimble were appointed guardians of the children, Dec. 1749. In 1761 the widow and children petitioned the Orphans' Court for a division of the property, which was accordingly ordered.

19. **William.** Edward Dutton devised to his son William Dutton "if living, the sum of Twenty pounds ; to be paid to him within the compass of three years after his coming here," from which it would appear that he had gone from home.

9 mo. 3, 1735, Concord meeting complained of William Dutton for not paying his just debts, and at the next meeting Henry Oborn and Robert Wilson were appointed to treat with him about absenting himself. 12 mo. 2, 1735, the friends appointed reported that William Dutton "did declare that he did not desire aney ways to belong to our Religious society ; therefore this meeting doth declare the said William Dutton to be no member of our society."

After this he is only incidentally mentioned in 1736, and all further trace of him is lost.

Children of Thomas (No. 5.) and Lucy Dutton.

20. **Thomas,** b. 3 mo. 1702 ; d. 10 mo. 1728, with the measles, unmarried.

21. **Rebekah,** b. 8 mo. 10, 1709; d. 10 mo. 1731, with the small-pox, unmarried.

22. **Richard,** b. 10 mo. 8, 1711 ; m. 8 mo. 7, 1733, at Middletown meeting, to Mary Martin, daughter of Thomas and Mary of Middletown township, She was born 6 mo. 30, 1711, and died 1 mo 26,1782. Her father was the only son of John and Elizabeth Martin, who came from Edgcott in Berkshire, Eng., and her mother was the daughter of Giles and Mary (English) Knight of Byberry, Philadelphia Co.

Richard inherited his father's part of the original Dutton tract in Aston, and built thereon a comfortable and substantial stone house, which is now in possession of Jacob Sides. A stone in the west gable bears the initials R. D. and M. D., and date 1749. Having purchased land in Chichester township, he removed thither, and in 1768 conveyed the above house with 109 acres of land to his son Thomas. Both he and his wife were active members of Chichester meeting, as well as among the most substantial citizens of the township. The present meeting house was built in 1769 and the date stone bears the initials R. D., which are said to be for Richard Dutton, and it is probable that he was the principal contributor to the expense of its erection. He died 2d mo. 18, 1795.

23. **David,** b. 12 mo. 28, 1713-4; d. 3 mo. 25, 1798. Although by birth a member of the Society of Friends, his name does not occur in their records nor was he considered a member; otherwise his marriage would have been noticed. His wife's name was Jane, but whose daughter she was is uncertain, unless we suppose her father was Joseph McClaskey, who in his will, dated 1753, mentions his daughter Jennett Dutton. David was a blacksmith and lived in Middletown on 50 acres of land devised to him by his father. Toward the close of his life he resided with his son in law, Jacob Yearsley, in Thornbury. He was a large and powerful man. In his will dated Mar. 21, 1798 he gave to his daughter Sarah Booth his silver shoe buckles, and directed his real estate in Middletown and Chester to be sold, and the proceeds divided between his four daughters; except that Lydia Mancil was to have £00 less than the others.

24. **Lydia,** b. 2 mo. 14. 1716; m. 6 mo. 30, 1739 at Chichester meeting to William Hewes, son of William and Mary of Chichester. She died 4 mo. 11, 1748,but it is not known that she left any children. William in his will dated 8 mo. 4, 1753, and proven the 18th of the same month,mentions his wife Rebecca and son Aaron ; also appoints his brother John Hewes and brother in law Richard Dutton his executors, and says, "I will that my executors shall cause grave stones to be made and set up at the head and feet of the graves of my father and mother and my deceased wife and children, and also at my own grave."

Whether the will of the testator was executed in these respects

has not been ascertained, but it is to be regretted that Friends have
so generally excluded from their burial places those marks by which
we might otherwise identify the last resting places of our ancestors.

25. Jonathan, b. 6 mo. 11, 1721 ; d. 10 mo. 18, 1745, intestate, unmarried, and without issue, and the land which his father had devised to him was inherited by his eldest brother Richard.

26. John, b. 7 mo. 6, 1721 ; d. 2 mo. 6. 1759. It is not known that
he was ever married. He died at the house of Mary Hewes in Chichester where he happened to fall sick, and in his will of the same
date devised nearly all his property to his brother David and sister
Sarah.

27. Mary, b. 7 mo. 6, 1721. At Concord Monthly Meeting 4 mo.
8, 1745, Chichester meeting informed that Mary Dutton, daughter of
Thomas Dutton, now Mary Grubb, had been married out to one who
was not a member. For this she made an acknowledgment. but be-
yond this nothing is known of her or her family, except that an old
record says that she died at the age of 38 yrs. 6 mo. 25 d.

28. Sarah, b. 8 mo. 22, 1725 ; m. John Power of Chichester, who
was not a member, and she was consequently disowned 6 mo. 3,1747.
He died 2 mo. 1, 1791, and she 2 mo. 20, 1795, "intestate and without
issue."

Children of Robert (No. 6,) and Ann Dutton.

29, Mary, b. 8 mo. 15, 1708: **30. Ann,** b, 10 mo. 10, 1711: **31.
Robert,** b. 8 mo. 26, 1713. Nothing further is known of these
three children.

32. Elizabeth, b. 1 mo. 25, 1722; m. 2 mo. 20, 1742, at East Not-
tingham meeting, to Joseph England of Kent Co. Md., son of Lewis
England. The meeting record of births states that Joseph England
"Livs at Joppa," but little has been ascertained respecting the family.

FOURTH GENERATION.

Children of John Dutton (No. 7,) and Prudence Reynolds.

33. Prudence, m. prior to 5 mo. 5, 1755, to ——— Shelley "by a
priest," for which she made an acknowlegment to the meeting.
Nothing is known of her descendants.

34. John. A complaint was made to Concord Monthly Meeting,
3 mo. 6th 1765,of his marriage by a priest,for which he was disowned
7 mo. 3, 1765. In this year he was assessed in Upper Chichester
with 74 acres and buildings, 2 horses, 3 cows, and 6 sheep ; also rents

received, £8 per annum.   Daniel Brown of U. Chichester in his will
dated Jan. 19, 1767, proven Dec. 12, 1767, mentions his granddaughter
Rachel Dutton, wife of John Dutton ;—probably the above John.
One John Dutton died Jan. 1, 1796, but whether the father, son, or a
cousin is unknown.   His descendants, if any, not ascertained.

35. **Elizabeth**, was disowned 8 mo. 5, 1766 for accompanying her
brother in his disorderly marriage, and for her own marriage subsequently by a priest, to —— Booth.

36. **Benjamin**, disowned 6 mo. 5, 1765, on complaint of card
playing, &c.,preferred by Chichester meeting.

37. **Isaac**, disowned 4 mo. 3, 1771 for his marriage by a priest.
This is supposed to have been the Isaac Dutton who married Elizabeth
Lampley, and owned the old Blue Ball tavern not far from Marcus
Hook ; since torn down by Jonathan Larkin.   He died Mar. 31, 1795.
In 1783 Isaac Dutton was assessed in Lower Chichester with 177
acres, 2 horses and 5 cattle.

38. **Henry**, a minor, petitioned Court, 1768, as a grandson of
Francis Reynolds, and Joseph Brown was appointed his guardian.
In 1772 Henry Dutton was disowned by the meeting for absconding
from his creditors.   Nothing further known of him.

Children of Hannah Dutton (No. 8,) and Nathaniel Scarlett.

39. **Elizabeth**, b. 5 mo. 17, 1731 ; probably died young or unmarried.

40. **Mary**, b. 12 mo. 23, 1733; m. 5 mo. 22, 1755, at Londongrove meeting, to John Cox of Mill Creek, Del., son of William.

41. **Joseph**, b. 11 mo. 29, 1735; died in infancy.

42. **John**, b. 2 mo. 15, 1737 ; m. 10 mo. 31, 1765, at Newgarden
meeting, to Mary, dau. of Joseph and Sarah Dixon of Newgarden.
They resided in Newgarden township about a mile west of Kennett
Square.   Mary died 11 mo. 8, 1803 in her 66th year, and he died 6 mo.
25, 1814.

43. **Hannah**, b. 4 mo. 18, 1739 ; d. 11 mo. 18, 1802.   She was married 4 mo. 17, 1765, at Londongrove meeting, to Isaac Baily, son of
Thomas Baily of W. Marlborough township, where they continued
to reside.   She was his second wife.   He died 1 mo. 16, 1826.

44. **Joseph**, b. 12 mo 24, 1740 ; was living in 1783, but no further
information has been obtained respecting him.

45. **Deborah**, b. 12 mo. 25, 1742 ; d, 2 mo. 9, 1783 ; married Caleb
Wiley.

46. **Nathaniel**, b. 11 mo. 26, 1744 ; probably died young.

47. **Lydia**, b. 7 mo. 12, 1746 ; d. 1767, unmarried.

Children of Kingsman Dutton (No. 10,) and Anne Routh,

48. **Francis,** married Hannah, dau. of Joseph and Hannah Talbot of Middletown township,. After several years he removed westward, and died at Shepherdstown, Belmont Co., O. His grandson thinks he died about 1840, and a nephew says he was 95 years old. He married a second wife, Lydia Booth.

49. **David,** b. about 1756; m. in 1777 to Hannah, dau. of Robert and Mary (Talbot) Rogers, and a niece of his brother Francis's wife. She was born in Chester County, Pa., in 1761, and died at Harrisville, O. Nov. 14, 1837. At the time of the battle of Brandywine they were living near, and in the evening David assisted in caring for the wounded, and afterward in burying the dead. After some years they removed to Berkley County, Va., and settled at the foot of North Mountain, about twelve miles from Winchester. Some of their children having migrated to Ohio, they followed them in 1830, and spent their few remaing years at Harrieville in Harrison Co.

There may have been other children of Kingsman Dutton, but the above two are all that have been reported definitely to the writer.

Child of Jacob Dutton (No. 11,) and Hannah ——.

50. **Rebecca.** Upon the petition of Charles Henzley, her stepfather, the Court appointed Abraham Carter to be her guardian, Dec. 19, 1752. Upon her own petition Joseph Cloud was appointed her guardian June 17, 1760. Her further history unknown.

Children of Joseph Dutton (No. 12,) and Elizabeth Smith.

51. **Mary.**

52. **Jacob,** millwright, m. Jane Bishop, and resided in Brandywine hundred, Del., where he died Aug. 31, 1791, in his 41st year. Jane died Aug. 24, 1828, in her 75th year. She was the daughter of Thomas and Margaret Bishop of Upper Providence.

53. **James.** 54. **Susanna.** 55. **Hannah.** 56. **Elizabeth.**

57. **Joseph,** b. Aug. 1763; m. Mary Davis who was born April 17, 1764,and died Mar. 15,1847. He was a millwright and lived in Brandywine hundred, where he died May 1827, aged 63 y. 8 m. 19 d.

The above children are mentioned in their father's will, but the records of some of them are wanting.

Children of Robert Dutton (No. 13,) and —— ——.

58. **Susanna.** 59. **Hannah.** John Crosby of Ridley in his will, dated Sept. 22, 1750, and proven Oct. 15, 1750, mentions his cousins (nieces?) Susanna and Hannah, daughters of Robert Dutton, which is all that is known of them.

Children of James Dutton (No. 14,) and Hannah ——

60. **John,** died July 5, 1799, aged 48 years; probably unmarried.

61. James, resided in Philadelphia on Front Street just above Coates, during the latter part of his life. It is not known that he was ever married. His death occurred Jan. 8, 1813, and in his will, dated Nov. 26, 1812, he devised £200 in trust to keep in repair the wall &c. of the Coates burying ground, where his father, mother, brother John, and aunt Sarah Evans had been buried, and where he wished to be buried. He also directed his executors to place a large stone across all their graves, with dates of births and deaths as in his old bible. This burying ground is now covered with buildings; the bodies having been removed several years ago to South Laurel Hill Cemetery. The inscriptions on the stones were copied into a book, but the Dutton stone was broken and not preserved. James Dutton also devised money to the guardians of the poor of the township of Northern Liberties;—the interest to be applied yearly to the benefit of the poor. This legacy is still in existence. His principal legatees were Maybury, Stephen and Nathan Witman.

Children of Isaac Dutton (No. 15,) and Mary Coates.

62. Elizabeth, probably died young or unmarried.

63. Sarah, m. April 30, 1778 to Peter Browne, and died Nov. 3, 1800, in the 57th year of her age. Her husband was born Sept. 1751, and died Dec. 1810. They were both interred in the Coates burying ground, and a stone erected by her husband sets forth her many virtues, but this is all that is known of her family.

Children of John Dutton (No. 18,) and Elizabeth Dunlap.

64. John. 65. Elizabeth, m. Thomas Casey of Lower Chichester, blacksmith. 66. **Mary. 67. Samuel,** "cordwainer," was living in 1767. No descendants of the foregoing have been obtained.

68. David, it is supposed, married in 1772, Lydia, dau. of Jacob and Ann Sharpless of Middletown; who was born 12 mo. 31, 1754, and died in 1799. She was disowned for her marriage, which was before a magistrate, but in 1781 made an acknowledgment to the meeting, and was again received into membership, with her children Benjamin and Ann.

Children of Richard Dutton (No. 22,) and Mary Martin.

69. Thomas, b. 11 mo. 7, 1734-5; m. Hannah, dau. of Francis and Sarah Routh, who was born 10 mo. 15, 1736. She was probably a niece of Kingsman Dutton's wife. Their marriage was "by a priest," for which they made an acknowledgment to the meeting 9 mo. 10, 1761. Thomas settled on the homestead in Aston, which his father conveyed to him in 1768. In 1765 he was assessed with 100 acres and buildings, 20 acres of woodland, 3 horses, 4 cattle, 8 sheep, and *one servant.* His death occurred 3 mo. 21, 1775.

At the time of the battle of Brandywine, Sept. 11, 1777, Hannah

Dutton was a widow with five children ; of whom the oldest was in his 19th year, and the youngest not yet three. Her son Thomas, then in his ninth year, said that he went to school that morning, but when the booming of the distant cannon was heard from the scene of conflict, the teacher dismissed the scholars, saying, "Go home, children, I can't keep school to-day." A few days after the battle the British army arrived in the neighborhood, and encamped on the hills to the westward ;—a part of the camp being on the Dutton farm. Little Tommy marched boldly up to the camp, and drove the cows home lest they should be killed by the soldiers. An officer noticed him, and thinking no doubt there must be something good to eat where the cows belonged, ordered four soldiers to follow, and accompanied him home. As they walked along, the officer made various inquiries about the family, asking Tommy if his father was a rebel, —whether his older brother had a gun, and what he did with it, &c. Arriving at the house the four soldiers were stationed around it to prevent a surprise from any lurking rebels who might be in the neighborhood, while the officer entered. Hannah Dutton was somewhat alarmed at first, but was assured that the family would not be molested, with the exception that she must produce all the butter, cheese, milk, and other fresh provisions, that she could possibly spare; for all of which the officer paid her, saying, they did not come to rob the people. She remarked that he had but one hand, to which he replied that he had lost the other in Flanders. Before leaving he informed her that the army would probably move from their encampment in a few days, and that she had better bolt and bar every door and window, to keep out the stragglers or camp followers, who, under plea of wishing to get a drink, or light a pipe, would try to gain admittance in order to steal whatever they could lay their hands upon. This timely warning was of use as events proved.

While the army was still encamped here, Thomas Dutton and another boy of the neighborhood strolled into the camp, when some of the soldiers, to tease them, prevented their return for a little time, and told them they were going to shoot the old men of the country, and hung the boys. Thomas thinking he certainly had a friend in the one handed officer, decided in case of trouble to inquire for him.

Hannah Dutton was married a second time 12 mo. 11, 1783, to Thomas Wilson of Chichester. Her death occurred 3 mo. 25, 1825. She was active in meeting affairs, and filled the station of overseer in Chichester meeting.

70. **Hannah**, b. 8 mo. 19, 1736, was married "by a priest," to Jonathan Richards, son of Joseph Richards of Aston. For this she made an acknowledgment to the meeting 10 mo. 3, 1757. She died 11 mo. 30, 1791.

71. **Joseph**, b. 8 mo. 31, 1741 ; d. 5 mo, 1742.

72. **Rebekah,** b. 1 mo. 28, 1743; m. 5 mo. 24, 1764, at Chichester meeting, to Vincent Pilkington, of Wilmington, Del.; son of Thomas and Rose of Middletown (now) Del. Co. Pa. They resided for some time in Wilmington, but afterwards removed to the neighborhood of York, Pa. Vincent died 4 mo. 30, 1813, and his widow on the 6th of the following month. Their descendants not ascertained.

73. **Mary,** b. 7 mo. 11, 1745; m. 6 mo. 26, 1766, at Chichester meeting, to William Booth of Aston, son of Robert. She died 10 mo. 28, 1767, and it does not appear that she left any child. William married again.

74. **Jonathan,** b. 11 mo. 3, 1747-8; m. in 1772, his first cousin, Martha, dau. of John and Alice (Martin) Beeson; for which he was disowned. In 1774 he made an acknowledgment, which was accepted by the meeting. In 1780 he became feoffee in trust of 200 acres of land in Kennett township, originally devised by John Packer for the benefit of the poor of Concord Monthly Meeting. He removed thither, and in 1781 conveyed the land to five persons appointed by the meeting, from whom in turn he took a lease for 999 years. He afterwards disposed of the lease and in 1789 returned to Chichester, where by the will of his father he became possessed of over 200 acres. He died 5 mo. 9, 1820, and his widow, 1 mo. 30, 1830. She was born 5 mo. 25, 1750.

75. **Richard,** b. 1 mo. 14, 1752; d. 4 mo. 21, 1756.

Children of David Dutton (No. 23,) and Jane ———.

76. **Mary,** m. to Jacob Yearsley of Thornbury.

77. **Sarah,** m. to ——— Booth: 78. **Elizabeth,** m. to ——— M'Clellan. The descendants of these three have not been traced, and it is supposed that Sarah and Elizabeth went south.

79. **Lydia,** m. to John Mancil son of William dec. of Newlin township Chester Co.

Children of Elizabeth Dutton (No. 82,) and Joseph England.

80. **Robert,** b. 7 mo. 7, 1743: 81. **William,** b. 8 mo. 22, 1745; d. 9 mo. 23, 1745: 82. **Hannah,** b. 9 mo. 12, 1746. These dates are from the Records of Nottingham Monthly Meeting, and are all that is known of the family.

FIFTH GENERATION.

Children of Isaac Dutton (No. 37,) and Elizabeth Lampley.

83. **Prudence,** m. Feb. 20, 1806, to Charles Cheyney.

84. **Mary,** m. to Joseph Worrall.

85. **Isaac,** m. Nov. 26, 1803, to Susan Price, and resided in Philadelphia, where he died Nov. 22, 1838.

86. **Benjamin,** died young.

87. **Elizabeth,** b. 1781; m. Jan. 5, 1804 to William Hannum of Concord, son of William Hannum. She died Oct. 4, 1824, and he Jan. 13, 1852.

88. **Joseph L.,** b. July 27, 1787; the only surviving one of the family, and now almost blind. He has been a carpenter and builder in Philadelphia where he resides, and has been twice married, but his family have neglected to furnish their records.

89. **Rachel,** m. to Frederick Shull, and they resided at Marcus Hook, where he had charge of the Lazaretto for some years.

Children of Mary Scarlett (No. 40,) and John Cox.

90. **Nathaniel,** the only one whose name has been obtained, was a legatee of his grandfather Nathaniel Scarlett.

Children of John Scarlett (No. 42,) and Mary Dixon.

91. **Hannah,** and 92. **Joseph,** died unmarried.

93. **Sarah,** m. 6 mo. 19, 1806, at Newgarden meeting, to Eli Thompson of White Clay Creek, Del. She died 3 mo. 1, 1859.

94. **Lydia,** m. 12 mo. 24, 1801, at Newgarden meeting, to Ephraim Scarlett of Robinson, Berks Co. Pa., son of William and Susanna (Jackson) Scarlett. She died 12 mo. 20,1843,aged near 72,and he 6 mo. 26, 1850, near 82. William Scarlett was the son of John and Sarah (Humphrey), and grandson of John Scarlett, the settler in Berks Co., who may have been the son of Humphrey Scarlett of Chichester; p. 42.

95. **John,** m. 12 mo. 2, 1801, at Hockessin meeting, to Ann, dau. of John and Susanna (Lamborn) Marshall of Kennett. They resided near Kennett Square. He died 8 mo. 11, 1814. She was born 8 mo. 22, 1778, and died 5 mo. 26, 1862.

96. **Mary,** b. 8 mo. 13, 1774; m. 4 mo. 19, 1798, at Newgarden meeting, to James Thompson of Mill Creek, Del., son of Daniel and Elizabeth. He was born 7 mo. 10, 1768, and died 7 mo. 29, 1846. She died 12 mo. 30, 1840.

97. **Nathaniel,** b. 1779 ; m. 11 mo, 22, 1810, at Londongrove meeting to Lydia, dau. of John and Sarah (Taylor) Baily of E. Marlborough. She died 3 mo. 11, 1850, and he 2 mo. 2, 1863.

98. **Deborah,** d. 2 mo. 10, 1819, aged 38, unmarried.

Children of Hannah Scarlett (No. 43,) and Isaac Baily.

99. **Nathaniel,** b. 12 mo. 18, 1765 : 100. **Eli,** b. 1 m. 18, 1767 ; d. 4 mo. 14, 1807 : 101. **Jesse,** b. 2 mo. 17, 1769 : 102. **Hannah,** b. 9 mo. 3, 1770 ; m. 11 mo. 12, 1794, at Londongrove meeting, to Joshua Baily of Kennett, son of Isaac and Sarah Baily.

103. **Benjamin,** b. 6 mo. 11, 1772 ; m. 4 mo. 27, 1797, at Bradford meeting, to Edith, dau. of Nathan and Amy Cope of East Bradford.

104. **Ellis,** b. 6 mo. 29, 1775 : 105. **Sarah,** b. 2 mo. 8, 1776 : 106. **Deborah,** b. 6 mo, 15, 1777 ; m. 12 mo. 17, 1800, at Londongrove meeting, to Jacob Trego of Honeybrook township, son of William and Rachel.

107. **Mary,** b. 10 mo. 18, 1779 ; m. 1 mo. 14, 1801, at Londongrove meeting, to Abraham Vernon of West Caln, son of Edward and Mary.

108. **Isaac,** b. 8 mo. 26, 1782 ; d. 9 mo. 28, 1827.

These dates are from the meeting records, no information having been furnished by any of the family, and they will not be traced further.

Child of Deborah Scarlett (No. 45,) and Caleb Wiley.

109. **Hannah,** the only one whose name has been obtained, was a legatee of her grandfather Nathaniel Scarlett.

Children of Francis Dutton (No. 48,) and Hannah Talbot.

110. **John T.,** b. 2 mo. 27, 1776 ; m. Mary, dau. of Jacob and Rachel Hewes of Lower Chichester, who was born 7 mo. 1, 1775, and died 5 mo. 9, 1801 ; leaving one child. He married again 8 mo. 9, 1802, Sarah Walter, and died 2 mo. 13, 1805. A child by the second marriage died in infancy.

111. **Joseph,** m. Mary Morris, who was the mother of his children. 2nd wife Joanna Smith. 3rd wife Sarah Mendenhall. He removed from Washington Co. Pa. to Ohio in 1816, and probably resided at Hanoverton until his death, Dec. 26, 1865.

112. **David,** of whom there is no account.

113. **Elisha,** d. 11 mo. 12, 1799, aged about 16.

By second wife, Lydia Booth.

114. **Francis,** cooper, and 115. **Jacob,** farmer, probably resided in the neighborhood of Shepherdstown, Belmont Co. O. It is said there was another child. whose daughter is the wife of John Green of that place, but no particulars received.

Children of David Dutton (No. 40,) and Hannah Rogers.

116. **William,** b. 11 mo. 5, 1780, in Penna; m. in Berkley Co. Va. to Ann Garnet and afterward settled near Uniontown, Fayette Co. Pa.

117. **Susan,** b. 2 mo. 24, 1785, in Penna. ; m. in Berkley Co. Va. to James Cowarden. They removed to Ohio in 1823. He died of cholera in 1834, and she died about 1850, near Harrisville, Ohio.

118. **Mary,** b. 1 mo. 15, 1787, in Berkley Co. ; m. about 1815 to James Larry, and in 1817 they removed to Ohio. She died in Harrisville 1835.

119. **Robert,** b. 9 mo. 2, 1788, in Berkley Co. ; m. 6 mo. 13, 1811, at Harrisville O., to Abigail, dau. of Nehemiah Matson. She died 3 mo. 2, 1831, aged 41, and he married again 10 mo. 2, 1833, Anna, dau. of Ezra and Martha Wharton ; formerly of Bucks Co. Pa. Robert died 4 mo. 20, 1845, after which his widow m. Levi Townsend,and lived with him until her death, 10 mo. 28, 1860, aged 69 yrs. 6 m. Robert was a wagon maker and farmer, and one of the founders of Harrisville : was a Quaker and known as a decided Abolitionist.

120. **Sarah,** b. 1 mo. 20, 1790 ; m. William Matson, and they lived and died at Harrisville, Ohio,

121. **David,** b. 1 mo. 20, 1792; m. in 1816 his first cousin, Mary, dau. of John Rogers of Washington Co. Pa. He continued to reside in Berkley Co. Va. for about three years, when he removed to Washington Co. Pa.,and there died Jan. 1834. When his parents removed from Virginia to Ohio in 1830, they spent the winter with this son on their way.

122. **Hannah,** b. 2 mo. 19, 1793; m. in Va. 1817, to Daniel Hensil, and they removed to Ohio in 1828 : afterward to Griggsville Illinois, where she died in 1858. Daniel still resides there.

123. **Nancy,** b. 2 mo. 18. 1795; m. Josiah Mills and resides near Mt. Pleasant Jefferson Co. O. Her husband died about 1864. No children.

124. **Asa,** living with his sister Nancy, unmarried.

125. **Francis R.,** b. Feb. 20, 1801 in Berkley Co. Va. ; m. Sept. 1822 to Catharine Davis, and in 1834 removed to Harrisville O. : now living at Jerseyville, Illinois.

Children of Jacob Dutton (No. 52,) and Jane Bishop.

126. **Thos. Bishop,** b. Jan. 1, 1776 ; d. Oct. 14, 1777.

127. **Elizabeth,** b. Jan. 19, 1778 ; died Oct. 4, 1783.

128. **Margaret,** born May 18, 1780; m. Joseph Gould, and died Aug. 11, 1820. He died Sept. 1859, in his 76th year.

129. **Jacob,** b. Sep. 3, 1782; married and left children, some of whom live in Brandywine hundred, Del., but their records not obtained.

130. **Joseph,** m. 10 mo. 8, 1818, Jane, widow of Joshua Kirk, and dau. of William and Mary Harvey of Birmingham. She was born 7 mo. 2, 1782, and died 7 mo. 13, 1846. Joseph resided at Wilmington, Del., where he lost his life by the washing away of the Brandywine bridge in a freshet 2 mo. 20, 1822. His body was found 4 mo. 7th, and interred at Chichester meeting.

131. **Jane,** d. 1847, unmarried.

132. **James,** m. Mary Gould and resided in Brandywine hundred, where he died Jan. 9, 1837, and she Oct. 25, 1852, in her 62nd year.

Children of Joseph Dutton (No. 57,) and Mary Davis.

133. **Elizabeth,** b. Aug. 10. 1789; d. Nov. 28, 1865.

134. **Ann,** b. May 2, 1791; m. Edward Carter Johnson, and is deceased. Her children, if any, not ascertained.

135. **Joseph,** b. Jan. 10. 1793; m. Jan. 21, 1819, Ann Bell, who was born Feb. 1, 1800, and died in Milford, Del., Dec. 27, 1862. He died Oct. 20, 1831.

136. **George,** of whom no further account.

137. **Jacob,** b. May 1796; d. in Michigan Mar. 9, 1848; m. Elizabeth Smith and Elmira ——. No further records.

138. **Mary,** b. April 6, 1800; m. Nov. 16, 1828, to Lindsey Pierce, and resides on Concord Road, 9th ward, Wilmington, Del.

139. **Sidney Ann,** b. May 18, 1811; m. Dec. 19, 1833, to James Downing, and resides at 421 E. Third St. Wilmington, Del.

Children of David Dutton (No. 68,) and Lydia Sharpless.

140. **Benjamin,** m. in 1795 Hannah, dau. of Peter and Ann Vickers of Solebury, Bucks Co. Pa., and settled in E. Whiteland, Chester County, Pa.

141. **Anne,** b. 10 mo. 22, 1775; became addicted to the use of opium, and died in Friends' Asylum at Frankford, Pa., 9 mo. 15, 1854, unmarried.

142. **Caleb,** died young or unmarried.

Children of Thomas Dutton (No. 69,) and Hannah Routh.

143. **Richard,** b. 11 mo. 20, 1758; m. 4 mo. 19, 1787, at Chichester meeting, to Margaret, dau. of Isaac and Sarah Larkin of Bethel; who was born 6 mo. 14, 1767, and died 3 mo. 18, 1837. Richard obtained the homestead by purchase from the other heirs of his father, who died intestate, and his grandfather bequeathed some additional land to him. He died 11 mo. 5, 1832.

144. **Sarah,** b. 12 mo. 7, 1760 ; d. 2 mo. 9, 1841 ; m. 11 mo. 19, 1778, at Chichester meeting, to Jacob Hibberd, son of John and Mary of Willistown ; who was born 10 mo. 3, 1752, and died 9 mo. 13, 1827. They resided in Middletown township, Del. Co. Pa.

145. **George,** b. 8 mo. 27, 1763 ; d. 7 mo. 12, 1775.

146. **Mary,** b. 5 mo. 30, 1766 ; d. 11 mo. 6, 1771.

147. **Thomas,** b. 2 mo. 2, 1769 ; d. 9 mo. 12, 1869, having lived to the unusual age of more than a century. He was but little more than six years old when his father died. When about fifteen years of age he obtained a situation with Thomas Marshall of Concord, as an apprentice to the tanning trade. After spending three years at this place, his master, being about to decline the business, took steps to provide another situation for him, and he accordingly went to Daniel Maule's in Radnor to finish his apprenticeship. Three years more being spent at this place he was now of age, and immediately began to make preparations for establishing himself in the tanning business. Finding that he could bring the water of a small rivulet to a favorable site on his grandfather's land in Aston, he obtained permission to build, and accordingly erected a dwelling house, partly of stone and partly of logs ; also a tan house, in the wall of which may be seen a stone bearing the initials T. D., and date 1790.

Being now established in business he was married at Radnor meeting, 11 mo. 24, 1791, to Sarah, daughter of John and Mary Jones of Lower Merion township, with whom he had made acquaintance during the latter part of his apprenticeship. Her father was the son of Robert Jones, and her mother the daughter of William and Ann Rowland.

Richard Dutton of Upper Chichester, now conveyed to his grandson Thomas Dutton of Aston, tanner, two acres of ground on which the latter had erected his buildings, by deed dated 12 mo. 20, 1791 : " in consideration of the natural love and affection which he has and do bear unto his said grandson, Thomas Dutton, and for his better advancement and preferment in this world." Thomas also obtained by the will of this grandfather a considerable tract of land surrounding these two acres, a part of which he continued to hold until his death.

He carried on the tanning business till the fall of 1808, when he was solicited to undertake the management of a farm at Tunessasa in Cattaraugus Co. N. Y., adjoining a Reservation on the Alleghany river, belonging to the Seneca Nation of Indians. This farm had been purchased by Friends of Philadelphia Yearly Meeting, under a concern for the improvement and gradual civilization of the Indians, by giving them instruction in farming, as well as school education. Benjamin Cope had been there for some time, but having lost his wife was now about to relinquish the situation and return to his home in Chester County Pa. Thomas having consented to take his place, sat out in a carriage with his wife and children, and after an arduous journey, much of it through a wilderness, arrived at Tunessasa about the 18th of 10th month. On the way they were sometimes obliged to sleep by a fire in the woods, which, owing to snow and rain, was not always pleasant.

After a four years residence among the Indians they returned to their old home, but owing to the unsettled state of the country, from the breaking out of a war with England, it was thought unadvisable to resume the tanning business at that time. In the Spring of 1813, Thomas took charge of the County Poor-house in Upper Providence, and continued in that situation for four years.

His wife Sarah died 7 mo. 25, 1814, and on the 25th of 12 mo. 1816, he was married again, at West Chester meeting, to Amy, widow of Samuel Trimble, and daughter of Isaac and Hannah (Cope) Pim, deceased, of East Caln township, Chester County. She was the mother of Dr. Isaac P. Trimble, now of Newark, N. J. She was descended from the old and highly respectable family of Pim, who settled in Ireland more than two hundred years ago, and from whence came her great grandfather William Pim, in 1730; who settled in East Caln township. She was born 1 mo. 8, 1785, and died 2 mo. 26, 1825; leaving four children of her second marriage.

In 1817 Thomas Dutton resumed the tanning business, which he carried on with his usual energy for several years. He introduced a steam engine into his works, which is said to have been the first in the County, and various were the speculations throughout the neighborhood as to the feasibility of the experiment.

On the 15th of 11 mo. 1827, he was married a third time, to Mary, dau. of William and Sarah Yarnall of Thornbury. She was born 2 mo. 6, 1782, and died 3 mo. 11, 1857, leaving no children.

Thomas was joined in his business by his son Edmund, but did not continue it after the death of the latter in 1846. Having arrived at the age of seventy seven years he ceased to take an active part in any business, and slowly journeyed down the hill of life, yet not free from the ills and infirmities to which the human family is subject. His hearing became dull, his sight much impaired, and for some time before his death he was unable to walk without assistance, which, however, was partly owing to his corpulence. On the day of the Presidential election in 1868 he was taken to the polls in a carriage, and there deposited his ballot in favor of a brother tanner for the highest office in our government. He remembered hearing the firing of cannon on the occasion of the Declaration of Independence, and would often talk of incidents connected with the Revolutionary War, some of which have been previously mentioned. He voted for George Washington at his second election, and at every Presidential election since, except in 1808, when he was absent from home.

A few weeks before he completed his one hundredth year it was decided to have a meeting of his descendants and relatives to celebrate the anniversary of his birth, and about two days before the event he was asked by some of his family if he had any objections. After a short pause he replied, "I have no objection provided it is orderly conducted, and if so it will be a credit to me, and to you afterward." The writer was requested to prepare an outline of the family history, to be read on the occasion, and thereby unfortunately involved himself to some extent in the labor of its subsequent publication, with such additions as could conveniently be obtained, in the present form. An account of the meeting will be given hereafter. See Appendix.

Thomas Dutton was buried 9 mo. 15, 1869, at Chichester meeting, where doubtless lay his ancestors of three or four generations.

His widowed daughter Susan was his principal care taker during his last years, but we must not forget to mention Sarah Carpenter, who for several years presided over the domestic arrangements, and was as a daughter to the aged patriarch. She possesses the unusual ability to understand conversation by watching the speaker's lips, being deaf herself. Another foster child was Rachel Morrison, who came with the family on their return from Tunessasa, then a little child, and now the wife of Daniel Husted, of West Chester, Pa.

148. **Hannah**, b. 6 mo. 21, 1771; m. 10 mo. 11, 1798, at Chichester meeting, to James Broomall, son of Daniel and Martha (Talbot) Broomall of Thornbury, and uncle to Hon. John M. Broomall of Delaware Co. He died 3 mo. 12, 1838, aged 73 y. 1 mo. 6 d., and was buried at Middletown meeting. She died 3 mo. 2, 1846.

149. **Susanna**, b. 10 mo. 29, 1774; m. 11 mo. 8, 1798, at Chichester meeting, to Andrew Steel, son of Andrew and Mary of Newtown, Del. Co. Pa. She died 6 mo. 18, 1857.

Children of Hannah Dutton (No. 70,) and Jonathan Richards.

150. **Thomas.** 151. **Jehu**, millwright, m. Jan. 31, 1794 to Susanna Worrall, who died Mar. 23, 1814, aged about 45. He died May 31, 1836, in his 73d year.

152. **Jonathan.** 153. **Joseph**, m. June 26, 1806, to Mary Patterson. 154. **Richard**, m. Nov. 24, 1803 to Rachel Paiste. 155. **Josiah**, m. Jan. 4, 1798 to Betsey Vernon. 156. **Lucy**, d. Dec. 7, 1799, unmarried. 157. **Hannah**, m. William Plowman, and died Jan. 24, 1817. 158. **Lydia**, m. Mar. 14, 1797 to William Price. 159. **Dutton**, m. Sept. 3, 1807 to Mary Vernon, and died Feb. 5, 1819. She lives in Baltimore, Md. No records received of the descendants of any of the above except Jehu.

Children of Jonathan Dutton (No. 74,) and Martha Beeson.

160. **Mary**, b. 12 mo. 14, 1772; d. 9 mo. 3, 1777.

161. **John**, b. 8 mo. 16, 1774: m. 5 mo. 19, 1802 to Ann, dau. of Isaac and Esther Pennell of Upper Chichester; who was born 11 mo. 14, 1772, and died 9 mo. 12, 1851. They were both members of Chichester meeting but were married by a magistrate, and conse-

quently disowned. He was a miller on Chester creek where his son Jonathan now lives, in Chester township. He died 3 mo. 19, 1840.

102. **Richard**, b. 8 mo. 12, 1776; m. 5 mo. 22, 1790, at Concord meeting, to Lydia Larkin, dau. of Isaac and Rachel of Bethel; who was born 7 mo. 2, 1777, and died 7 mo. 27, 1840: a half sister to his cousin Richard Dutton's wife Margaret. They resided in Middletown township, where he died 2 mo. 15, 1854.

103. **Alice**, b. 7 mo. 5, 1778; m. 1 mo. 24, 1805, at Chichester meeting, to William Paiste, son of William and Ann of Springfield township; being his second wife. She died 4 mo. 16, 1837.

104. **Lucy**, b. 6 mo. 3, 1780; d. 2 mo. 17, 1782.

105. **Martha**, b. 3 mo. 10, 1782; d. 3 mo. 13, 1803; m. 3 mo. 11, 1802, at Chichester meeting, to Joseph, son of Isaac and Esther Pennell of Upper Chichester. Isaac was the son of Caleb and grandson of John and Mary (Morgan) Pennell of Aston. Joseph died 9 mo. 13, 1812.

106. **Jonathan**, b. 1 mo. 9, 1784: m. 9 mo. 21, 1809, at Chichester meeting, to Rachel, dau. of Nathan and Susanna (Talbot) Pennell of Lower Chichester. Nathan Pennell was descended from Robert Pennell, an early settler in Middletown, through William and James. Rachel was born 2 mo. 26, 1789, and died 8 mo. 3, 1850. Her son Nathan was killed by lightning, and although it was not supposed that she was struck, yet the shock to her system was so great that it terminated her life within an hour. Jonathan resided on a farm in U. Chichester near the S. W. corner of Aston; it being a part of his father's land. He died 7 mo. 27, 1861.

107. **Thomas**, b. 3 mo. 31, 1786; m. 6 mo. 15, 1809, at Chichester meeting, to Susan, dau. of Robert and Susanna (Lukens) Robinson of Upper Chichester; who was born 2 mo. 8, 1787, and died 1 mo. 21, 1870. Thomas was a farmer and resided in U. Chichester on the eastern part of his father's land.

108. **Amor**, b. 7 mo. 19, 1788; d. 10 mo. 10, 1790.

109. **Rebecca**, b. 10 mo. 16, 1790; d. 1 mo. 30, 1857, unmarried.

Children of Lydia Dutton (No. 79,) and John Mancil.

170. **William**, b. 1777; m. Susanna (Worrall) Eyre, who died Mar. 18, 1850, aged 82. He died Oct. 21, 1845.

171. **John**, m. Oct. 8, 1807 to Jane Griswold, and died Oct. 16, 1857, in his 79th year. Jane died Feb. 2, 1857, in her 79th year. He was a farmer and lived in Brandywine hundred, Del., near Talleyville.

172. **Ann**, b. Feb. 17, 1781; m. May 14, 1812 to Daniel Thompson, who was born July 29, 1765, and died July 17, 1847. She died Dec. 22, 1857.

173. **Joseph**, m. Feb. 4, 1805 to Mary Squibb, who died Nov. 12, 1856, in her 74th year, and he died Mar. 30, 1855, in his 82d year.

SIXTH GENERATION.

Child of Prudence Dutton (No. 83,) and Charles Cheyney.

174. **David**, lost his mother in infancy ; is married and living in Bethel township, but his records not obtained.

Children of Mary Dutton (No. 84,) and Joseph Worrall.

175. **Joseph**, living in Del. Co. Pa., and others whose names are not obtained.

Children of Isaac Dutton (No. 85,) and Susan Price.

170. **Samuel P.**, residing on Washington Avenue Philadelphia, has neglected to furnish records of his own or his father's family.

Children of Elizabeth Dutton (No. 87,) and William Hannum.

177. **Isaac D.**, b. 1804; is married and lives in Delaware Co. Pa. 178. **John**, b. 1806; died young. 179. **Ruth E.**, b. 2 mo. 2, 1808; m. Samuel H. Bennett, son of James and Hannah, and died 6 mo. 24, 1838. 180. **John**, b. 1809. 181. **Samuel E.**, b. 1811. 182. **Elizabeth**, b. 6 mo. 2, 1813; d. 2. mo. 7, 1840; was the second wife of Samuel H. Bennett, who lives in Columbiana Co. O. 183. **Evalina**, b. 1815. 184. **Jane**, b. 1817. 185. **William**, b. 1819; is married and living in Concord township. 186. **Philip E.** 187. **Rachel.** 188. **Joseph D.**, b. 1824; d. 12 mo. 15, 1824. No further records received of this family.

John Hannum was a settler in Concord as early as 1688, and perhaps earlier. His wife Margery was the daughter of Robert Southery, who was one of the first purchasers of land from William Penn. They had children, *James*, who died unmarried 1717; *Robert, George, John; Mary* m. to Thomas Smith ; *Elizabeth*, m. to Thomas Brown ; *Margery*, m. to Anthony Baldwin ; *Ann*, m. to John Way ; *Sarah*, m. to Jacob Way. The father died in 1730 and the mother about 1742.

The son John married Mary Gibbons in 1731, but she is not known to have left children, and he married again in 1741 Jane Neild ; see page 34. He had sons William, John and James, and some daughters. William was the father of *William*, who married Elizabeth Dutton ; *Samuel*, who married Susan Pennell ; *John, Joseph, Aaron, Evan, Norris, Elizabeth* and *Jane.*

Children of Rachel Dutton (No. 89,) and Frederick Shull.

It is said that two sons went west some years ago, and that a daughter married George Churchman, and lives near Wilmington, Del., but no particulars have been obtained.

Child of Sarah Scarlett (No. 93,) and Eli Thompson.

189. **Mary,** b. 5 mo. 15, 1810; m. 10 mo. 11, 1827, to Jeremiah Starr of Newgarden, son of Jeremiah and Ann. He was born 7 mo. 5, 1798, and they reside in Newgarden township, Chester Co. Pa.

Children of Lydia (No. 94,) and Ephraim Scarlett.

190. **James,** b. 10 mo., 6 1802; m. Sarah, dau. of Enos and Lydia Morris of Robeson, Berks Co. Pa. She died 9 mo. 14, 1848, and he married a second wife Matilda Kurtz. Address, Geiger's Mills, Berks Co. No children.

191. **William,** b. 2 mo. 21, 1804; m. Justina, daughter of Henry and Catharine Warren of Robeson, and they both died in 1850.

192. **Mary,** b. 8 mo. 28, 1805; m. Isaac Dickinson, son of Isaac and Mary of Robeson. He died 4 mo. 1848, and she 7 mo. 7, 1861.

193. **John,** b. 3 mo. 15, 1807; m. 4 mo. 2, 1840, to Catherine S., dau. of John and Elizabeth M. James of Reading, Pa. They removed from Robeson to West Chester, Pa., 1870.

194. **Ephraim,** b. 1 mo. 30, 1809; m. Sarah Lee of Oley, Berks Co. Address, Scarlett's Mill, Berks Co. Pa.

195. **Susanna,** b. 6 mo. 29, 1814; m. Levi, son of Jacob and Susan Miller of Robeson, and died 5 mo. 28, 1854. He is also deceased.

Children of John Scarlett, (No. 95,) and Ann Marshall.

196. **Susanna,** b. 11 mo. 18, 1802; m. 1870 to Cyrus Chambers of Kennet Square, Pa., son of William and Susanna.

197. **Mary,** b. 10 mo. 26, 1804; m. 12 mo. 16, 1830, at Kennett Square meeting, to Samuel Way of Kennett, son of John and Hannah. They settled in West Chester, Pa., where they still reside.

198. **Martha,** b. 11 mo. 26, 1806; m. 11 mo. 13, 1828. at Kennett Square, to Caleb Heald of Mill Creek, Del., son of Joseph and Hannah. They live near Hockessin meeting, Del.

199. **Marshall,** b. 10 mo. 4, 1809; d. 12 mo. 21, 1843, unmarried.

200. **John,** b. 9 mo. 29, 1811; unmarried.

201. **Ann,** b. 7 mo. 24, 1814; m. 10 mo. 19, 1842, at her mother's, to Enoch Passmore of Kennett, son of James and Martha. They reside in Kennett Square.

Children of Mary Scarlett (No. 96,) and James Thompson.

202. **Hannah,** b. 2. mo. 2, 1799; m. 5 mo. 15, 1817, at Newgarden meeting, to John P. Chambers of Kennett, son of William and Susanna (Pusey) Chambers. He was born 10 mo. 28, 1798, and died 12 mo. 21, 1870.

203. **Mary,** b. 8 mo. 14, 1801; d. 6 mo. 21, 1805.

204. **Elizabeth**, b. 4 mo. 7, 1803; d. 5 mo. 28, 1820, unmarried.

205. **John**, b. 2 mo. 4, 1806; unmarried.

206. **Mary D.**, b. 4 mo. 12, 1808; m. 11 mo. 17, 1825, at Newgarden meeting, to James M. Hughes of Londongrove, son of Samuel and Lydia. He was born 1 mo. 12, 1795. They resided for several years in West Chester, Pa., but he is now living with his brother Jesse in Londongrove township. She is deceased.

207. **Sarah**, b. 5 mo. 5, 1811; m. 11 mo. 14, 1833, at Newgarden meeting, to William Johnson, son of Joshua and Ann of Mill Creek, Del. She is deceased and he resides at Toughkenamon, Newgarden township.

Children of Nathaniel Scarlett (No. 97,) and Lydia Baily.

208. **Sarah**, b. 9 mo. 15, 1811; m. 11 mo. 25, 1841, at Kennett Square meeting, to William Johnson (above) then of West Marlborough township. She has no children.

209. **Mary**, b. 1 mo. 23, 1813; m. 4 mo. 17, 1851, at her father's, to Ellis P. Marshall of Concord, Del. Co., son of Samuel and Philena (Pusey) Marshall. She died 2 mo. 22, 1852.

210. **Abiah**, b. 8 mo. 5, 1816; m. Sarah D., dau. of John P. and Elizabeth Hoopes of Londongrove, who was born 12 mo. 20, 1822. They reside in Newgarden township, near Kennett Square.

211. **Deborah**, b. 12 mo. 19, 1820; d. 5 mo. 14, 1856; m. 11 mo. 12, 1840, at Kennett Square, to Jasper C. Way of Pennsbury, son of Moses and Susanna.

- 212. **Ann**, b. 9 mo. 20, 1822; d. 11 mo. 27, 1866; m. 11 mo. 18, 1847, at her father's, to Elias Hicks of Londongrove, son of Thomas and Amy.

213. **Joel**, b. 6 mo. 24, 1828; m. 2 mo. 15, 1855, at her father's, to Anna, dau. of William and Ruthanna Chandler of Newgarden. She was born 10 mo. 26, 1829, and died 6 mo. 15, 1857. He was married again 2 mo. 18, 1864, at her father's, to Jane, dau. of John and Phebe Richards of Newgarden. She was born 1 mo. 20, 1834. They reside in Kennett township, west of Kennett Square.

Child of John T. Dutton (No. 110,) and Mary Hewes.

214. **Jacob**, b. 7 mo. 7, 1800; left an orphan when quite young, and taken by his father's uncle John Talbot, a wealthy member of Chichester meeting, who raised him until old enough to learn a trade. He was married 3 mo. 6, 1822, to Susan, dau. of James and Sarah Mendenhall. She was born 4 mo. 16, 1803. They now reside at No. 743, St. Clair Street, Cleveland, O.

Children of Joseph Dutton (No. 111,) and Mary Morris:

215. **Elisha.** 216. **Hannah.** 217. **Maria.** 218. **Sarah.** 219. **Eliza.** 220. **Phebe.** 221. **Matilda.** 222. **Deborah.** 223. **David.**

These have all been married, but three of them are deceased. Elisha and David live at the homestead near Hanoverton, O. Those who might have furnished the records of the family have neglected to do so.

Children of William Dutton (No. 116,) and Ann Garnet.

224. **John.** 225. **Martin,** and eleven others whose records have not been obtained. John is supposed to be living near Uniontown, Pa.

Children of Susan Dutton (No. 117,) and James Cowarden.

226. **Samuel,** supposed to be living near St. Louis, Mo., and 227. **David,** in Wheeling, W. Va. Two others whose names are unknown.

Children of Mary Dutton, (No. 118,) and James Larry, (or Lawry.)

228. **Louisa,** m. —— Rhodes, and went to Henderson, Ky. 229. **David,** and 230, **Robert,** supposed to be in Frankford, Ky. The names of five other sons and three daughters have not been obtained.

Children of Robert Dutton (No. 119,) and Abigail Matson.

231. **William,** b. 1 mo. 9, 1813 ; m. Jan. 13, 1840, to Sarah Elizabeth Matson : is a silversmith at Chester Hill, Morgan Co., O.

232. **David,** b. 12 mo. 14, 1814 ; m. 8 mo. 8, 1839, to Huldah, dau. of John and Albina Strode, who removed from Chester Co., Pa., to Ohio about 1820. She was born 8 mo. 24, 1815. They resided at Harrisville, O. until 1858, except one year in northern Illinois, and then removed to Richland, Keokuk Co. Iowa, where they now reside. He is a farmer.

233. **Rachel M.,** b. 11 mo. 3, 1817 ; m. May 23, 1839, to Levi Beck of Harrisville, O., blacksmith, and member of the M. E Church.

234. **John,** b. 5 mo. 1, 1820 ; d. 12 mo. 5, 1833.

235. **Hannah,** b. 3 mo. 3, 1822 ; d. 8 mo. 24, 1839.

236. **Rees,** b. 1 mo. 28, 1825 ; a wagon maker and unmarried.

237. **Robert,** b. 3 mo. 10, 1827 ; m. 1st Alcinda, dau. of Uriah Matson (No. 243,). 2nd wife Eliza Jane Henshaw, who died in 1857, leaving one child who died soon after. 3rd wife Eliza Jane Saylor. Robert lives on Long Run in Jefferson Co. O., and is a coal miner.

238. **Nehemiah,** b. 12 mo. 27, 1830 ; m. Phebe Huntsman ; is a blacksmith and living near Mt. Pleasant, Jefferson Co., O. His family records not obtained.

By second wife, Anna Wharton.

239. **Martha A.,** b. 12 mo. 22, 1834 ; d. 1 mo. 16, 1852, unmarried.

240. **Cynthia**, b. 2 mo. 14, 1837; is married and living in Tuscarawas Co. O. Her husband follows the occupations of wagon making and farming.

241. **Ezra**, b. 1 mo. 7, 1839; m. Philena Hartly and lives near Alliance, O

242. **Hannah**, b. 12 mo. 15, 1840; is married and living near Harrisville, O. Her husband is a cooper but farms some.

Children of Sarah Dutton (No. 120,) and William Matson.

There were ten of these and all are now deceased. The names of but three have been furnished, the others not having left any issue.

243. **Uriah**, the eldest child lived at Harrisville, O.

244. **Elizabeth**, second child, m. to Robert Wade of Harrisville.

245. **Morris**, eighth child, left one son.

Children of David Dutton (No. 121,) and Mary Rogers.

246. **Victoria**, m. in. 1840 to Isaiah Linton, civil engineer, and died four years after, leaving one daughter whose name is not obtained.

247. **John Rogers**, settled in Brownsville, Pa., in 1845, and engaged in the mercantile business, which he still continues. He was married Sept. 8, 1847, to Sarah A. Crider, a niece of Robert Rogers, Esq. of Brownsville.

248. **Isabel M.**, m. in 1841 Isaac N. Cleaver, who died in 1864, leaving six children whose names are not given.

249. **Franklin**, m. Susan Shuman of Brownsville in 1846, and died in 1861 in California, leaving a widow and four children whose names are not obtained.

250. **Thomas L.**, and 251. **Hannah Jane**, of whom there is no further account.

Children of Hannah Dutton (No. 122,) and Daniel Hensil.

252. **Sarah A.**, m. —— Downing, and lives at Griggsville, Illinois.

253. **Robert F.** 254. **David.** 255. **Rebecca.** 256. **Louisa.** The following are deceased: 257. **Mary.** 258. **Hester.** 259. **Susan.** 260. **Almy.** 261. **Elizabeth.** No further records obtained.

Children of Francis R. Dutton (No. 125,) and Catharine Davis.

262. **Sarah V.**, b. Oct. 23, 1823; m. in Belmont Co. O. 1849, to John Patton, who died in 1864.

263. **Franklin A.**, b. Oct. 23, 1824; m. in Wheeling, W. Va., 1850, to Mary E. Florence, and removed to Illinois the same year; now living at Jerseyville.

264. **Julia A.**, b. Feb. 22, 1826; m. in 1845 to Rev. L. M'Guire, and died at Martinsville. O. in 1850. No children.

265. **Effinety Ann**, b. Sept. 24, 1827; m. 1845 to William Smith, who died in 1848. She lives at Jerseyville.

266. **Joseph D.**, b. April 9, 1829; d. in Martinsville, O. 1849.

267. **Mary J.,** b. Oct. 21, 1830; m. May, 1849, to Harvey Pratt of Zanesville, O., now of Delavan, Ill. She died in 1854 when on a visit to her father; had one child who died at Delavan, aged about six years.

268. **Hannah,** b. Mar. 31, 1832; m. in 1851 to Francis Peverly, and they removed to Whitehall Ill.; thence to Iowa in 1863. He died in 1866.

269. **Catharine M.,** b. Oct. 5, 1833; m. in 1852 to George W. Gurd, and they lived at Shanesville, O. till 1864; thence to Jerseyville, Ill., where she died Sept. 12, 1869. They had eight children, of whom five are living with their father in Jerseyville.

270. **Harriet A.,** b. Jan. 1, 1836, in Harrison Co. O.; m. in 1853, to Wesley Brown and they removed to Pike Co. Ill., where she died in 1867. They had ten children, of whom eight live in Milton, Ill.

271. **James W.,** b. Nov. 29, 1838, in Jefferson Co. O.; went to Delavan, Ill., in 1858, and was married there to Alice, dau. of Uriah Parke of Zanesville, O.; moved to Jerseyville, Ill. 1864, but now living at Kane, Green Co., Ill.

272. **Maria H.,** b. May 22, 1840 in Jefferson Co., O.; m. in 1861 to Louis Smallwood, and now living at Steubenville, O., with three children.

273. **David D.,** b. April 10, 1842 in Belmont Co. O.; enlisted in the army in 1862 and was in the battles of Perryville, Franklin and Chickamauga : wounded in the leg and went home to Jerseyville on furlough : returned to the army at Chattanooga and was in the principal battles until the taking of Atlanta : marched through with Sherman to the sea, and died at Savannah, Feb 5, 1865, with typhoid fever.

Two other children died in infancy.

Children of Margaret Dutton (No. 128,) and Joseph Gould.

274. **Rachel,** b. about 1806 : m. Dec. 1830 to William Campbell. and died June 6, 1836. No further records.

275. **Jane,** m. James Campbell and is deceased.

276. **Elizabeth,** m. Aug. 23, 1834 to Granville Crosley, and 2nd to Richard Cox ; died Aug. 1848. No further records.

277. **Joseph,** b. Oct. 2, 1812 ; m. April 2, 1835 to Mary, dau. of Joshua and Ann Hutton, who was born May 1, 1819. He is a butcher and resides at 4th and Poplar Streets, Wilmington, Del.

278. **Samuel,** d. Sept. 1859, aged about 40 yrs.

279. **Jacob D.,** b. about 1820 ; d· June 25, 1843, unmarried.

280. **Mary,** living, unmarried.

Children of Joseph Dutton (No. 130,) and Jane Harvey.

281. **Margaretta B.,** b. 7 mo. 30, 1819 : d. 8 mo. 30, 1843 ; buried at Center meeting, Del., unmarried.

282. **Elizabeth Jane,** b. 6 mo. 4, 1822; m. in 1842 to John H.

Walter son of John and Rebecca, who was born 7 mo· 30, 1819. He is a miller and lives in Birmingham, Del, Co. Pa., near Chadd's Ford.

Children of James Dutton (No. 132,) and Mary Gould.

283. **Ethan Gould,** m. Sept. 17, 1831 to Martha Bullock : is a wheelwright but now engaged in building cars. Residence 211, Poplar St., Wilmington, Del.

284. **Margaret E.,** b. Dec. 20. 1814 ; m. Jan. 31, 1831 to Hiram Tulley, wheelwright. Residence 223, Poplar St., Wilmington.

285. **Jacob,** m. Sarah Cuddington and is deceased. His children supposed to live in Ohio.

286. **Susan Jane,** b. Mar. 11, 1818 ; m. Mar. 17, 1836 to John· Foulk, farmer, of Brandywine hundred, Del.; who was born Dec. 20, 1816, and died April 7, 1864.

287. **Hicklen Gould,** m. Jane Cuddington, and died May 13, 1852, in his 32nd year. His children, if any, supposed to live in Ohio.

288. **James Barnard,** m. Angerett Glasby, and a second time June 5, 1856 to Harriet Shaw. He died Nov. 13, 1864, in his 42nd year.

289. **Thomas Bishop,** d. Oct. 9, 1839, in his 17th year.

290. **Rachel Ann,** b. July 19, 1825 ; m. July 3, 1851 to Frederick Bowker, ship joiner, and they reside on Second St. and Concord Avenue, Chester, Pa.

291. **Mary Ellen,** b. July 29, 1827 ; m. May 4, 1866 to Olof Crohan and resides on French Street, Wilmington, Del. No children.

Children of Joseph Dutton (No. 135,) and Ann Bell.

292. **George,** b. Oct. 23, 1819 ; d. June 7, 1822.

293. **Elizabeth Bell,** b. Dec. 28, 1824 ; m. April 22, 1841 to James Henry M'Colley. He was a government officer on the Pacific coast for eight years, and at the time of his death, April 17, 1869, was U. S. Consul at Callao, Peru ; to which station he was appointed by President Lincoln. He died at Lima of yellow fever, and his remains were brought to Milford, Del., and interred there Nov. 26, 1869.

Children of Mary Dutton (No. 138,) and Lindsey Pierce.

294. **Emeline H.,** b. Dec. 2, 1829 ; m. Lewis Bullock.

295. **Edgar C.,** b. Sept. 8, 1831 ; m. Mary Ann Hill, and resides in Wilmington, Del.

296. **Mary Matilda,** b. Mar. 12, 1833 : m. William Lane, and lives on Adams Street, Wilmington.

297. **Sidney Ann,** b. Aug· 5, 1835 ; d. Nov. 1835.

298. **Lindsey Lewis,** b. Mar. 8, 1839 : m. Margaret Jane Pyle.

299. **John Tyler,** b. April 22, 1843.

Children of Sidney Ann Dutton (No. 139,) *and James Downing.*

300. **Mary Emma,** b. Oct. 30, 1834 ; d. July 23, 1837.
301. **Elizabeth Julia,** b. Aug. 20, 1836 ; d. Feb. 6, 1840.
302. **James Nelson,** b. Mar. 1, 1839 ; m. April 28, 1862 to Elizabeth Neely, and lives at 421 E. Third St., Wilmington, Del.
303. **Edward J.,** b. Dec. 29, 1842 ; d. Aug. 3, 1854.
304. **William S.,** b. Mar. 7, 1847 ; m. June 18, 1867 to Mary Charlotta Wilson, and lives at No. 11 Quarry St., Philadelphia, Pa. : is a steamboat engineer.
305. **Charles W.,** b. Nov. 21, 1850 ; d. Feb. 5, 1853.

Children of Benjamin Dutton (No. 140,) *and Hannah Vickers.*

306. **William J.** 307. **Benjamin V.** 308. **Hannah,** died young. *See Sharpless Family Record,* 1810.

Children of Richard Dutton (No. 143,) *and Margaret Larkin.*

309. **Sarah,** b. 2 mo. 18, 1788 ; d. 9 mo. 11, 1819, unmarried.
310. **Thomas,** b. 9 mo. 5, 1790 ; m. Hannah Cotman of Philadelphia, where they resided.   He died 3 mo. 26, 1827 and was buried at Chichester meeting. She died 12 mo. 25, 1836 and was buried at Holmesburg. ·
311. **Isaac,** b. 7 mo. 22, 1792 ; m. Jan. 14, 1817, in Philadelphia, to Catharine, dau. of Lewis and Catharine Taylor, who was born April 19, 1797. They resided in Philadelphia, where Isaac died Feb. 26, 1829, and was buried at Christ Church burying ground.   His widow survives.
312. **Richard,** b. 7 mo. 1, 1790 ; studied medicine, and died at sea 9 mo. 16, 1829, unmarried.   His body was brought home in spirits and interred at Chichester 10 mo. 29, 1829.
313. **Larkin,** b. 5 mo. 15, 1798 ; d. 5 mo. 10, 1837 and was buried at Chichester : m. 11 mo. 30, 1819 to Maria Norris, who died 3 mo. 15, 1825, and he was married again 2 mo 21, 1828 to Ann, dau. of Simeon and Elizabeth Matlack of Radnor.   He lived in Aston, and died in the house which was said to have been built by the first Thomas Dutton.   His widow resides near Concordville, Del. Co., Pa.
314. **John Brinton,** b. 7 mo. 12, 1806 ; d. 6 mo. 20, 1848, unmarried.

´ *Children of Sarah Dutton (No.* 144,) *and Jacob Hibberd.*

315. **Mary,** b. 7 mo. 17, 1779 ; died unmarried.
316. **Hannah,** b. 1 mo. 9, 1781 ; m. 4 mo. 19, 1817, to Israel Lobb of Upper Darby, Del. Co., and is deceased.
317. **John,** b. 1 mo. 4, 1783 ; m. 5 mo. 16, 1810 to Amy (Lobb) Thomas, who died 4 mo. 19, 1836,   Second marriage 11 mo. 28, 1839, to Rebecca, dau. of George and Elizabeth Maris of Pikeland, Chester County.   She was born 12 mo. 13, 1804, and died 3 mo. 24, 1845.   He died in Nether Providence township, Del. Co. Pa.

318. **Thomas,** b. 10 mo. 14, 1785; m. 4 mo. 12, 1820, at Chester meeting, to Margaret, dau. of John and Amelia Powell of Chester; who was born 9 mo. 14, 1790, and died 2 mo. 5. 1853. He is also deceased.

319. **Jacob,** b. 1 mo. 11, 1787; m. Hannah Baker, and removed to Ohio.

320. **Phinehas,** b. 12 mo. 11, 1792: d. 8 mo. 24, 1808.

321. **Phebe,** b. 9 mo. 12, 1794; d. 5 m. 20, 1808.

322. **Samuel,** b. 1 mo. 8, 1797; m. 1 mo. 1, 1829, at Middletown meeting, to Lydia, dau. of Jesse and Elizabeth Reece of Upper Providence. They resided in Middletown.

323. **Jesse,** b. 10 mo. 10, 1801; d. 8 mo. 28, 1808.

324. **Susanna M.,** b. 9 mo. 27, 1803; d. 12 mo. 4, 1851; m. 5 mo. 3, 1827, at Middletown meeting, to Levi Cox of Willistown, son of William and Lydia. He was born 11 mo. 8, 1795; now deceased.

325. **Sarah D.,** b. 9 mo. 27, 1808; m. 4 mo. 7, 1825, at Middletown meeting, to Maris Hall of Willistown, son of John and Susanna. He was born 9 mo. 20, 1794, and died 12 mo. 1, 1805. Sarah resides in Willistown township.

326. **Abraham,** b. 6 mo. 21, 1806; d. 1 mo. 25, 1807.

Children of Thomas Dutton (No. 147,) and Sarah Jones.

327. **Hannah,** b. 2 mo. 20, 1793; d. 4 mo. 10, 1794.

328. **Susanna,** b. 4 mo. 2, 1795; m. 11 mo. 3, 1815, at Providence meeting, to Isaac Powell of Nether Providence, son of John and Amelia of Chester. He was born 10 mo. 4, 1789, and died 11 mo. 20, 1835. She now resides in West Chester, Pa:

329. **John,** b. 2 mo. 23, 1797; went south on account of his health and died with consumption at Savannah, Ga., 2 mo. 3, 1822, unmarried.

330. **Rowland,** b. 2 mo, 4, 1799: d. 9 mo. 5, 1820, unmarried.

331. **Thomas,** b. 1 mo. 7, 1803; d. 4 mo. 6, 1849; settled in Burlington, N. J., and followed the mercantile business: m. 10 mo. 10, 1828 Hannah E., dau. of William and Mary Ridgway, who died 2 mo. 17, 1837, and he married again 4 mo. 1840 Elizabeth, dau. of Charles Spencer. She was born 7 mo. 15, 1812, and now living at Burlington.

332. **Edmund,** b. 4 mo. 12, 1805; d. 2 mo. 12, 1846; m. 11 mo. 20, 1828 to Tacy, dau. of Simeon and Elizabeth Matlack of Radnor, who was born 2 mo. 8, 1803. He joined his father in the tanning business in Aston.

333. **Mary,** b. 4 mo. 5, 1808; m. 4 mo. 7, 1831, at Chichester meeting, to Jared Darlington of Middletown, Del. Co. Pa., son of Jesse and Amy; who was born 8 mo. 15, 1799, and died 12 mo. 7, 1802. He was a farmer and lived close by the rail road at what is called after him, *Darlington's Station.* Mary now lives in West Chester, Pa.

By second wife, Amy Pim.

334. **Samuel**, b. 11 mo. 16, 1817; m. 9 mo. 16, 1841 to Mary J. Worrall of Middletown, who died 4 mo. 30, 1851. 2nd wife Mary E. Young of West Chester. He resides in Media, Del. Co., Pa. No children.

335. **Nathan C.**, b. 7 mo. 26, 1819; m. 7 mo. 30, 1840 to Maria, dau. of Joshua and Elizabeth Butler of Chester Co., who died 5 mo. 21, 1846. 2nd wife Hannah, dau. of George and Elizabeth Smedley of Middletown, Delaware Co. 3rd wife Anne, dau. of James and Sarah Shearer of Springfield township, Del. Co., where he resides. He is a farmer.

336. **Ruthanna**, b. 3 mo 26, 1822; d. 2 mo. 11, 1847; m. 5 mo. 30, 1844 to Thomas W. Cassin of Providence township, son of Thomas and Rachel, and brother of the late John M. Cassin of Philadelphia. He now resides in Iowa.

337. **Amy Pim**, b. 3 mo. 9, 1824; m. 4 mo. 19, 1848 to John Williamson, who died 1 mo. 10, 1861. She resides at Media, Del. Co. Pa.

Children of Hannah Dutton (No. 148,) and James Broumall.

338. **Thomas D.**, b. 8 mo. 5, 1799; married and left two children.

339. **John**, b. 7 mo 6, 1800; has been married three times.

340. **Abraham**, b. 7 mo. 20, 1801. 341. **Daniel**, b. 6 mo. 23, 1802. 342. **Susanna**, b. 8 mo. 20, 1803; unmarried.

343. **James**, b. 4 mo. 29, 1805; died young. 344. **James**, b. 10 mo. 30, 1806, d. 11 mo. 19, 1825. 345. **Hannah D.**, b. 6 mo. 4, 1813 : m. Eli Baker and is deceased.

Some of these reside in Middletown township Del. Co. Pa., but have neglected to furnish the records of their families·

Children of Susanna Dutton (No. 149,) and Andrew Steel.

346. **Mary**, m. Jesse Horton and William Jones.

347. **Thomas**, d. unmarried. 348. **Hannah**, d. unmarried.

349. **Susanna M.**, m. John Leedom and resides at Norristown, Pa., the only one of the family now living.

850. **Andrew**, m. Margaret Johnson. 351. **Margaretta**, m. John Davis. 352. **Anne**, d. unmarried·

The descendants of this family have not been ascertained.

Children of Jehu Richards (No. 151,) and Susanna Worrall.

353. **Hannah**, b. Sept. 14, 1795; d. Dec. 19, 1864; m. Oct. 1, 1829 to Seth Thomas, who died Jan. 21, 1848, in his 64th year. No children.

354. **Nathaniel**, b. Oct. 23, 1797; m. May 1, 1834 to Jane Giffen, who was born Nov. 14, 1814. He is a millwright, living in Mill Creek Hundred, Del.

855. **Mary Ann**, b. Aug. 14, 1799; m. Nov. 29, 1821 to Joseph Dizer, farmer, who was born Mar. 1, 1792, and died July 28, 1852. She lives at Village Green, Del. Co., Pa.

356. **Lydia**, b. Aug. 26, 1801 ; m. Oct. 10, 1822 to John Slawter, cooper, who died Oct. 29, 1863. She lives in Chester, Pa.

357. **Joseph**, b. Oct. 26, 1803 ; m. in 1830 to Mary Fields, who was born Oct. 3, 1805, and died Nov. 2, 1845. Second marriage Feb. 3, 1866 to Lydia (White) Brady. He is a blacksmith and lives in Ridley township, Del. Co., Pa.

358. **Sarah**, b. Sept. 17, 1805 ; d. Mar. 10, 1848 ; m. Mar. 23, 1838 to Lewis Slawter.

Children of John Dutton (No. 161,) and Ann Pennell.

359. **Mary Ann**, b. 2 mo. 22, 1803 ; d. 4 mo. 18, 1867 ; m. 3 mo. 24, 1831 to Samuel P. Harrison, who died 12 mo. 3, 1860 : both buried at East Caln meeting, Chester Co., Pa.

360. **Elizabeth**, b. 8 mo. 29, 1804 ; m. 3 mo. 13, 1851 to Jethro Johnson, and they live near Village Green, Del. Co. Pa. No children.

361. **Susanna**, b. 10 mo. 29, 1806 ; m. 3 mo. 24, 1831 to Isaac R. Jones, and lives near Sugartown, Chester Co., Pa. No children.

362. **Esther P.**, b. 3 mo. 3, 1808 ; m. 11 mo 29, 1827 to Joseph Pennell Hannum, son of Samuel and Susan,(see page 61). He was born .3 mo. 29, 1801, and died 9 mo. 6, 1860, in East Marlborough, Chester Co. She lives in Wilmington, Del.

363. **Jonathan**, b. 10 mo. 19, 1810 ; m. 4 mo. 30, 1835 to Lydia Ann Fell, who died 5 mo. 11, 1849. Second marriage, 3 mo. 9, 1854 to Lydia Fairlamb. He is a miller and owns the mills on Chester Creek which belonged to his father and grandfather.

364. **Isaac Pennell**, b. 6 mo. 14, 1812 ; m. 9 mo. 23, 1841 to Anna Maria, dau. of Humphrey Johnson of Middletown, Del. Co. Pa.: is a miller and owns mills on Ridley creek, near Sugartown, Chester Co. Pa.

Children of Richard Dutton (No. 162,) and Lydia Larkin.

365. **John**, b. 4 mo. 9, 1800 ; m. 10 mo. 30, 1823 to Lydia Vernon, who was born 1803 and still living. He died 10 mo. 20, 1849 at Buffalo N. Y., and his remains were brought home and buried at Chichester meeting on the 25th.

366. **Ann**, b. 12 mo. 5, 1801 ; d. 3 mo. 6, 1802.

367. **Isaac,** b. 3. mo. 18, 1803 ; d. 1 mo. 12, 1837, unmarried.

368. **Rachel**, b. 8 mo. 20, 1805 ; d. 8 mo. 27, 1835 ; m. 1 mo. 17, 1833 to William H. Grubb, son of Nathaniel Grubb and Elizabeth Hannum ; page 61. He now resides in Wilmington, Del.

369. **Hannah**, b. 5 mo. 23, 1807 ; living at Sugartown Chester Co. Pa., unmarried.

370. **Joseph**, farmer, b. 8 mo. 4, 1810 ; m. 12 mo. 24, 1834 to Sarah, dau. of William and Beulah Thatcher. They live in East Goshen township. Chester Co. Pa.

371. **Martha**, b. 10 mo. 22, 1812 ; d. 9 mo. 24, 1854 ; m. 12 mo. 11, 1834 to Bennett Temple, son of Caleb and Rachel. He and his son keep a store at Thorntonville, Del. Co. Pa.

372. **Jonathan**, b. 7 mo. 16, 1814; m. 2 mo. 13, 1840 to Elizabeth J. Bullock, who died 12 mo. 3, 1848. 2nd marriage, 3 mo. 1860 to Maggie ——. He lives near the Brick Meeting, Cecil Co., Md.

Children of Alice Dutton (No. 163,) and William Paiste.

373. **Jonathan**, b. 10 mo. 23, 1806; m. 2 mo. 14, 1828 to Priscilla Cloud, and died 8 mo. 1, 1852.

· 374. **Sarah**, b. 2 mo. 10, 1809 ; m. 3 mo. 4, 1835, at Chester meeting, to Joseph Priestman Baynes of Wilmington, Del. ; son of John B. and Miriam, formerly of England. They live in Baltimore, Md.

375. **Mary**, b. 5 mo. 12, 1812 ; d. 9 mo. 9, 1812.

Child of Martha Dutton (No. 165,) and Joseph Pennell.

376. **Jonathan**, b. 12 mo. 8, 1802 in Lower Chichester ; m. Nov. 26, 1828 to Sarah Jane Bright of Wilmington, Del., who was born in Salem Co. N. J., Sept. 11, 1810. He was a shoemaker. His widow resides at 1529 Carpenter Street, Philadelphia, Pa.

Children of Jonathan Dutton (No. 166,) and Rachel Pennell

377. **Martha**, b. 3 mo 7, 1811 ; m. 1 mo. 14, 1836, at Chichester meeting, to William West of Chester township, son of Samuel and Mary. They live near Chester, Pa.

378. **Nathan P.**, b, 3 mo. 2, 1813 ; m. 4 mo. 25, 1850 to Sidney Larkin. He was killed by lightning when attending a public sale at Village Green 8 mo. 3, 1850. His widow married again but died soon after. No children.

379. **Susanna**, b. 2 mo. 14, 1815 ; m. 2 mo. 13, 1834 to Mahlon Mancil, (No. 398,) and now living at Chester, Pa.

380. **Hannah H.**, b. 8 mo. 13, 1817 ; m. 4 mo. 3, 1851 to John Valentine, who died 11 mo. 2, 1855, in his 48th year. They lived in Upper Chichester, and she is now with her brother at the homestead.

381. **Gulielma**, b. 2 mo. 20, 1819 ; living at the homestead, un-married.

382. **Sarah**, b. 2 mo 24, 1821 ; d. 5 mo. 10, 1841, unmarried.

383. **Beulah**, b. 3 mo. 31, 1823 ; d. 3 mo. 29, 1830.

384. **Rebecca Ann**, b. 4 mo. 26, 1825 ; m. 5 mo. 26, 1849 to Cloud Elliott, son of Mark and Rachel. They reside at Fairville, Chester County, Pa.

385. **David H.**, b. 1 mo. 8, 1829 ; m. May 15, 1856 to Elizabeth R. Moore, and lives on a part of his father's land in U. Chichester.

386. **William Henry**, b. 7 mo. 12, 1831 ; living at the homestead, unmarried.

Children of Thomas Dutton (No 167,) and Susan Robinson.

387. **Robert R.**, b. 4 mo. 13, 1810; m. 12 mo. 11, 1833 to Ann, dau. of Benjamin and Phebe Bartram. He was elected sheriff of Delaware Co. Pa.. in 1846 : resides in Chester.

388. Aaron L., b. 5 mo. 28, 1813; m. 12 mo. 30, 1847 to Anne G., dau. of Joseph and Elizabeth James of New Jersey. They reside in Chester, Pa.

389. Jesse, b. 3 mo. 28, 1816; m. 5 mo. 31, 1849 to Emily L., dau. of Thomas and Eliza Horne; living in Ridley township, Delaware Co. Pa.

390. Emily, b. 5 mo. 10, 1818; m. 9 mo. 20, 1848 to Garrett Hannum, son of Evan (p. 61,) and Elizabeth of Concord township. Address, Booth's Corners, Del. Co. Pa.

391. Charles, b. 9 mo. 13, 1821; m. 4 mo. 4, 1850 to Hannah H., dau. of Thomas and Eliza Horne, who died 3 mo. 15, 1851. Second marriage 12 mo. 25, 1855 to Jane W., dau. of Joseph H. and Elizabeth Johnson. He resides in Upper Chichester on land which belonged to his ancestors of three generations.

392. Sidney, b. 8 mo. 9, 1824; m. 3 mo. 3, 1853 to Lewis B. Hickman and they live near Brick Meeting, Cecil Co. Md.

393. Susan Ann, b. 4 mo. 13, 1827; m. 3 mo. 14, 1855 to William B. Hannum of Chichester, son of Isaac D. (No. 177).

Children of William Mancil (No. 170,) and Susanna Worrall.

394. Lydia, b. Feb. 21, 1800; d. Oct. 24, 1850; m. Mar. 28, 1822, to Joseph Griffith.

395. Elizabeth, b. Sept. 25, 1803; m. Nov. 15, 1820, to Samuel Vernon, who died June 8, 1869, aged 78 y. 2 m. 22 d. She lives in Chester, Pa.

396. David D., b. Dec. 30, 1804; m. Jan. 7, 1829 to Sarah Hinkson, and they live in Philadelphia, Pa.

397. Susan, b. Jan. 9, 1807; d. July 30, 1846; m. March 29, 1827 to Jesse Griswold. They removed westward, and after her death he married again. He lives at Mecca, Trumbull Co., Ohio.

398. Mahlom, d. May 28, 1845; m. Feb. 13, 1834 to Susanna Dutton, (No. 379,) who now lives at Chester, Pa.

Children of John Mancil (No. 171,) and Jane Griswold.

399. Edward, b. July 3, 1808; d. July 24, 1808.

400. Mary J, b. Feb. 12, 1810; m. Mar. 3, 1828 to Eli Baldwin Talley, and resides near Talleyville, in Brandywine hundred, Del.

401. Ellen, b. July 10, 1812; m. July 14, 1836 to William T. M'Kee, who died Dec. 4, 1851, in his 45th year. She resides in Wilmington, Delaware.

402. Abigail, b. July 31, 1814; m. Jehu Chandler of Beaver Valley, Del., blacksmith, son of Jehu and Lydia.

403. Lydia, b. Dec. 5, 1815; living with her sister Mary, unmarried.

Children of Ann Mancil (No. 172,) and Daniel Thompson.

404. William, b. Feb. 2, 1813; m. Jan. 9, 1838 to Elizabeth Brunner, and Feb. 11, 1847 to Mary Hansell: resides in Chester, Pa.

10

405. **Mary,** b. Oct. 5, 1814; living, unmarried.
406. **Lydia,** died young. 407. **Emeline,** b. Dec. 1818; m. William Peterson and is deceased.
408. **Susan,** died young.

Children of Joseph Manoil (No. 173,) and Mary Squibb.

409. **Hannah,** b. June 8, 1805; m. John Winterbottom. No statement received as to her family. 410. **Jesse,** b. July 12, 1807; d. Aug. 20, 1869. 411. **Ann,** b. July 17, 1810; d. Nov. 11, 1824. 412. **Eliza,** b. May 4, 1812; d. July 22, 1823. 413. **John,** b. Feb. 3, 1815; d. July 21, 1823. 414. **Lydia D.,** b. July 8, 1817; d. Feb. 19, 1859; m. John P. Sager, miller, who resides at Sagerville, (Lenape,) Chester Co. Pa., and has children but no data have been furnished.
415. **Mary S.,** b. Mar. 8, 1820; m. Mar. 10, 1842 to Charles Johnson, farmer, son of Humphrey of Middletown, Del. Co. Pa., where they reside. No records of their family furnished.
416. **Susan,** b. Sept. 25, 1822; d. July 11, 1823. 417. **Joseph,** b. April 13, 1826; m. April 13, 1850 to Anna Mary Mahoney and lives in Wilmington, Del. No children. 418. **William,** b. Oct. 19, 1831; living.

SEVENTH GENERATION.

Children of Isaac D. Hannum (No. 177).

419. **William B.,** the only one whose name has been furnished, married Susan Ann Dutton. See No. 893.

Children of Mary Thompson (No. 189,) and Jeremiah Starr.

420. **Sarah,** m. Robert L. Walter, son of William and Margaret of Kennett township, who was born 10 mo. 23, 1820. They live in Newgarden township, Chester Co. Pa.
421. **Jeremiah,** b. 4 mo. 27, 1830; m. Rebecca, dau. of Jesse and Jane Hallowell, who was born 3 mo. 15, 1830.
422. **Eli,** b. 1mo. 7, 1834; m. Carrie Jefferis.
423. **Anna,** b. 10 mo. 5, 1836; d. 6 mo. 24, 1842.
424. **Samuel,** b. 7 mo. 22, 1839; unmarried. 425. **Mary Anna,** b. 12 mo. 22, 1842; m. William Haines. 426. **Charles T.,** b. 8 mo. 23, 1846.

Children of William Scarlett (No. 191,) and Justina Warren,

427. **Rowland G,,** m. 1871 to —— Seidel, and is living in Philadelphia, Pa. There were several others who are deceased.

Children of Mary Scarlett (No. 192,) and Isaac Dickinson.

428. **Ephraim**, b. 11 mo. 28, 1829; m. Hannah Fries who is deceased. His address, Geiger's Mills, Berks Co., Pa.
429. **Benjamin**, b. 4 mo. 23, 1842; m. Sarah Seifert of Reading, Pa., where she now resides. He died 11 mo. 14, 1869.
430. **Elwood**, b· 6 mo. 30, 1845; m. Hannah Fox. Several other children died young.

Children of John Scarlett (No. 193,) and Catharine James,

431. **Anna Lydia**, b. 9 mo. 8, 1841: d. 5. mo. 17, 1842.
432. **Mary D.**, b. 4 mo. 9, 1843; d. 11 mo. 6, 1869, unmarried.
433. **James Miller**, b. 9 mo. 6, 1847; keeps a Flour and Feed store in West Chester, Pa.; unmarried. 434. **William Penn**, b. 2 mo. 9, 1853; d. 2 mo. 20, 1859.

Children of Ephraim Scarlett (No. 194,) and Sarah Lee.

435. **Lydia Ann**, b. 2 mo. 6, 1835: m. William Harts, son of Elias and Lydia and they reside at Robeson, Berks Co. Pa.
436. **Eli**, b. 10 mo. 1, 1837: m. Margaret, dau. of John and Sidney Peters of Indiana and resides at Ft. Wayne, Ind.
437. **James**, b. 2 mo. 9, 1842; m. Rachel Ann, dau. of John and Elizabeth M. James of Reading, Pa., where they also reside.
438. **Lee**, b. 1 mo. 24, 1850.
The parents have lately removed to Reading.

Children of Susanna Scarlett (No. 195,) and Levi Miller.

439. **Ephraim**, m. Amelia Seifert of Reading where they reside.
340. **Elizabeth**, d. about 1865.

Children of Mary Scarlett (No. 197,) and Samuel Way.

441. **Ann S.**, b. 6 mo. 5, 1832; d. 10 mo. 24, 1848.
442. **Hannah M.**, b. 4 mo. 7, 1834; m. 6 mo. 19, 1861 to John Windle M. D. of Hamorton, Chester Co. Pa.
443. **Susan S.**, b· 2 mo. 23, 1839; d. 8 mo. 14, 1864, unmarried.
444. **Ellen D.**, b. 12 mo. 1, 1841; d. 12 mo. 20, 1868; m. Thomas D. Ingram, son of Wm. Torbert and Elizabeth of East Bradford, Chester Co., Pa. Their child died in infancy.
445. **Marshall S.**, b. 2 mo. 12, 1845; m. Annie Smedley and resides in West Chester, Pa. He is of the firm of Way and Mendenhall, dealers in Lumber and Coal.
446. **Samuel E.**, b. 8 mo. 19, 1849; living in West Chester with his parents.

Children of Martha Scarlett (No. 198,) and Caleb Heald.

447. **John**, b. 10 mo. 18, 1829; d. 7 mo. 21, 1830. 448. **Anna**, b. 4 mo. 30, 1831; d· 7 mo. 28, 1831. 449. **Joseph**, b. 7 mo. 16, 1832; living with his parents, unmarried. 450. **Jacob**, b. 1833; d. 8 mo.

1834.   451. **Hannah M.**, b. 3 mo. 9, 1830; d. 11 mo. 22, 1836.   452.
William, b. 8 mo. 17, 1838; d. 10 mo. 11, 1838.   453. **Mary R.**, b.
10 mo. 1, 1846; living with her parents, unmarried.

Children of Ann Scarlett (No. 201,) and Enoch Passmore.

454. **Elizabeth W.**, b. 1 mo. 20, 1844.   455. **James D.**, b. 12 mo.
11, 1845.

Children of Hannah Thompson (No. 202,) and John P. Chambers.

456. **William**, b. 4 mo, 15, 1818; m. Annie J. Anderson.
457. **Mary**, b. 12 mo. 19, 1819 ; d. 2 mo. 24, 1844, unmarried.
458. **James**, b. 4 mo. 5, 1822 ; m. Amy Thompson who is deceased.
459. **Pusey**, b. 1 mo. 4, 1824; d. 10 mo. 30, 1844.
460. **Edwin**, b. 12 mo. 23, 1825; m. Martha, dau. of Simon and
Sarah Barnard, of West Chester, Pa., and resides in Philadelphia, Pa.
461. **Susanna P.**, b. 3 mo. 1, 1828.   462. **Maris**, b. 3 mo. 9, 1830.
463. **Sarah P.**, b. 1 mo. 5, 1832; d. 3 mo. 19, 1841.
464. **Hannah T.**, b. 3 mo. 30, 1835 ; m. 9 mo. 27, 1854 to Jeremiah
Croasdale of Philadelphia, who is now deceased.
465. **Ruth Ann**, b. 12 mo. 14, 1837 ; m. Davis Huey.
466. **Elizabeth**, b. 1 mo. 6, 1840; d. 7 mo. 11, 1842.
467. **John T.**, b. 3 mo. 11, 1842; m. Alice Jackson.

Children of Mary D. Thompson (No. 206,) and James M. Hughes.

468. **Lydia**, unmarried.   469. **James T.**, d. unmarried.
470. **Henry C.**, died young.   471. **Sallie**, unmarried.
472. **Alfred**, m. —— Maxon.   473. **Mary Emma**, unmarried.

Child of Sarah Thompson (No. 207,) and William Johnson.

474. **Sarah**, m. Edward S. Marshall, son of Samuel and Philena
of Concord, and they live in W. Marlborough, Chester Co. Pa.

Child of Mary Scarlett (209,) and Ellis P. Marshall.

475. **Mary S.**, b. 1 mo. 19, 1852.

Children of Abiah Scarlett (No. 210,) and Sarah D. Hoopes,

476. **Anna Mary**, b. 4 mo. 6, 1845 ; m. Thompson Richards, son
of John and Phebe of Newgarden township, Chester Co., Pa.
477. **William H.**, b. 3 mo. 17, 1848.   478. **Taylor**, b. 2 mo. 3,
1851.   479. **Elizabeth H.**, b. 5 mo. 15, 1852.

Children of Deborah Scarlett (No. 211,) and Jasper C. Way.

480. **Charles C.**, b. 8 mo. 9, 1842.   481. **Nathaniel S.**   482.
George B.   483. **Alfred.**   484. **Francis**, b. 6 mo. 1, 1852.

Children of Ann Scarlett (No. 212,) and Elias Hicks.

485. **Sarah J.**, b. 11 mo. 11, 1848 ; m. William H. Phillips, miller.
486. **Mary B.**, b. 9 mo. 11, 1850 ; m. Eugene P. Mercer of Kennett
Square, Pa.

487. **Lydla S.,** b. 1 mo. 22, 1853 ; d. 10 mo. 15, 1862. 488. **Amle,** b. 7 mo. 19, 1855.

Child of Joel Scarlett (No. 213,) and Anna Chandler.

489. **Mary M.,** b. 1 mo. 20, 1856.

By second wife, Jane Richards.

490. **Annie C.,** b. 1 mo. 20, 1865. 491. **Phebe.**

Children of Jacob Dutton (No. 214,) and Sarah Mendenhall.

492. **Edwin,** b. Feb. 13, 1823 ; m. in 1851 to Elizabeth Clark, and resides at Hanoverton, O.

493. **Mary J.,** b. Jan. 28, 1826; m. May 4, 1843, to Samuel Logue. Second husband Isaac Johnson, and they reside at Marietta, Iowa.

494. **Jonathan P.,** b. Jan. 5, 1830; m. May 25, 1854 to Emeline Glass. Residence, Cleveland, O.

495. **Sallie Ann,** b. Aug. 8, 1832; m. Feb. 27, 1856 to John J. Pettit, and lives at Allegheny City, Pa.

496. **William P.,** b. Feb. 24, 1835 ; m. Mar. 27, 1856 to Almira Carver, and lives at Cleveland, O.

497. **Frank,** b. Dec. 14, 1838; m. Nov. 16, 1865 to Ella Stilman ; d. Nov. 14, 1868. He was in the army during the late war.

Children of Elisha Dutton (No. 215).

498. **Joseph.** 499. **John.** 500. **Emma,** and one deceased.

Child of David Dutton (No. 223).

501. **Josephine.**

Children of William Dutton (No. 231,) and Sarah Elizabeth Matson.

502. **Robert M.,** b. Mar. 15, 1841. 503. **Alice A.,** b. Mar. 1, 1843. 504. **John E.,** b. Feb. 13, 1845. 505. **Mary S.,** b. Nov. 28, 1847. 506. **Benjamin F.,** b. Apr. 24, 1850. 507. **Susan E.,** b. Sept. 20, 1852. 508. **Sarah L.,** b. Mar. 28, 1856. 509. **William H.,** b. June 21, 1859.

Children of David Dutton (No. 232,) and Huldah Strode.

510. **Victoria,** b. Jan. 5; 1841 ; m. Isaac Hutchins, and they live at Fountain, eighty miles south of Denver, where he follows farming and cattle raising. 511. **Sereno,** b. Feb. 4, 1843; m. and has two sons living and one deceased. He was in the 7th Iowa regiment and at the battles of Ft. Donaldson, Pittsburg Landing, Atlanta, and with Sherman to Savannah, near which he was mustered out and returned home. 512. **Robert S.,** b. Feb 13, 1845; living with his parents. 513. **John W.,** b. May 18, 1847 ; d. Sept. 18, 1850. 514. **Nehemiah,** b. Dec. 22, 1849 ; d. Dec. 29, 1849. 515. **Joseph,** b. Jan. 11, 1851. 516. **Mary E.,** b. Aug. 10, 1853. 517. **David,** b. Jan. 13, 1856 ; d. Oct. 31, 1859. 518. **Rachel L.,** b. July 17, 1861.

Children of Rachel M. Dutton (No. 238,) and Levi Beck.

519. **Hannah M.**, b. Feb. 3, 1840; d. July 7, 1854. `520. **Abigail**, b. May 22, 1841; m. Thomas B. Hill and lives at Cadiz, O.; a member of the M. E. Church. She has four children living and one deceased. 521. **George R.**, b. Dec. 8, 1842; m. Maria ——, and has a son and a daughter. 522. **Robert W.**, b. Aug. 2, 1844; m. Martha ——, and has had three daughters, two deceased. He and George were both in the army and now live at Harrisville, O., where they follow marketing and shipping produce: members of the M. E. Church. 523. **Anna**, b. July 24, 1846. 524. **Adazilla**, b. Feb. 11, 1848; m. David Murdock and has a son and a daughter: members of M. E. Church. 525. **Alana Ann**, b. Sept. 31, 1849. 526. **Rachel L.**, b. Dec. 4, 1851; m. George Wilson. 527. **Frances L.**, b. May 29, 1854. 528. **John L.**, b. Oct. 10, 1860.

Children of Robert Dutton (No. 237,) and Alcinda Matson.

529. **Uriah M.**, b. Jan 26, 1852. Another son died in 1854.

By third wife, Eliza Jane Saylor.

530. **Mary Elma**, b. Sept. 3, 1859. 531. **Elmer Ellsworth**, b. April 20, 1861. 532. **James Clement**, b. Mar. 2, 1863. 533. **Cora Maud**, b. Dec. 6, 1864. 534. **Netta Blanch**, b. Oct. 5, 1866. 535. **Elizabeth L.**, b. Nov. 20, 1869.

Children of Uriah Matson (No. 243).

536. **Alcinda**, m. Robert Dutton. See No. 237. 537. **John**, m. and has four children. 538. **Caroline**, unm. 539. **Morris**, d. leaving one daughter. 540. **Robert**, unm. 541. **Amanda**, m. James Clark, and lives in Marshall Co., Iowa.

Children of Elizabeth Matson (No. 244,) and Robert Wade.

542. **Sarah**, unm. 543. **N Allen**, a lawyer living in Butler, Bates Co., Mo., unm. 544. **Rowena**, unm. 545. **Adelaide**, unm. 546. **Martha**, m. and has one child: lives at Harrisville, O. 547. **Genevra**, unm.

Child of Morris Matson, (No. 245).

548. **Morris**, living in Bureau Co., Illinois.

Children of J. Rogers Dutton (No. 247,) and Sarah A. Crider.

549. **Elizabeth R.** 550. **Mary.** 551. **Linton R.**, 552. **Alvin J.** 553. **William S.** 554. **Robert R.** 555. **Blanch.** 556. **Maud.** 557. **Harry.**

Children of Sarah V. Dutton (No. 262,) and John Patton.

558. **Hannah**, m. William Sedwick. 559. **Robert.** 560. **Matthew.** 561. **Jennie.** 562. **Wilson.** 563. **Frank.**

Children of Franklin A. Dutton (No. 263,) and Mary E. Florence.
564. **George.** 565. **Mary Bella,** d. 1868, aged about 11 years.

Child of Effinety Ann Dutton (No. 265,) and William Smith.
566. A daughter, married Edward Reynolds.

Children of James W. Dutton (No. 271,) and Alice Parke.
567. **Maggie.** 568. **Fanny.** 569. **Parke.**

Child of Jane Gould (No. 275,) and James Campbell.
570. **Lorenzo D.,** b. Jan. 23, 1831; m. April 14, 1852 to Rebecca A. Crosgrove, and resides at No. 820 Poplar St., Wilmington, Del.

Children of Joseph Gould (No. 277,) and Mary Hutton.
571. **Bennett,** b. Nov. 17, 1836; d. Nov. 18, 1836. 572. **Margaret Ann,** b. June 23, 1838; d. Mar. 23, 1839. 573. **Joseph Harrison,** b. May 17, 1840; m. April 2, 1862 to Lottie, dau. of David and Elizabeth Shaw, and resides on West St., Wilmington, Del. 574. **Pierce,** b. May 15, 1843; m. Jan. 8, 1868 to Elizabeth, dau. of John and Elizabeth Barber, and resides on E. Third St., Wilmington. 575. **Adaline Chandler,** b. April 9, 1846; d. Jan. 6, 1851. 576. **Joshua,** b. Aug. 22, 1849; d. Aug. 24, 1863. 577. **Lola M.,** b. May 25, 1858.

Children of Elizabeth Jane Dutton (No. 282,) and John H. Walter.
578. **William H.,** b. Oct. 14, 1842. 579. **Townsend H.,** b. Oct. 18, 1843. 580. **Joseph D.,** b. Aug. 25, 1845. 581. **Samuel M.,** b. Sept. 9, 1847; d. Jan. 29, 1848. 582. **Thomas C. L.,** b. Oct. 27, 1849; d. Dec. 28, 1849. 583. **Granville W.,** b. April 15, 1851. 584. **Edwin P.,** b. May 14, 1854. 585. **Abby Rebecca,** b. Aug. 22, 1857. 586. **Mary Ann,** b. April 23, 1859. 587. **Evans,** b. Feb. 3, 1863. 588. **Edith W.,** b. April 22, 1867.

Children of Ethan G. Dutton (No. 283,) and Martha Bullock.
589. **Jacob J.,** b. Jan. 10, 1833; m. Eliza M'Cracken, and is Superintendent of the banks on League Island below Philadelphia. 590. **John F.,** b. Aug. 15, 1835; d. Sept. 5, 1835. 591. **Sarah Elizabeth,** b. Oct. 30, 1836; m. Jan. 14, 1858 to William Leonard Bowers, and they reside in Wilmington, Del. 592. **Mary Jane,** b. Aug. 25, 1839; d. Aug. 30, 1843. 593. **Joseph Chandler,** b. Oct. 14, 1841; m. Rebecca Hansley and resides at Ninth and Poplar Sts., Wilmington, Del.; is a brickmaker. 594. **Enoch G.,** b. Oct. 29, 1844; is a blacksmith. 595. **Martha Ann,** b. Mar. 31, 1850; d. Dec. 7, 1857. 596. **Florence E.,** b. Mar. 1, 1853. 597. **Willamina,** b. Aug. 19, 1856; d. April 30, 1865.

Children of Margaret E. Dutton (No. 284,) and Hiram Talley.
598. **Willamina,** b. Nov. 17, 1831; d. Dec. 3, 1832. 599. **Joseph**

G., b. Aug. 18, 1834; d. June 5, 1847. 600. **Mary Elizabeth,** b. Jan. 12, 1837; m. Dec. 6, 1859 to Charles Henry Heath and resides on E. Third St., Wilmington, Del. 601. **Hiram D.,** b. June 12, 1839; d. Feb. 9, 1864, unmarried.

Children of Susan Jane Dutton (No. 286,) and John Foulk.

602. **Elthera C.,** b. Feb. 3, 1837; m. April 9, 1868 to William W. Hickman, and they live in Wilmington, Del. 603. **Anna Mary,** b. Jan. 20, 1839; d. Mar. 26, 1859. 604. **John,** b. Sept. 12, 1840; d. in the army Mar. 8, 1862. 605. **Sue H.,** b. Jan. 21, 1843. She and the younger children live with their mother. 606. **James K.,** b. Feb. 11, 1845. 607. **Thomas H.,** b. July 16, 1847. 608. **Nelson C.,** b. June, 24, 1850. 609. **William R.,** b. Sept. 20, 1852. 610. **Harlan B.,** b. Nov. 2, 1854.

Children of James Barnard Dutton(No.288,)and Angerett Glasby.

611. **Joseph Alphonso,** b. Mar. 26, 1846; is a machinist and lives in Wilmington, Del., unmarried. 612. **Mary E. M.,** b. Sept. 10, 1847; m. Mar. 29, 1866 to John Nicholson Kates, and lives on E. Third St., Wilmington, Del.

By second wife, Harriet Shaw.

613. **Emma Jones,** b. July 29, 1857; living with her aunt M. E. Talley.

Children of Rachel Ann Dutton(No. 290,) and Frederick Bowker.

614. **Mary G.,** b. April 10, 1852. 615. **Emily B.,** b. Mar. 9, 1855. 616. **Levi Watts,** b. May 9, 1858. 617. **George,** b. Dec. 14, 1861. 618. **Harry Ethan,** b. Oct. 8, 1864. 619. **Frank,** b. Dec. 12, 1866.

Children of Elizabeth Bell Dutton (No. 298,) and J. H. M'Colley.

620. **Annie Bell,** b. June 13, 1842; m. Nov. 10, 1864 to Alexander C. Hyer, Jr., who was for some time consular clerk at Callao, Peru. 621. **Hester E.,** b. Jan. 28, 1844; d. Nov. 14, 1846. 622. **Joseph D.,** b. Sept. 28, 1845; d. Mar. 13, 1846. 623. **Theodosia E. H. B.,** b. April 14, 1849; d. in Philadelphia, Pa., Mar. 7, 1858.

Children of James N. Downing (No. 302,) and Elizabeth Neely.

624. **Anna Bell,** b. Nov. 15, 1863. 625. **Emma,** b. Jan. 7, 1866. 626. **Charles Edward,** b. Oct. 10, 1868.

Children of William S. Downing (No. 304,) and Mary C. Wilson.

627. **William J.,** b. June 15, 1868. 628. **Rebecca J.,** b. Mar. 4, 1870.

Children of Thomas Dutton (No. 810,) and Hannah Cotman.

629. **Mary Ann**, m. Charles Pearson, and went to Reading, Pa., where she died. No further records. 630. **William**, left Philadelphia many years ago and nothing further known of him. 631. **Harriet**, went to Reading with her sister and there married a widower. She is deceased and no further records obtained.

Children of Isaac Dutton (No. 811,) and Catharine Taylor.

632. **Lewis Taylor**, b. Dec. 2, 1817; m. Jan. 11, 1844 to Mary, dau. of Thomas and Martha Moore, and resides at 1226 Ogden Street, Philadelphia.
633. **Sarah Mary**, b. Nov. 19, 1819; m. by Rev. Benj. Dorr of Christ Church, June 21, 1855, to Joseph Eves Hover of Philadelphia, where they reside. He is well known as an ink manufacturer.
634. **Richard Routh**, b. Mar. 4, 1822; m. May 1, 1851 to Margaret Elizabeth Boyle, dau. of Peter Oxholum and Mary Smith Boyle. They reside at 625 N. Eighth St., Philadelphia.
635. **Alexander Lafayette**, b. May 23, 1824; living in Philadelphia, unmarried. 636. **Augustus Paul**, twin brother of the last, lives with his brother Richard, unmarried. A. L. and A. P. Dutton are dealers in boots and shoes at 927 Market Street.
637. **Catharine Matilda**, b. Aug. 27, 1827; d. Oct. 29, 1843.

Children of Larkin Dutton (No. 813,) and Maria Norris.

638. **Norris**, enlisted in the army and it is supposed that he died at Andersonville, Ga., unmarried. 639. **George**, was married, and died 1 mo. 25, 1846, but no further records have been obtained. 640. **John Richard**, was married and is deceased.

By second wife, Ann Matlack.

641. **Anna Maria**, b. 12 mo. 14, 1828; unmarried. 642. **Simeon M.**, m. Mar. 15, 1859 to Ruth Anna Davis, dau. of John and Margaretta, No. 351. They live at Norristown, Pa. No children.

Child of Hannah Hibberd (No. 316,) and Israel Lobb.

643. **Esther**, m. Samuel G. Levis.

Child of John Hibberd (No. 317,) and Rebecca Maris.

644. **Amy Ann**, b. 5 mo. 27, 1843; d. 9 mo. 13, 1851.

Children of Thomas Hibberd (No. 318,) and Margaret Powell.

645. **John**, b. 5 mo. 31, 1821; is a lawyer and lives in Chester, Pa., unmarried.
646. **Hannah**, b. 8 mo. 17, 1823; d. 10 mo. 19, 1870, unmarried.
11

Children of Jacob Hibberd (No. 819,) and Hannah Baker.

647. **Phebe,** m. Christopher Bailey. 648. **Lydia,** m. David Sheehan. 649. **Mary Ann,** m. Adamier Reed. 650. **Jesse,** m. Caroline Stansell. 651. **Sarah.** 652. **Dutton.**

Children of Samuel Hibberd (No. 822,) and Lydia Reece.

653. **Jacob,** b. 12 mo. 11, 1829; m. 12 mo. 31, 1863 to Sarah R., dau. of Richard T. and Mary Ann Worrall, of Nether Providence, Delaware county, Pa., where he resides. 654. **Jesse,** b. 12 mo. 28, 1834; m. Mary Ann Levis and lives in Middletown, Delaware county, Pa., near Lima. 655. **Mary,** b. 10 mo. 9, 1836; unm. 656. **Elizabeth,** b. 6 mo. 17, 1841; unm. 657. **John,** b. 6 mo. 17, 1841; unm.

Children of Susanna M. Hibberd (No. 324,) and Levi Cox.

658. **Sarah D.,** b. 12 mo. 31, 1830; unm. 659. **J. Hibberd,** b. 12 mo. 23, 1834; d. 11 mo. 28, 1862, unm. 660. **William G.,** b. 11 mo. 21, 1836; m. Sallie Jones. 661. **Levi,** b. 9 mo. 3, 1842; dec. 662. **Gulielma,** b. 2 mo. 18, 1847; unm.

Children of Sarah D. Hibberd (No. 325,) and Maris Hall.

663. **Jacob H.,** b. 1 mo. 16, 1827; m. Johanna Pugh, and is dec'd. 664. **Susanna,** b. 12 mo. 18, 1828; m. David Eldridge, son of Joseph and Abigail, of E. Goshen, Chester Co. Pa., and they settled in Harford Co. Md., where she died. 665. **Jesse,** b. 8 mo. 28, 1830. 666. **Barclay,** b. 8 mo. 29, 1833; m. Ella Cline. 667. **Mary,** b. 7 mo. 3, 1836; d. 4 mo. 27, 1846. 668. **Clarkson,** b. 1 mo. 23, 1838; m. 3 mo. 14, 1867 to Margaret L., dau. of Joseph L. and Jane M. Garrett of E. Goshen. Second wife, —— M'Dowell. 669. **Hannah,** b. 10 mo. 18, 1840; unm. 670. **Maris,** b. 1 mo. 22, 1844; d. 1 mo. 17, 1845.

Children of Susanna Dutton (No. 328,) and Isaac Powell.

671. **Sarah D.,** b. 6 mo. 29, 1817; d. 7 mo. 31, 1861; m. 3 mo. 28, 1849 at 12th Street meeting, Philadelphia, to Isaac Leeds of Moorestown, N. J., son of Samuel and Ruth. 672. **Benjamin Rush,** b. 7 mo. 28, 1819; d. in Philadelphia 2 mo. 19, 1851, unmarried.

Children of Thomas Dutton (No. 331,) and Hannah E. Ridgway.

673. **Sarah Jones,** b. 7 mo. 22, 1829; living at Burlington, N. J. unmarried. 674. **William R.,** b. 12 mo. 10, 1830; m. 8 mo. 30, 1853 to Sarah H., dau. of Thomas and Rebecca Scattergood: is a bank teller and lives at Frankford, Pa. His children were born in West Philadelphia, Pa. 675. **Rowland Jones,** b. 9 mo. 6, 1832; m. 6 mo. 8, 1863 to Helen

E., dau. of William and Mercy Ann Burr of Burlington, N. J.,
where he is engaged in the mercantile business.
676. **Mary**, b. 12 mo. 12, 1834; m. 4 mo. 13, 1854 to Richard J.
Allen, son of George and Sidney of Springfield, Del. Co. Pa. He
was a teacher for several years but now a merchant in Philadelphia,
Pa. Two of their children were born in Westtown, Pa., three in
Haddonfield, N. J., and the sixth in Philadelphia.
677. **Charles Ridgway**, b. 11 mo. 28, 1836; d. 4 mo. 12, 1838.

By second wife, Elizabeth Spencer.

678. **Charles Spencer**, b. 12 mo. 8, 1842; d. 10 mo. 12, 1867, unm.
679. **Hannah**, b. 12 mo. 29, 1843; d. 3 mo. 21, 1869; m. 9 mo. 5,
1867 to Henry C. Ellis of Milford, Mass., now of Philadelphia, Pa.   .
680. **Thomas**, b. 6 mo. 16, 1846; m. 6 mo. 19, 1867 to Emma F.·
Kinsey of Philadelphia, Pa., where he resides.
681. **George**, b. 8 mo. 24, 1848; d. 10 mo. 27, 1848.

Children of Edmund Dutton (No. 332,) and Tacy Matlack.

682. **Sallie J.**, b. 10 mo. 4, 1829; d. 5 mo. 22, 1853, unmarried.
683. **Elizabeth M.**, b. 12 mo. 12, 1835; m. 2 mo. 26, 1857 to J.
Hibberd Bartram, son of Israel and Mary Ann. He is a farmer in
Westtown township, Chester Co. Pa.
684. **Thomas Dillwyn**, b. 1 mo. 10, 1842; m. 11 mo. 3, 1867 to
Lydia, dau. of Randall and Mary G. Pratt, who was born 2 mo. 3,
1843. They live in Newtown township, Del. Co. Pa.

Children of Mary Dutton (No. 333,) and Jared Darlington.

685. **Edward**, b. 1 mo. 22, 1832; m. 3 mo. 12, 1856 to Mary F., dau.
of Charles Palmer of Concord, Del. Co. Pa. He is a farmer in Middletown township.
686. **Sarah J.**, b. 8 mo. 31, 1833; living in West Chester, Pa., unmarried.   .
687. **Albert**, b. 5 mo. 12, 1835; m. Charlotte Kitts, who was born
Oct. 21, 1838. He is a farmer in Middletown, Del. Co., Pa.
688. **Amy**, b. 2 mo. 20, 1837; m. 3 mo. 16, 1859 to Henry Pratt, son
of Nathaniel and Susan, who was born 10 mo. 7, 1832. They live in
Concord township, Del. county.
689. **Frances**, b. 2 mo. 13, 1839; a school teacher, unm.
690. **Jesse**. b. 7 mo. 8, 1841; m. 10 mo. 25, 1866 to Hannah W., dau.
of Thomas and Mary Pratt of Middletown, who was born 9 mo. 9,
1841. He is a farmer in Middletown.
. 691. **Thomas**, b. 7 mo. 16, 1843; d. 7 mo. 20, 1843.
. 692. **Jared**, b. 8 mo. 16, 1844; living at the homestead, unmarried.
He and his brothers carry on the dairy farming business extensively
and successfully.
693. **Mary**, b. 3 mo. 15, 1846; living in West Chester, unm.
694. **Ruthanna**, b. 12 mo. 8, 1848 : a school teacher.

Children of Nathan C. Dutton (No. 335,) and Maria Butler.

695. **Mary E.**, b. 2 mo. 2, 1841; m. Charles Leech, 1870.
696. **Thomas E.**, b. 10 mo. 1844; now in the oil business in Venango Co. Pa. 697. **Edmund**, b. 2 mo. 14, 1846; m. and teaching school at Omaha, Neb.

By second wife, Hannah Smedley.

698. **Lewis G.**, store keeper at Green Tree, Chester Co. Pa. 699. **George S.**, machinist, living in Philadelphia, Pa.

Children of Ruthanna Dutton (No. 336,) and Thomas W. Cassin.

700. **Mary**, died young. 701. **Charles L.**, b. 5 mo. 9, 1846; a graduate of Penn'a University, and now physician on the U. S. Steamer Colorado; unmarried.

Children of Amy P. Dutton (No. 337,) and John Williamson.

702. **Jane R.**, b. 3 mo. 8, 1849; d. 2 mo. 6, 1852.
703. **Sidney B.**, b. 2 mo. 7, 1850; d. 2 mo. 11, 1852.
704. **Mary D.**, b. 3 mo. 10, 1851.
705. **Ruthanna**, b. 8 mo. 10, 1853; d. 9 mo. 15, 1853.
706. **Rebecca**, b. 1 mo. 7, 1855.
707. **Charles**, b. 11 mo. 6, 1856.

Children of Nathaniel Richards (No. 354,) and Jane Giffen.

708. **Thomas**, farmer, b. Feb. 9, 1835; unm. 709. **Edward**, b. Dec. 24, 1836; m. Dec. 13, 1860 to Catharine A. Pierce, who was born Aug. 27, 1834. Residence on E. Third St., Wilmington, Del. 710. **Joseph**, b. April 23, 1839; d. Nov. 8, 1842. 711. **Jane W.**, b. June 28, 1844; m. April 19, 1860 to David B. Ridgway, who was born Oct. 9, 1838. They reside at or near Harmony Mills, Del. 712. **Dutton**, b. Nov. 26, 1845; m. Dec. 23, 1869 to Laura Whiteman, who was born Dec. 21, 1849: resides near Drummond's Hill, Del. 713. **Susanna**, b. Dec. 6, 1848; m. Mar. 21, 1867 to George W. Currinder, who was born Jan. 30, 1845: resides at or near Harmony Mills. 714. **Franklin**, b. June 3, 1853. 715. **Anna Maria**, b. Jan. 7, 1857.

Children of Mary Ann Richards (No. 355,) and Joseph Dizer.

716. **James R.**, b. Aug. 26, 1823; d. Aug. 12, 1824. 717. **Joseph**, b. Jan. 26, 1825; d. Sept. 7, 1826. 718. **Mary Ann**, b. Oct. 15, 1826; m. Oct. 11, 1848 to Philip Nelling, shoemaker, who died April 6, 1864, and she lives with her mother at Village Green, Del. Co. Pa. 719. **Susanna R.**, b. Sept. 29, 1828; living with Jonathan Dutton, (No. 363,) unmarried. 720. **William**, b. Aug. 17, 1830; d. Dec. 6, 1831. 721. **Abby Ann**, b. May 18, 1833; living in Chester, Pa., unm. 722. **Tho. Jefferson**, b. Dec. 14, 1834; living in Wilmington, Del., unm. 723. **Geo. Washington**, b. Sept. 16, 1837; living with his mother, unmarried.

Children of Lydia Richards (No. 356,) and John Slawter.

724. **Susanna,** b. June 2, 1823; d. May 7, 1848, unm. 725. **Jemima,** b. Nov. 11, 1824. 726. **John,** b. June 29, 1826; m. Mar. 1, 1849 to Rachel Griffith, (No. 859,) and lives in Chester, Pa. 727. **Mary,** b. Feb. 3, 1828; m. April 4, 1855 to Edward Conn, who died Jan. 4, 1870, and she lives in Chester. 728. **Lydia Ann,** b. Oct. 1, 1830; living in Chester, unm. 729. **Jehu Dutton,** b. Aug. 5, 1833; m. Dec. 18, 1866 to Caroline Mancil, (No. 877,) and lives at Mosesville, Chester Co. Pa.; is a blacksmith. 730. **Lewis,** painter, b. Jan. 6, 1836; m. Lydia Lyons, and lives in Wilmington, Del. 731. **Humphrey J.,** b. Sept. 9, 1839; d. Aug. 19, 1840. 732. **Charles Edwin,** b. Feb. 13, 1842; d. Sept. 21, 1865. 733. **Hannah Ann,** b. Nov. 17, 1844; living in Chester, unm.

Children of Joseph Richards (No. 357,) and Mary Fields.

734. **Jonathan,** b. July 11, 1831; d. May 25, 1850. 735. **Susanna,** b. Oct. 3, 1833; m. March 29, 1854 to John Plumley, farmer, of Ridley, Del. Co., Pa. 736. **Sarah,** b. Feb. 19, 1836; d. Dec. 24, 1858, unm. 737. **Elizabeth,** b. Oct. 27, 1838; m. April 27, 1861 to George E. Johnson, stone mason, and they live at 213 Pennell St., Chester, Pa. 738. **Louisa,** b. July 3, 1841; unm.

There are children of the second marriage but their names not obtained.

Children of Mary Ann Dutton (No. 859,) and Samuel P. Harrison.

739. **Eleanor,** b. May 27, 1832; living with her brother, unm. 740. **John D.,** b. Sept. 29, 1835; m. May 2, 1861 to Emma, dau. of Isaac and Amy Larkin of Newgarden, and lives at the homestead near Guthrieville, Chester Co., Pa. 741. **Samuel,** and 742, **Joshua,** twins, b. June 5, 1837; died in infancy.

Children of Esther P. Dutton (No. 302,) and Joseph Pennell Hannum.

743. **Mary Elizabeth,** b. July 3, 1828; m. Ezra L. Baily, farmer, son of Ezekiel Baily, and they live in E. Marlborough, Chester Co. Pa. 744. **John Alfred,** b. May 13, 1830; d. Sept. 10, 1858, unm. 745. **Susan D.,** b. Sept. 11, 1831; m. Oct. 31, 1851 to Joseph H. Peters, who was born June 14, 1827, and died Aug. 14, 1861. 746. **Samuel P.,** b. May 31, 1833; d. Oct. 15, 1835. 747. **Lewis,** b. April 17, 1835; d. Mar. 13, 1862. 748. **Samuel Pennell,** farmer, b. Aug. 14, 1836; m. Susan, dau. of George and Susan Darlington of Pocopson, and lives in E. Marlborough. 749. **Jane,** b. Sept. 4, 1838; d. Oct. 4, 1838. 750. **Anna Eliza,** b. Nov. 26, 1839; d. June 1, 1843. 751. **Eleanor,** b. May 28, 1842; d. Nov. 30, 1843. 752. **Esther Anna,** b. Jan. 20, 1845; unm. 753. **Emma Louisa,** b. July 15, 1848; m. Mar. 3, 1870 to Mark L. Garrett of Wilmington, Delaware.

Children of Jonathan Dutton (No. 363,) and Lydia A. Fell.

754. **Jane T.**, m. Powell Clayton, and lives in Philadelphia, Pa. 755. **Annie G.**, unm. 756. **John**, m. April 23, 1862 to Harriet Beatty, and lives near his father. 757. **George G.**, m. Jan. 1866 to Mary L. James, and lives near his father. 758. **Elizabeth**, d. Jan. 29, 1848.

Children of Isaac Pennell Dutton (No. 364,) and Anna M. Johnson.

759. **Henry Harrison**, m. Mar. 25, 1866 to Sallie Kearney, and resides near Sugartown, Chester Co. Pa. 760. **Mary E.**, unm. 761. **Henrietta**, unm. 762. **J. Elwood**, m. Mar. 17, 1870 to S. Fanny Bunting. 763. **Maurice.** 764. **Eugene.**

Children of John Dutton (No. 365,) and Lydia Vernon.

765. **Hannah E.**, b. Sept. 10, 1824; m. April 28, 1852 to Joseph Tree, and lives in Philadelphia. No children. 766. **Tho. Vernon**, b. July 30, 1826; m. June 21, 1849 to Elizabeth Smedley, who died in 1868. He lives in Aston township near Village Green, Del. Co., Pa. 767. **Samuel E.**, b. April 2, 1828; d. Aug. 14, 1850, at St. Louis, Mo. 768. **Sarah V.**, b. June 1, 1830; d. Nov. 11, 1851, unm. 769. **Richard Henry**, b. April 5, 1832; d. Oct. 10, 1862; m. April 14, 1857 to Caroline Galley, who lives in Philadelphia. 770. **Sidney F.**, b. Aug. 25, 1834; m. Jan. 2, 1862 to David D. Thompson. No children. 771. **Rachel**, b. May 8, 1836; living at Village Green, unm. 772. **Emma**, b. Oct. 13, 1838; d. Sept. 21, 1858. 773. **Martha**, b. Sept. 11, 1840; d. Feb. 10, 1866, unm.

Children of Rachel Dutton (No. 368,) and William H. Grubb.

774. **Mary Elizabeth**, b. March 13, 1834; unm. 775. **William H.**, b. Nov. 12, 1840; d. May 30, 1859.

Children of Joseph Dutton (No. 370,) and Sarah Thatcher.

776. **William T.**, b. 7 mo. 9, 1836; m. 12 mo. 22, 1859 to Anna Mary Heyburn. 777. **Isaac L.**, b. 3 mo. 21, 1838; m. 2 mo. 18, 1863, to Caroline S., dau. of Thomas and Ruth Ann Hickman, and lives near West Chester, Pa. 778. **Henry S.**, b. 3 mo 18, 1840, unm. 779. **Beulah T.**, b. 9 mo. 10, 1842; m. 11 mo. 15, 1865 to William H. Sager. 780. **Rebecca**, b. 12 mo. 24, 1844; m. 7 mo. 4, 1866 to Washington W. James. 781. **Richard**, b. 6 mo. 11, 1847; m. 2 mo. 1, 1871 to Mary Green of Radnor. 782. **Edward**, b. 9 mo. 25, 1850. 783. **Lydia Ann**, b. 4 mo. 23, 1853. 784. **Sallie**, b. 8 mo. 0, 1856. 785. **Emma**, b. 3 mo. 12, 1859.

Children of Martha Dutton (No. 371,) and Bennett Temple.

786. **Lydia Ann**, b. 2 mo. 19, 1836; m. Alfred Mancil, (See No 892). 787. **Thomas Riley**, b. 7 mo. 6, 1838; m. 2 mo. 14, 1858 to Sallie

L. **Briggs**: is a store-keeper at Thorntonville, Del. Co. Pa. 788. **Rachel B.,** b. 10 mo. 13, 1841 ; d. 11 mo. 14, 1842.

Children of Jonathan Dutton (No. 372,) and Elizabeth J. Bullock.

789. **Richard Smith,** b. Dec. 6, 1840; m. Rachel Armitt. 790. **Reece R.,** b. Dec. 20, 1841. 791. **Alfred B.,** b. Feb. 11, 1843. 792. **Thomas H.,** b. Dec. 2, 1844. 793. **Isaac Larkin,** b. Mar. 4, 1846.

By second wife.

794. **Henry Lincoln,** b. June 8, 1862.

Children of Jonathan Paiste (No. 373,) and Priscilla Cloud.

795. **William.** 796. **Alice Ann.** 797. **Lydia.** 798. **Ann.** 799. **Jesse.** 800. **Elizabeth.** 801. **Sarah.** 802. **Jonathan D.** No further records obtained.

Child of Sarah Paiste (No. 374,) and Joseph P. Baynes.

803. **Alice P.,** b. 9 mo. 25, 1836 in U. Chichester; m. 12 mo. 14, 1865 in Baltimore, Md., to D. Hull Twining.

Children of Jonathan Pennell (No. 376,) and Sarah Bright.

804. **Ann Eliza,** m. Dec. 24, 1847 to Charles J. F. Henry, carpenter. 805. **Joseph,** m. Aug. 1859 to Rebecca Mickey of Patterson, Juniata Co. Pa., where he is a Dry Goods merchant. 806. **John,** m. Mar. 1856 to Mary A. Gray of Wilmington, Del., and is a cigar manufacturer. 807. **Mary Jane,** m. Oct. 15, 1861 to George B. Hinkson, of Chester, Pa., carpenter; now living in Philadelphia, Pa. 808. **Sarah Emma,** m. Oct. 5, 1861 to William Hatton, of Chester, and lives in Philadelphia. 809. **Isaac James,** deceased.

Children of Martha Dutton (No. 377,) and William West.

810. **Samuel,** b. 11 mo. 20, 1836; unm. 811. **Jonathan D.,** b. 10 mo. 14, 1838 ; d. 2 mo. 24, 1839. 812. **William Pusey,** b. 2 mo. 6, 1840; m. 9 mo. 6, 1866 to Margaret D. Pidgeon, and resides in Philadelphia. 813. **Elias Hicks,** b. 2 mo. 24, 1842; unm. 814. **Rachel P.,** b. 2 mo. 24, 1842; m. 2 mo. 7, 1867 to James F. Leys, who is deceased, and she lives with her parents. 815. **Keziah,** (Kate D.) b. 2 mo. 24, 1842; unm.

Children of Hannah H. Dutton (No. 380,) and John Valentine.

816. **Anna Regina,** b. 3 mo. 9, 1853; d. 3 mo. 3, 1863. 817. **Harry W.,** b. 6 mo. 10, 1855 ; d. 8 mo. 3, 1861.

Children of Rebecca Ann Dutton (No. 384,) and Cloud Elliott.

818. **Joseph T.,** b. Sept. 26, 1850. 819. **Melinda,** b. Jan. 31, 1853. 820. **Jonathan D.,** b. Mar. 26, 1854.

Children of David H. Dutton (No. 385,) *and Elizabeth Moore.*

821. **Horace Hervey**, b. 4 mo. 13, 1857. 822. **Rachel Pen-nell**, b. 5 mo. 27, 1859.   823. **Bessie**, b. 12 mo. 13, 1864; d. 9 mo. 20. 1865.

Children of Robert R. Dutton (No. 387,) *and Ann Bartram.*

824. **Emily Frances**, b. June 12, 1834 ; m. April 8, 1856 to John M. Larkin.   825. **Caroline**, b. April 5, 1836 ; m. April 24, 1861 to John Lewis Garrett.   826. **Hannah Booth**, b. June 30, 1839 ; m. Oct. 20, 1863 to Wm. George Randle.   827. **Arabella**, b. Feb. 11, 1841 ; m. May 23, 1860 to Charles Hinkson.   828. **Julius Augustus**, b. Feb. 11, 1843.   829. **Albert**, b. June 23, 1844.   830. **Henry B.**, b. April 24, 1846 ; d. June 6, 1849.   831. **Benjamin B.**, b. May 8, 1850 ; d. Aug. 16, 1851.   832. **Howard**, b. Dec. 16, 1852 ; d. Jan. 11, 1857.

Children of Aaron L. Dutton (No. 388,) *and Anne G. James.*

833. **Clara Sanford**, b. April 1, 1849 ; d. Dec. 20, 1852.   834. **James Mortimer**, b. Nov. 8, 1850 ; clerk, living in Chester, Pa. He has shown much interest in this work, and collected a large part of the information herein presented.   835. **Thomas**, b. Feb. 6, 1853 ; salesman in a store at Glenloch, Chester county, Pa.   836. **Clarence Bird**, b. Nov. 11, 1855 ; d. July 1, 1867.

Children of Jesse Dutton (*No.* 389,) *and Emily L. Horne.*

837. **Eliza Lamela**, b. 3d mo. 25, 1850.   838. **Anna Louisa**, b. 7 mo. 17, 1853 ; accidentally killed on the rail road 9 mo. 2, 1865.   839. **Thomas Elwood**, b. 7 mo. 19, 1856.   840. **Laura E.**, b. 11 mo. 23, 1859.   841. **Susan Emma**, b. 8 mo. 31, 1862.

Children of Emily Dutton (*No.* 390,) *and Garrett Hannum.*

842. **Susan D.**, b. July 11, 1849.   843. **Charles Elwood**, b. Aug. 17, 1851.   844. **Clara Emma**, b. Feb. 12, 1854 ; d. Jan. 10, 1857.

Child of Charles Dutton (*No.* 391,) *and Hannah Horne.*

845. **Hannah E.**, b. 2 mo. 19, 1851.

By second wife, Jane W. Johnson.

846. **Howard J.**, b. 12 mo. 23, 1856.   847. **Elizabeth W.**, b. 7 mo. 6, 1858.   848. **Charles L.**, b. 4 mo. 9, 1861 ; d. 2 mo. 20, 1869.   849. **William Worrall**, b. 7 mo. 8, 1864.   850. **Jesse Alfred**, b. 7 mo. 12, 1866.

Children of Sidney Dutton (*No.* 392,) *and Lewis B. Hickman.*

851. **George Washington**, b. Aug. 25, 1854.   852. **Robert R.**, b. July 16, 1856 ; d. Dec. 28, 1858.   853. **Sidney Emma**, b. Nov. 7, 1858.   854. **Anna Mary**, b. Aug. 17, 1864.   855. **Thomas Elwood**, b. Mar. 22, 1866.

Child of Susan Ann Dutton (No. 393,) and Wm. B. Hannum.

850. **Susan Anna Willa,** b. Dec. 16, 1865.

Children of Lydia Mancil (No. 894,) and Joseph Griffith.

857. **Susanna,** b. Feb. 22, 1823. 858. **Ann Eliza,** b Jan. 20, 1825; d. July 9, 1826. 859. **Rachel,** b. Feb. 18, 1827; d. Nov. 6, 1868; m. John Slawter, (See No. 726). 860. **William M.,** b. Nov. 4, 1828; d. Jan. 29, 1849. 861. **Maria H.,** b. Oct. 19, 1830; m. Aug. 1, 1809 to George Clark, and lives at Rowlandsville, Md. 862. **Frederick P.,** b. Oct. 13, 1832; d. Aug. 28, 1833. 863. **Isaac M.,** b. June 5, 1834; d. Aug. 20, 1834. 864. **Abigail E.,** b. Dec. 21, 1836; m. Jan. 23, 1859 to Joseph G. Faulkner, spinner, and they live in Chester, Pa. 865. **Joseph H.,** b. Dec. 2, 1839; m. Feb. 23, 1865 to Rachel S. Fairlamb, and lives in Willistown, Chester Co. Pa. ; farmer. 866. **Jesse Lewis,** b. Feb. 18, 1842; killed in the battle of the Wilderness May 6, 1864.

Children of Elizabeth Mancil (No. 395,) and Samuel Vernon.

867. **Lydia Ann,** b. June 16, 1823 ; m. Oct. 16, 1807 to J. Wesley Ottey. 868. **Susan M.,** b. Feb. 26, 1826 ; m. Jan. 29, 1852 to William Craig. 869. **William Mancil,** b. Feb. 1, 1828; m. Mar. 15, 1853, to Eliza Stevens, who lives in Chester, Pa. He died May 29, 1865. 870. **Elizabeth Caroline,** b. May 9, 1830; m. Simon Wilmot. 871. **Martha P.,** b. Jan. 13, 1834; unm. 872. **Sarah Ann,** b. Jan. 6, 1836 ; m. June 18, 1856 to John Hinkson, carpenter, and lives in Chester, Pa. 873. **Emma,** b. July 23, 1840; d. Sept. 1, 1840.

Children of David D. Mancil (No. 396,) and Sarah Hinkson.

874. **Mary T.,** b. July 5, 1830 ; m. Dec. 22, 1852 to Aaron King of E. Pikeland, Chester county, Pa. 875. **Susanna,** b. Jan. 13, 1832 ; m. Dec. 22, 1853 to Joseph Phillips, and lives near Pottstown, Pa. 876. **Morris H.,** b. Feb. 18, 1834 ; m. Jan. 11, 1860 to Mary Anna Chrisman, who died Dec. 25, 1867. Second marriage Feb. 10, 1870, to Emma M. Johnson. He is Superintendent of carpentry for P. & B. C. R. R., at Oxford, Chester county, Pa. 877. **Caroline,** b. Feb. 28, 1836 ; m. Jehu Dutton Slawter (See No. 729). 878. **Harriet B.,** b. Nov. 20, 1837 ; d. April 30, 1865 ; unm. 879. **Samuel Barton,** b. Feb. 3, 1840 ; d. Aug. 26, 1840. 880. **William,** b. Nov. 14, 1841 ; d. Mar. 3, 1850. 881. **George Elwood,** b. April 8, 1844 ; m. Martha R. Hinkson, and lives at 3512 Green St., Philadelphia, Pa. 882. **Mahlon,** b. Aug. 12, 1847; carpenter, residing in Philadelphia. 883. **David D.,** b. Sept. 16, 1849 ; carpenter, living in Phila.

Children of Susan Mancil (No. 397,) and Jesse Griswold.

884. **Elisha,** M. D., b. Mar. 14, 1828 ; m. Miss Cook of Vermont, in 1856, and lives at Sharon, Mercer Co. Pa. No children. 885. **Mary Elizabeth,** b. Aug. 26, 1829 ; m. Aug. 16, 1849 to

12

Leavit R. Simpkins of Vernon, Trumbull Co. Ohio, and now lives near Gardner, Grundy Co. Ill.

886. **David M.**, b. Aug. 13, 1831 ; m. Aug. 15, 1858 to Melissa C. Wate, and lives near Gardner, Ill.

887. **William P.**, b. May 6, 1834.

888. **Lydia Sarah**, b. July 31, 1836 ; m. May 6, 1855 to Hiram L. Hilyer of Mecca, Trumbull Co. O., and now lives at Gardner, Ill.

889. **Laura**, b. Sept. 16, 1836 ; m. Sept. 21, 1859 to David Callahan, and lives at Greenville, Mercer Co. Pa.

890. **Margaret Ann**, b. June 18, 1841 ; m. Jan. 1, 1861 to William H. Downs and lives near Gardner, Illinois.

891. **Clarinda**, b. Sept. 23, 1843 ; m. Jan. 26, 1862 to Truman D. Phelps of Mecca, O., and lives near Gardner, Ill. No children.

Children of Mahlon Mancil (No. 398,) and Susanna Dutton.

892. **Alfred**, blacksmith, b. Feb. 11, 1835 ; m. Oct. 8, 1857 to Lydia Ann Temple, (No. 786,) and lives at Sugartown, Chester Co. Pa. 893. **Nathan P.**, b. July 23, 1836 ; d. Feb. 23, 1838. 894. **Rachel A.**, b. Oct. 6, 1837 ; m. April 4, 1860 to Jonathan Johnson. 895. **Sarah D.**, b. Aug. 21, 1841 ; m. Feb. 12, 1861 to Edward Barton. 896. **Arabella**, b. June 23, 1844 ; m. Jan. 12, 1870 to James E. Miller.

Children of Mary J. Mancil (No. 400,) and Eli B. Talley.

897. **Curtis**, b. Nov. 20, 1828 ; d. Sept. 18, 1851, unm. 898. **William**, b. May 6, 1830 ; m. Feb. 9, 1860 to Sarah Elizabeth Langley, and is a farmer living near Talleyville, Del. 899. **John Wesley**, b. May 3, 1832 ; d. April 12, 1864, unm. 900. **Eli B.**, b. Mar. 27, 1834 ; d. May 5, 1835. 901. **Mary Jane**, b. April 27, 1836 ; d. Feb. 24, 1843. 902. **Elihu**, b. May 29, 1838 ; m. Nov. 17, 1868 to Ann Haubey, and is a farmer near Talleyville. 903. **James A. Bayard**, b. Oct. 21, 1840 ; d. Aug. 28, 1852. 904. **Lydia Ann**, b. April 4, 1843 ; d. Mar. 8, 1867 ; m. Mar. 22, 1864 to Martin V. Palmer, who d. Nov. 18, 1860. 905. **Caroline Elizabeth**, b. May 11, 1845 ; m. Dec. 21, 1868 to Lewis R. Springer, and lives in Wilmington, Del. 906. **Harriet Ellen**, b. May 29, 1848 ; unm.

Children of Ellen Mancil (No. 401,) and William T. M'Kee.

907. **Sarah Jane**, b. June 10, 1838 ; m. April 22, 1858 to John Black, cabinet maker, and they reside in Wilmington, Del. 908. **John Wesley**, b. Sept. 26, 1840 ; d. July 22, 1841. 909. **Mary Ellen**, b. Sept. 4, 1842 ; m. April 24, 1863 to George W. Churnside, and they live at Delaware Iron Works, near Newport, Del. 910. **Lydia Amanda**, b. Mar. 11, 1845 ; unm. 911. **Juliet**, b. Feb. 19, 1848 ; unm. 912. **Keziah Emma**, b. Jan. 3, 1851.

Children of Abigail Mancil (No. 402,) and Jehu Chandler.

913. **Barton**, b. Dec. 10, 1828 ; died same date. 914. **Amor H.**, b. Dec. 27, 1829 ; m. Rebecca ———. 915. **Susanna S.**, b. Jan. 4, 1832 ;

d. Sept. 25, 1833.   916. **Mary E.**, b. Mar. 19, 1833; m. Joseph L.
Pyle.   917. **Rachel Ann**, b. Aug. 3, 1835; m. John A. Graves.
918. **William T.**, b. Sept. 18, 1839; m. Mary ——.

Child of William Thompson (No. 404,) and Elizabeth Brunner.
919. **George D.**, b. Feb. 13, 1845.

By second wife, Mary Hansell.
920. **Josephine**, b. Mar. 17, 1850.   921. **Ann Elizabeth**, b.
Oct. 5, 1851 ; d. Feb. 28, 1869.   922. **Mary Emma**, b. Mar. 13, 1853.
923. **Leonard B.**, b. April 20, 1855.   924. **Ruth Hannah**, b.
Mar. 12, 1862.

EIGHTH GENERATION.

Such dates as have been obtained respecting the descendants in
this generation are here given, with their corresponding numbers,
and the names will be found in the succeeding pages.

925 b. 1 mo. 11, 1858.
926 b. 2 mo. 7, 1857.
927 b. 11 mo. 1860.
952 b. 8 mo. 1, 1863.
961 b. 8 mo. 14, 1855.
973 b. Nov. 1854.
974 b. May, 1861.
975 b. April 14, 1844 ;
    d. Mar. 7, 1858.
976 b. Oct. 30, 1845.
978 b. Mar. 22, 1855.
979 b. June 6, 1850.
980 b. July 16, 1864.
981 b. Jan. 1857.
982 b. Aug. 1863.
983 b. Sep. 3, 1857.
984 b. Aug. 15, 1859.
985 b. Aug. 24, 1866.
987 b. Aug. 6, 1854.
988 b. June 16, 1866;
    d. July 4, 1860.
989 b. Dec. 24, 1859.
990 b. Nov. 5, 1862.
991 b. May 3, 1867.
992 b. June 19, 1870
993 b. Feb. 25, 1864.
994 b. Aug. 2, 1869.
995 b. Oct. 12, 1869.
996 b. April 10, 1853.
997 b. Sept. 6, 1860.
998 b. Mar. 2, 1864.
999 b. Oct. 9, 1860.
1000 b. Aug. 27, 1863.
1001 b. Oct. 31, 1869.
1002 b. Dec. 24, 1866.
1003 b. April 19, 1869.
1004 b. Oct. 17, 1865;
    d. May 21, 1868.

1005 b. Oct. 7, 1866.
1006 b. Feb. 2, 1845.
1007 b. Jan. 17, 1847.
1008 b. Oct. 4, 1848.
1009 b. Nov. 1, 1850.
1010 b. April 17, 1853 ;
    d. Nov. 30, 1856.
1011 b. Sep. 27, 1855.
1012 b. Nov. 5, 1862.
1013 b. July 12, 1858.
1014 b. Feb. 4, 1860.
1015 b. Dec. 18, 1861.
1016 b. July 13, 1863.
1017 b. Feb. 7, 1852.
1018 b. Oct. 23, 1854 ;
    d. July 25, 1859.
1019 b. Oct. 27, 1856.
1020 b. Jan. 7, 1859.
1058 b. 7 mo. 30, 1850.
1059 b. 10 mo. 22, 1851.
1060 b. 4 mo. 8, 1853.
1061 b. 11 mo. 29, 1854 ;
    d. 1 mo. 7, 1855.
1062 b. 5 mo. 6, 1856.
1063 b. 9 mo. 6, 1858.
1064 b. 6 mo. 2, 1854.
1065 b. 2 mo. 16, 1858.
1066 b. 5 mo. 31, 1864.
1067 b. 6 mo. 13, 1855.
1068 b. 9 mo. 3, 1857.
1069 b. 3 mo. 26, 1860.
1070 b. 4 mo. 5, 1862 ;
1071 b. 7 mo. 1, 1863 ;
    d. 8 mo. 11, 1864.
1072 b. 1 mo. 31, 1869.
1073 d. 3 mo. 21, 1869.
1074 b. 1 mo. 26, 1868.

1075 b. 6 mo. 10, 1858 ;
    d 10 mo. 15, 1862.
1076 b. 10 mo. 2, 1862.
1077 b. 3 mo. 9, 1864.
1078 b. 7 mo. 28, 1869.
1079 b. 3 mo. 15, 1869.
1080 b. 4 mo. 2, 1857.
1081 b. 8 mo. 4, 1858.
1082 b. 2 mo. 12, 1860.
1083 b. 10 mo. 10, 1862.
1084 b. 7 mo. 3, 1864.
1085 b. 6 mo. 3, 1866.
1086 b. 6 mo. 2, 1870.
1087 b. 4 mo. 1, 1860.
1088 b. 8 mo. 2, 1861.
1089 b. 12 mo. 1, 1863.
1090 b. 9 mo. 19, 1865 ;
    d. 9 mo. 21, 1865.
1091 b. 5 mo. 3, 1867.
1092 b. 9 mo. 14, 1867.
1093 b. 10 mo. 21, 1870.
1094 b. Dec. 24, 1863.
1095 b. July 29, 1864.
1096 b. Sept. 19, 1866.
1097 b. Jan. 4, 1869.
1098 b. Mar. 3, 1867;
    d. July 19, 1868.
1099 b. Nov. 12, 1868.
1100 b. Sept. 28, 1870.
1101 b. Jan. 16, 1868.
1102 b. Sept. 22, 1849 ;
    d. Aug. 7, 1852.
1103 b. Sept. 10, 1851.
1104 b. Mar. 30, 1850 ;
1105 b. June 23, 1853.
1106 b. Nov. 15, 1859.
1107 b. April 9, 1863.
1108 b. April 26, 1866.

1109 b. Oct. 28, 1868.	1168 b. Sept. 15, 1870.	1217 b. June 15, 1859.
1110 b. Oct. 9, 1856.	1169 b. Feb. 11, 1863.	d. Nov. 20, 1859.
1111 b. July 19 1858 ;	1170 b. Nov. 28, 1865.	1218 b. Aug. 7, 1860.
d. Oct. 2, 1858.	1173 b. Oct. 24, 1863.	1219 } b. Dec. 3, 1863.
1112 b. Mar. 4, 1860 ;	1174 b. Oct. 17, 1865.	1220 }
d. June 30, 1860.	1175 b. Dec. 26, 1867.	1221 b. Nov. 4, 1868.
1113 b. May 7, 1861.	1177 b. Dec. 22, 1856.	1222 b. Mar. 3, 1856.
1114 b. Oct. 11, 1863.	1178 b. Jan. 8, 1859.	1223 b. Nov. 10, 1861 ;
1115 b. Dec. 24, 1868.	1179 b. June 10, 1867.	d. Dec. 18, 1861.
1116 b. Feb. 5, 1855.	1180 b. Feb. 8, 1862.	1224 b. April 27, 1863.
1117 b. Mar. 8, 1857.	1181 b. Nov. 1, 1863.	1225 b. Mar. 14, 1866.
1118 b. May 26, 1859.	1182 b. Aug. 7, 1866.	1226 b. Jan. 12, 1869.
1119 b. May 12, 1861.	1183 b. Oct. 5, 1864 ;	1227 b. Sept. 21, 1860 ;
1120 b. Aug. 1, 1863.	d. May 14, 1870.	d. June 2, 1862.
1121 b. Mar. 17, 1867.	1184 b. May 23, 1866 ;	1228 b. Dec. 16, 1862.
1122 b. Dec. 23, 1869.	d. April 10, 1867 ;	1229 b. June 19, 1865.
1123 b. Nov. 24, 1862 ;	1185 b. Feb. 29, 1868.	1230 b. Aug. 14, 1862.
d. June 10, 1863.	1186 b. Dec. 21, 1860.	1231 b. June 18, 1864.
1124 b. Dec. 17, 1864.	1187 b. Feb. 8, 1862.	1232 b. June 15, 1866.
1125 b. Feb. 23, 1868.	1188 b. Oct. 4, 1865.	1233 b. Aug 7, 1870.
1126 b. April 17, 1866.	1189 b. June 18, 1868.	1234 b. Feb. 1, 1859.
1127 b. Jan. 2, 1850.	1190 b. July 9, 1866.	1235 b. June 11, 1864.
1128 b. Jan 29, 1852 ;	1191 b. Jan. 2, 1853.	1236 b. April 22, 1869.
d. Sept. 1, 1858.	1192 b. Aug. 17, 1856 ;	1237 b. Jan. 15, 1865 ;
1129 b. Jan. 31, 1854.	d. Oct. 9, 1857.	d. Oct. 8, 1866.
1130 b. Jan. 17, 1853.	1193 b. Oct. 9, 1862.	1238 b. Nov. 4, 1869.
1131 b. Feb. 22. 1858.	1194 b. Nov. 12, 1854.	1239 b. June 7, 1860.
1132 b. Jan. 28, 1863.	1195 b. Nov. 2, 1856 ;	1240 b. Sept. 4, 1865.
1133 b. Sept. 27, 1866.	d. Nov. 1, 1864.	1241 b. Nov. 17, 1867 ;
1134 b. Sept. 25, 1868.	1196 b. Sept. 4, 1858.	d. Nov. 19, 1867.
1137 b. Aug. 26, 1850.	1197 b. Feb. 20, 1861.	1242 b. May 28, 1869.
1138 b. July 2, 1852.	1198 b. July 31, 1857.	1243 b. July 7, 1864 ;
1139 b. 1859.	1199 b. May 10, 1859 ;	d. Oct. 21, 1864.
1140 b. July, 1862.	d. Dec. 7, 1860.	1244 b. Sept. 15, 1867 ;
1142 b. Nov. 4, 1860.	1200 b. April 4, 1861.	d. Mar. 26, 1868.
1143 b. Oct. 1869.	1201 b. Aug. 8, 1862.	1245 b. Sept. 20, 1868 ;
1144 b. Dec. 12, 1863.	1202 b. May 4, 1864 ;	d. July 13, 1869.
1145 b. Aug. 25, 1866.	d. May 8, 1864.	1246 b. Jan. 18, 1870.
1146 b. Feb. 7, 1870.	1203 b. May 15, 1865 ;	1247 b. Feb. 1, 1855.
1147 b. Jan. 19, 1867.	d. July 15, 1865.	1248 b. April 20, 1856 ;
1148 b. Sept. 1868.	1204 b. Mar. 28, 1867 ;	d. Oct. 1, 1856.
1149 b. April 1870.	d. July 5, 1867.	1249 b. Aug. 7, 1857.
1150 b. Nov. 1869 ;	1205 b. Mar. 15, 1868.	1250 b. Dec. 26, 1858.
d. Dec. 1869.	1206 b. Oct. 7, 1854.	1251 b. Sept. 28, 1863 ;
1151 b. Sept. 24, 1859.	1207 b. Dec. 10, 1856.	d. July 27, 1864.
1152 b. July 3, 1863.	1208 b. Sept. 17, 1861.	1252 b. April 17, 1865.
1153 b. Mar. 4, 1867.	1209 b. Mar. 9, 1863.	1253 b. Jan. 14, 1869.
1154 b. Sept. 13, 1868.	1210 b. Sept. 14, 1870.	1254 b. Feb. 22, 1861.
1162 b. Nov. 1, 1857.	1211 b. Jan. 20, 1852.	1255 b. Feb. 12, 1863.
1163 b. Dec. 6, 1859.	1212 b. Sept. 10, 1853.	1256 b. Aug. 15, 1868.
1164 b. July 9, 1862.	1213 b. Nov. 1, 1855.	1257 b. Oct. 9, 1870.
1165 b. Aug. 13, 1864.	1214 } b. Sept. 13, 1858.	1258 b. Sept. 18, 1865.
1166 b. Oct. 10, 1866.	1215 }	1259 b. Aug. 29, 1869 ;
1167 b. Aug. 20, 1868.	1216 b. Jan. 6, 1861.	d. Oct. 5, 1870.

The only name reported in the ninth generation is that of Clara Nellie Logan, b. Mar. 23, 1870 ; dau. of Lydia Ann Slawter (No. 1104,) and William Logan. Nos. 1026 and 1027 have children, but their names were not furnished.

RECAPITULATION.

The following table of the descendants, in brief, will show more readily the relationship of the different branches to each other. The numbers on the right refer to the descendants in the fifth generation.

SECOND GEN.	THIRD GENERATION.	FOURTH GENERATION.
(Children of John and Mary Dutton) 2. Elizabeth.	7. John	33. Prudence SHELLEY. 34. John. 35. Elizabeth BOOTH. 36. Benjamin. 37. Isaac. ....83-89. 38. Henry.
	8. Hannah SCARLETT.	39. Elizabeth. 40. Mary Cox.............90. 41. Joseph. 42. John.............91-98. 43. Hannah BAILY, ...99-108.
	9. Mary COBOURN.	44. Joseph. 45. Deborah WILEY.............109. 46. Nathaniel. 47. Lydia.
3. John	10. Kingsman	48. Francis.............110-115. 49. David.............116-125.
	11. Jacob	50. Rebecca.
	12. Joseph	51. Mary. 52. Jacob.............120-132. 53. James. 54. Susanna. 55. Hannah. 56. Elizabeth. 57. Joseph.............133-139.
	13. Robert	58. Susanna. 59. Hannah.
	14. James	60. John. 61. James.
	15. Isaac 16. Amy TALLEY.	62. Elizabeth. 63. Sarah BROWNE.
4. Edward	17. Mary DAVIS. 18. John.	64. John. 65. Elizabeth CASEY. 66. Mary. 67. Samuel. 68. David.............140-142.
	19. William.	
5. Thomas	20. Thomas. 21. Rebecca. 22. Richard	69. Thomas.............143-149. 70. Hannah RICHARDS.............150-159. 71. Joseph. 72. Rebecca PILKINGTON. 73. Mary BOOTH. 74. Jonathan.............160-169. 75. Richard.
	23. David 24. Lydia HEWES. 25. Jonathan. 26. John. 27. Mary GRUBB. 28. Sarah POWER.	76. Mary YEARSLEY. 77. Sarah BOOTH. 78. Elizabeth M'CLELLAN. 79. Lydia MANCIL.............170-173.
6. Robert	29. Mary. 30. Ann. 31. Robert. 32. Elizabeth ENGLAND.	80. Robert. 81. William. 82. Hannah.

5th GENERATION.	6th GENERATION.	7th GENERATION.	8th GENERATION.
83. Prudence............ CHEYNEY.	174. David.		
84. Mary............ WORRALL.	175. Joseph.		
85. Isaac............	176. Samuel P.		
	177. Isaac D............	419. William B.	
	178. John.		
86. Benjamin.	179. Ruth E.		
	180. John.		
87. Elizabeth............ HANNUM.	181. Samuel E.		
	182. Elizabeth.		
88. Joseph L.	183. Evalina.	420. Sarah............	925. Abigail T.
89. Rachel SHULL.	184. Jane.	R. L. WALTER.	926. Jennie H.
	185. William.		927. Mary T.
90. Nathaniel COX.	186. Philip E.		928. William.
	187. Rachel.	421. Jeremiah............	929. J. Hallowell.
	188. Joseph D.		
			930. Eugene.
91. Hannah.			931. Samuel E.
92. Joseph.		422. Eli............	932. R. Walter.
93. Sarah............	189. Mary............		933. Annie.
THOMPSON.	STARR.	423. Anna.	
		424. Samuel.	934. Mary Ella.
		425. Mary Anna............	
		HAINES.	
		426. Charles T.	
	190. James.		
	191. William............	427. Rowland G.	935. Samuel.
			936. Mary.
	192. Mary............	428. Ephraim............	937. James.
	DICKINSON.		
		429. Benjamin............	938. Annie.
		430. Elwood.	939. Daniel S.
		431. Anna Lydia.	
94. Lydia............	193. John............	432. Mary D.	
SCARLETT.		433. James Miller.	
		434. Wm. Penn.	940. William.
		435. Lydia Ann............	941. Lee.
		HARTS.	942. John.
	194. Ephraim............	436. Eli............	943. Sarah.
			944. Nallie, dec'd.
			945. William.
			946. Martha.
		437. James............	947. Anna.
		438. Lee.	948. John.
			949. Etna.
	195. Susanna............	439. Ephraim............	950. Elizabeth.
	MILLER.	440. Elizabeth.	951. Clyde.
	196. Susanna............	441. Ann S.	
	CHAMBERS.	442. Hannah M............	952. Anna M.
		WINDLE.	953. Samuel E.
	198. Mary............	443. Susan N.	
	SAM'L WAY.	444. Ellen B............	954. William.
		INGRAM.	
		445. Marshall S.	
		446. Samuel E.	
95. John............	197. Martha............	447. John.	
	O. HEALD.	448. Anna.	
		449. Joseph.	
	199. Marshall.	450. Jacob.	
		451. Hannah M.	
	200. John.	452. William.	
		453. Mary R.	
	201. Ann............	454. Elizabeth W.	
	E. PASSMORE.	455. James D.	
		456. William............	955. William.
		457. Mary.	

5th GENERATION.	6th GENERATION.	7th GENERATION.	8th GENERATION.
		458. James.	956. Mary R. 957. Howard. 958. Phebe. 959. George. 960. Arthur.
		450. Pusey.	
	202. Hannah. CHAMBERS.	460. Edwin. 461. Susanna P. 462. Maris. 463. Sarah P.	961. J. Barnard. 962. Paul. 963. Alice, dec'd. 964. Sarah.
96. Mary. THOMPSON.	203. Mary.	464. Hannah T. CROASDALE.	965. Robert. 966. Kate. 967. John P.
	204. Elizabeth.	465. Ruth Ann. HUEY.	968. Elsie. 969. Frederick.
	205. John.	466. Elizabeth. 467. John T.	
	206. Mary D. HUGHES.	468. Lydia. 469. James T. 470. Henry C. 471. Sallie. 472. Alfred. 473. Mary Emma.	
	207. Sarah. JOHNSON.	474. Sarah. MARSHALL.	970. William J. 971. Anna P. 972. Ellis.
	208. Sarah. 209. Mary. MARSHALL.	475. Mary S.	
	210. Abiah.	476. Anna Mary. 477. William H. 478. Taylor. 479. Elizabeth H.	
97. Nathaniel.	211. Deborah. WAY.	480. Charles C. 481. Nathaniel S. 482. George B. 483. Alfred. 484. Francis.	
98. Deborah.			
99. Nathaniel. 100. Eli. 101. Jesse. 102. Hannah. 103. Benjamin. 104. Ellis. 105. Sarah. 106. Deborah. 107. Mary. 108. Isaac.	212. Ann. HICKS.	485. Sarah J. 486. Mary B. 487. Lydia. 488. Amie.	
	213. Joel.	489. Mary M. 490. Annie C. 491. Phebe.	
109. Hannah.		492. Edwin.	973. Henry. 974. Mary S.
110. John T.	214. Jacob.	493. Mary J. LOGUE.	975. Jacob. 976. Henry. 977. Sallie Ann, dec.
112. David.		494. Jonathan.	978. William. 979. Flora. 980. Lillian.
113. Elisha.			
114. Francis.	216. Hannah. 217. Maria. 218. Sarah. 219. Eliza. 220. Phebe. 221. Matilda. 222. Deborah.	495. Sallie Ann. PETTIT.	981. Clarence. 982. Emily.
115. Jacob.		496. William P.	983. Alonzo. 984. Anna.
111. Joseph. (misplaced.)		497. Frank.	985. Willie S.
	215. Elisha. (misplaced.)	498. Joseph. 499. John. 500. Emma.	
	223. David.	501. Josephine.	

5th GENERATION.	6th GENERATION.	7th GENERATION.	8th GENERATION.
116. William............	224. John. 225. Martin.		
117. Susan............ COWARDEN.	226. Samuel. 227. David.	502. Robert M. 503. Alice A.	
118. Mary............... LAMEY.	228. Louisa. 229. David. 230. Robert.	504. John E. 505. Mary S. 506. Benjamin F. 507. Susan E.	
	231. William........	508. Sarah L. 509. William H.	
	232. David...............	510. Victoria. 511. Sereno............ 512. Robert S. 513. John W. 514. Nehemiah. 515. Joseph. 516. Mary E. 517. David. 518. Rachel L.	three children.
119. Robert............	233. Rachel M....... BECK.	519. Hannah M. 520. Abigail............ 521. George R........ 522. Robert W......... 523. Anna. 524. Adazilla...........	five children. two children. three children. two children.
	234. John. 235. Hannah. 236. Rees.	525. Alana Ann. 526. Rachel L. 527. Francis L. 528. John L.	
	237. Robert	529. Uriah M. 530. Mary Elma. 531. Elmer E. 532. James Clement. 533. Cora Maud. 534. Netta Blanch. 535. Elizabeth L.	
	238. Nehemiah. 239. Martha. 240. Cynthia. 241. Ezra. 242. Hannah.		
	243. Uriah..............	536. Alcinda............ 537. John............ 538. Caroline. 539. Morris............ 540. Robert. 541. Amanda.	529. Uriah M. four children. one child.
120. Sarah.............. MATSON.	244. Elizabeth........ WADE.	542. Sarah. 543. N. Allen. 544. Rowena. 545. Adelaide. 546. Martha............ 547. Genevra.	one child.
	245. Morris	548. Morris.	
121. David..............	246. Victoria. 247. John Rogers...... 248. Isabel M. 249. Franklin. 250. Thomas L. 251. Hannah Jane.	549. Elizabeth R. 550. Mary. 551. Linton R. 552. Alvin J. 553. William S. 554. Robert R. 555. Blanch.	
	252. Sarah A. 253. Robert F. 254. David. 255. Rebecca.	556. Maud. 557. Harry.	
122. Hannah............ MENSIL.	256. Louisa. 257. Mary. 258. Hester. 259. Susan.		
123. Nancy.	260. Almy. 261. Elizabeth.		

5th GENERATION.	6th GENERATION.	7th GENERATION.	8th GENERATION.
124 Asa	262 Sarah V............ PATTON	558 Hannah 559 Robert 560 Matthew 561 Jennie 562 Wilson 563 Frank	
	263 Franklin A........	564 George 565 Mary Bella	
125 Francis R.........	264 Julia A. 265 Effinety A .... SMITH	566 ...... REYNOLDS....	986 Lena
	266 Joseph B 267 Mary J .... 268 Hannah 269 Catharine M...... 270 Harriet A......... 271 James W .... 272 Maria H 273 David D	one child eight children ten children 567 Maggie 568 Fanny 569 Parke	
126 Tho. Bishop	274 Rachel		987 James Franklin 988 Mary E. 989 Annie T. 990 Lizzie A.
127 Elizabeth	275 Jane................ 276 Elizabeth CAMPBELL	570 Lorenzo D .... 571 Bennett 572 Margaret Ann	991 Laura G. 992 Maggie D.
128 Margaret........... GOULD	277 Joseph	573 J Harrison........	993 Adaline C. 994 Harrison
	278 Samuel 279 Jacob D. 280 Mary	574 Pierce .... 575 Adaline C. 576 Joshua 577 Lola M.	995 Joseph H.
129 Jacob			
130 Joseph	281 Margaretta B.	578 William H. 579 Townsend H 580 Joseph D. 581 Samuel 582 Thomas C. L. 583 Granville W.	
131 Jane	282 Elizabeth J ...... WALTER	584 Edwin P. 585 Abby Rebecca 586 Mary Ann 587 Evans 588 Edith W	
	283 Ethan G.............	589 Jacob J .... 590 John F. 591 Sarah E .... BOWERS 592 Mary Jane 593 Joseph C. 594 Enoch G. 595 Martha Ann 596 Florence 597 Willamina	996 Geo. Franklin 997 Edward E 998 Joseph
	284 Margaret E .... TALLEY	598 Willamina 599 Joseph 600 Mary F. .... HEATH 601 Hiram D.	999 Josephine 1000 Wm. Henry
	285 Jacob	602 Elthera C........... HICKMAN	1001 Lizzie
132 James	286 Susan J.............. FOULK	603 Anna Mary 604 John 605 Sue H. 606 James K. 607 Thomas H.	
	287 Hicklen G.	608 Nelson 609 William R. 610 Harlan B.	
	288 James B.............	611 Joseph A. 612 Mary E.............. KATES	1002 Harry Chester 1003 W. Thompson

13

5th GENERATION.	6th GENERATION.	7th GENERATION.	8th GENERATION.
	289 Thomas B.	613 Emma J. 614 Mary G. 615 Emily B. 616 Levi W.	
	290 Rachel Ann...... BOWKER	617 George 618 Harry E.	
	291 Mary E.	619 Frank	
133 Elizabeth 134 Ann	292 George	620 Annie Bell........ DYER.	1004 Elizabeth D. 1005 Sarah V.
135 Joseph,............ 136 George	293 Elizabeth B...... M'COLLEY	621 Hester F. 622 Joseph D. 623 Theodosia	
137 Jacob	294 Emeline M. 295 Edgar C. 296 Mary M.		
138 Mary .... PIERCE.	297 Sidney A. 298 Lindsey L. 299 John T.		
	300 Mary Emma 301 Elizabeth J.	624 Anna Bell 625 Emma	
139 Sidney A............ DOWNING	302 James N....... 303 Edward J. 304 William S. 305 Charles W.	626 Charles E. 627 William J. 628 Rebecca J.	
140 Benjamin......... 141 Anne 142 Caleb	306 William J, 307 Benjamin V. 308 Hannah		
	309 Sarah 310 Thomas............	629 Mary Ann 630 William 631 Harriet	1006 Isaac T. 1007 Adelaide V. 1008 Catharine T. 1009 Lewis T.
		632 Lewis T............	1010 Mary 1011 William M. 1012 Sophia T.
143 Richard	311 Isaac..................	633 Sarah M. .... HOVER	1013 Catharine 1014 Sarah 1015 Frances 1016 Howard D.
	312 Richard	634 Richard R....... 635 Alexander L. 636 Augustus P. 637 Catharine M.	1017 Richard R. 1018 Sarah O. 1019 Mary M. 1020 Alexander P.
	313 Larkin	638 Norris 639 George 640 John Richard 641 Anna M.	
	314 John B.	642 Simeon M.	

	315 Mary
	316 Hannah............
	     LONB
		643 Esther.............
		     LEVIS
			1021 Hannah H.
			1022 Anna
			1023 Albert

	317 John................	644 Amy Ann	
	318 Thomas.............	645 John 646 Hannah	
		647 Phebe............ BAILEY	1024 Jacob 1025 Walter
			1026 John D. 1027 Elmira M. 1028 Mary E. 1029 Jacob H.
	319 Jacob..............	648 Lydia............. SHEEHAN	1030 James A. 1031 Joseph A. 1032 Franklin 1033 Jesse P. 1034 George O.
144 Sarah............... HIBBERD			
		649 Mary Ann	1035 Arabell, dec. 1036 Phineas
		650 Jesse................. 651 Sarah 652 Dutton	1037 Roxanna} 1038 Albert 1039 Estella, dec. 1040 Taylor

5th GENERATION.	6th GENERATION.	7th GENERATION.	8th GENERATION.
	320 Phinehas 321 Phebe		1041 Perry 1042 Lettie
	322 Samuel	653 Jacob	1043 Bertha 1044 John 1045 Elwood
	323 Jesse	654 Jesse. 655 Mary 656 Elizabeth 657 John	1046 Samuel
	324 Susanna M. COX	658 Sarah D. 659 J. Hibberd 660 William G 661 Levi 662 Gulielma	1047 Eugene 1048 Susanna 1049 Harriet 1050 Gulielma S.
	325 Sarah D. HALL	663 Jacob H.	1051 Sarah 1052 Maria 1053 J. Barclay
145 George	326 Abraham	664 Susanna ELDRIDGE 665 Jesse 666 Barclay 667 Mary 668 Clarkson 669 Hannah 670 Maria	1054 Maria 1055 Jonathan 1056 Sarah 1057 Sarah
146 Mary	327 Hannah		1058 Susan P.* 1059 I. Powell*
	328 Susanna* POWELL	671 Sarah D. LEEDS 672 Benj. Rush	1060 B. Rush* 1061 Samuel 1062 Ruth Ann* 1063 Mary W.*
	329 John	673 Sallie J.* 674 William R.	1064 Mary Hillman* 1065 Anna S.*
	330 Rowland	675 Rowland J.*	1066 Edith Helen
	331 Thomas	676 Mary ALLEN	1067 Rowland D.* 1068 Wm. Charles* 1069 Richard J.* 1070 Mary 1071 George D. 1072 Henry D.
		677 Charles R. 678 Charles S. 679 Hannah ELLIS	1073 Bessie
	332 Edmund	680 Thomas* 681 George	1074 Charles S.
147 Thomas		682 Sallie J. 683 Elizabeth M.* BARTRAM	1075 Anna D. 1076 Mary T. 1077 Sarah D. 1078 George H.
		684 Thomas D.	1079 Randal P.
		685 Edward*	1080 Fannie* 1081 Deborah, dec. 1082 Charles* 1083 Mary* 1084 Jared* 1085 Anna*
		686 Sarah J.*	1086 Beulah
		687 Albert*	1087 Sue* 1088 Mary D.*
	333 Mary* DARLINGTON	688 Amy* PRATT	1089 Sarah D.* 1090 Emily 1091 Albert D.*
		689 Frances* 690 Jesse* 691 Thomas 692 Jared* 693 Mary* 694 Ruthanna	1092 Horace* 1093 Mary Ella

5th GENERATION.	6th GENERATION.	7th GENERATION.	8th GENERATION.
	334 Samuel*	695 Mary E.*	
	335 Nathan C.*	696 Thomas E.	
		697 Edmund	
		698 Lewis G.*	
		699 George S.*	
	336 Ruthanna	700 Mary	
	CASSIN	701 Charles L.*	
		702 Jane R.	
		703 Sidney B.	
	337 Amy P.*	704 Mary D.*	
	WILLIAMSON	705 Ruthanna	
		706 Rebecca*	
		707 Charles*	
	338 Thomas D.		
	339 John		
	340 Abraham		
148 Hannah	341 Daniel		
BROOMALL	342 Susanna		
	343 James		
	344 James		
	345 Hannah D.		
	346 Mary		
	347 Thomas		
	348 Hannah	708 Thomas	1094 Lewis Edward
	349 Susanna M.	709 Edward	1095 Sarah Jane
149 Susanna	350 Andrew		1096 Mary Ann
STEEL	351 Margaretta	710 Joseph	1097 Elizabeth E.
	352 Anne		
	353 Hannah	711 Jane W	1098 Charles
	354 Nathaniel	RIDGWAY	1099 Ella W.
		712 Dutton	1100 Arlina
		713 Susanna	1101 Estella
		CURRINDER	
150 Thomas		714 Franklin	
		715 Anna Maria	
		716 James R.	
		717 Joseph	
		718 Mary Ann	1102 Joseph D.
	355 Mary Ann	NELLING	1103 Abigail Jane
	DIZER	719 Susanna R.	
		720 William	
		721 Abby Ann	
		722 Tho. Jefferson	1104 Lydia Ann
		723 G. Washington	LOGAN
		724 Susanna	1105 John Elwood
		725 Jemima	1106 Susanna
		726 John	1107 Ida Maria
			1108 Charles Levis
151 Nathaniel			1109 Rachel Worrall
			1110 Albert
			1111 Henry
	356 Lydia	727 Mary	1112 Eliza
	SLAWTER	CONN	1113 John Edwin
			1114 Garrett L.
		728 Lydia Ann	
		729 Jehu D	1115 George E. M.
		730 Lewis	
		731 Humphrey J.	
		732 Charles E.	
		733 Hannah A.	
			1116 Morris W.
		734 Jonathan	1117 Lizzie
152 Jonathan		735 Susanna	1118 John
153 Joseph		PLUMLEY	1119 Anna Mary
154 Richard	357 Joseph	736 Sarah	1120 Harry
155 Josiah			1121 William
156 Lucy			1122 Louisa R.
157 Hannah			
158 Lydia	358 Sarah	737 Elizabeth	1123 Ell N.
159 Dutton		JOHNSON	1124 William C.
		738 Louisa	1125 Frank

5th GENERATION.	6th GENERATION.	7th GENERATION.	8th GENERATION.
160 Mary	359 Mary Ann.......... HARRISON	739 Eleanor 740 John D............... 741 Samuel 742 Joshua	1126 Mary Ellen
	360 Elizabeth 361 Susanna	743 Mary E............... BAILY 744 John Alfred 745 Susan D.............	1127 Joseph Henry 1128 Ezekiel Elwood 1129 Florence V.
	362 Esther P............. HANNUM	746 Samuel P. 747 Lewis 748 Samuel P. 749 Jane	1130 Eugene
161 John...............		750 Anna Eliza 751 Eleanor 752 Esther Anna 753 Emma Louisa	
	363 Jonathan...........	754 Jane............. ...... CLAYTON 755 Annie G. 756 John..................	1131 Maggie
		757 George G...........	1132 Clara B.
		758 Elizabeth.	1133 Laura J. 1134 William J.
	364 Isaac P.............	759 Henry H. 760 Mary E. 761 Henrietta 762 J. Elwood 763 Maurice 764 Eugene	1135 Kate 1136 Marey Pennell
		765 Hannah E. 766 Tho. Vernon...... 767 Samuel E. 768 Sarah V.	1137 Caroline G. 1138 Richard H. 1139 B. Franklin 1140 Lincoln
	365 John...............	769 Richard H.......... 770 Sidney F. 771 Rachel 772 Emma 773 Martha	1141 William
	366 Ann 367 Isaac	774 Mary Elizabeth 775 William H.	
	368 Rachel .... GRUBB. 369 Hannah	776 William T..........	1142 Albert 1143 George
		777 Isaac L...............	1144 Joseph H. 1145 Howard 1146 Arthur Pratt
		778 Henry S.	
		779 Beulah T......... ... SAGER.	1147 Elmer E. 1148 John P. 1149 Joseph Henry
	370 Joseph...............	780 Rebecca.......... JAMES	1150 Joseph Henry
162 Richard............		781 Richard 782 Edward 783 Lydia Ann 784 Sallie 785 Emma	
		786 Lydia Ann......... MANCIL	1234 Edwin Bennett 1235 Thomas Wilder
	371 Martha............... TEMPLE	787 Thomas R......... 788 Rachel B.	1151 Lydia Martha 1152 Wm. Clemson
	372 Jonathan...........	789 Richard S. 790 Reece R. 791 Alfred B. 792 Thomas H. 793 Isaac L. 794 H. Lincoln	

5th GENERATION.	6th GENERATION.	7th GENERATION.	8th GENERATION.
163 Alice..... .... PAISTE	373 Jonathan...........	795 William 796 Alice A. 797 Lydia 798 Ann 799 Jesse 800 Elizabeth 801 Sarah 802 Jonathan D.	
164 Lucy	374 Sarah.............. BAYNES 375 Mary	803 Alice P.............. TWINING	1153 Joseph B. 1154 Horace B.
165 Martha............. PENNELL	376 Jonathan..........	804 Ann Eliza.......... HENRY	1155 Isaac James 1156 Joseph J. 1157 Sarah E. 1158 Laura W. 1159 William H.
		805 Joseph.............	1160 Francis 1161 William
		806 John............	1162 Sarah J. 1163 Hannah V. 1164 John H. 1165 Isaac James 1166 Ida Mary 1167 Grace Ann 1168 Parrish P.
		807 Mary Jane........ HINKSON	1169 Ella Baker 1170 Howard R. 1171 William S.,dec. 1172 Rosannna, dec.
		808 Emma .... HATTON 809 Isaac James	1173 Rebecca Krug 1174 Wm. Baker 1175 Roseanna, dec.
166 Jonathan...........	377 Martha............. WEST 378 Nathan P. 379 Susanna............. MANCIL 380 Hannah H......... VALENTINE 381 Gulielma 382 Sarah 383 Beulah 384 Rebecca Ann.... ELLIOTT 385 David H............. 386 Wm. Henry	810 Samuel 811 Jonathan D. 812 Wm. Pusey 813 Elias Hicks 814 Rachel P........... LEYS 815 Kate D.	1176 James F.
		802-806	
		816 Anna Regina 817 Harry W.	
		818 Joseph T. 819 Melinda 820 Jonathan D.	
		821 Horace H. 822 Rachel P. 823 Bessie	
	387 Robert R....	824 Emily F............. LARKIN	1177 Laura C. 1178 Horace Finch 1179 John Morton
		825 Caroline........... GARRETT	1180 Howard Lee 1181 John Lentz 1182 Carrie Lewis.
		826 Hannah B......... RANDLE	1183 Henry B. 1184 Hattie Bell
		827 Arabella .... HINKSON	1185 Hannah H.
		828 Julius A. 829 Albert 830 Henry B. 831 Benjamin B. 832 Howard	

5th GENERATION.	6th GENERATION.	7th GENERATION.	8th GENERATION.
167 Thomas	388 Aaron L.	833 Clara Sanford 834 James Mortimer 835 Thomas 836 Clarence B.	
	389 Jesse	837 Eliza Lamela 838 Anna Louisa 839 Tho. Elwood 840 Laura E. 841 Susan E.	
	390 Emily HANNUM	842 Susan D. 843 Charles E. 844 Clara E.	
168 Amor	391 Charles	845 Hannah E. 846 Howard J. 847 Elizabeth W. 848 Charles L. 849 Wm. Worrall 850 Jesse Alfred	
	392 Sidney HICKMAN	851 Geo. Washington 852 Robert R. 853 Sidney Emma 854 Anna Mary 855 Tho. Elwood	
169 Rebecca	393 Susan Ann HANNUM	856 Susan Anna W.	
170 William	394 Lydia GRIFFITH	857 Susanna 858 Ann Eliza 859 Rachel 860 Willam M. 861 Maria H. 862 Frederick P. 863 Isaac M. 864 Abigail E. FAULKNER 865 Joseph H. 866 Jesse L. 867 Lydia Ann 868 Susan CRAIG	1104-1109 1186 Annie 1187 Josephine 1188 James 1189 Wm. Henry 1190 Isaac S. 1191 Albert M. 1192 Lizzie V. 1193 Harry D.
	395 Elizabeth VERNON	869 William M. 870 Elizabeth C. 871 Martha P. 872 Sarah Ann HINKSON 873 Emma 874 Mary T. KING 875 Susanna PHILLIPS	1194 Sarah E. 1195 Emma 1196 Charles 1197 Lewis 1198 Annie 1199 Lizzie C. 1200 Lewis L. 1201 Lillian 1202 Clara 1203 Ulysses 1204 Sallie M. 1205 Medora 1206 Sallie K. 1207 Dayton
	396 David D.	876 Morris H. 877 Caroline (in. 729) 878 Harriet B. 879 Samuel B. 880 William 881 George E. 882 Mahlon 883 David D. 884 Elisha 865 Mary E. SIMPKINS	1208 Emma Lee 1209 William H. 1210 Horace L. 1211 Judson B. 1212 Allen A. 1213 Lizzie S. 1214 Wm. Choe 1215 Mary C. 1216 Claire Ida

5th GENERATION.	6th GENERATION.	7th GENERATION.	8th GENERATION.
			1217 Claire E.
			1218 Clarence E.
	397 Susan.............	886 David C.	1219 Lettie A.
	ORISWOLD		1220 Hettie P.
			1221 Libby M.
		887 William P.	1222 Florence E.
			1223 Maverot A.
			1224 Carrie D.
		888 Lydia S.	1225 Minia E.
		HILYER	1226 Hiram E.
			1227 Theodore S.
		889 Laura...............	1228 Charles C.
		CALLAHAN	1229 William
			1230 Curtis J.
			1231 Elve H.
		890 Margaret A........	1232 Jesse E.
		DOWNS	1233 William H.
		891 Clarinda	1234 Edwin B.
		892 Alfred..............	1235 Thomas W.
		893 Nathan P.	
		894 Rachel A.	
	398 Mahlon...............	895 Sarah D.	
		896 Arabella	
		897 Curtis	
		898 William	
	399 Edward	899 John Wesley	
		900 Eli It.	
		901 Mary Jane	
		902 Elihu...............	1236 Eli D.
		903 J. A. Bayard	
	400 Mary J.............	904 Lydia Ann.........	1237 Mary T.
	TALLEY	PALMER	
		905 Caroline E........	1238 Ellen T.
		SPRINGER	1239 Ella T.
		906 Harriet E.	1240 Mary A.
		907 Sarah Jane.......	1241 William A.
		BLACK	1242 Harlan G.
		908 John W.	1243 Flora Meade
171 John...............		909 Mary Ellen.......	1244 Lydia Emma
		CHURNSIDE	1245 John W.
	401 Ellen	910 Lydia A.	1246 Howard C.
	M'KEE	911 Juliet	
		912 Keziah E.	1247 Theodore T.
			1248 Mary Emma
		913 Barton	1249 Anna F.
		914 Amor H...........	1250 Sarah E.
			1251 Martha Jane
			1252 Margaret M.
		915 Susanna S.	1253 Harriet A.
			1254 Jno. Chandler
	402 Abigail.............		1255 Elizabeth
	CHANDLER	916 Mary E......	1256 Joseph L.
		PYLE	1257 William G.
		917 Rachel A.	
	403 Lydia	918 William T.........	1258 Franklin E.
			1259 James E.
		919 George D.	
	404 William............	920 Josephine	
172 Ann	405 Mary	921 Ann Elizabeth	
THOMPSON	406 Lydia	922 Mary Emma.	
	407 Emeline	923 Leonard B.	
	408 Susan	924 Ruth Hannah	
	409 Hannah		
	410 Jesse		
	411 Ann		
	412 Eliza		
	413 John		
173 Joseph...............	414 Lydia D.		
	415 Mary S.		
	416 Susan		
	417 Joseph		
	418 William		

APPENDIX.

NOTE A.—page 59.

A CENTENNIAL BIRTH-DAY CELEBRATION.

From the "American Republican" of Feb. 9, 1869.

On the 2nd inst. the descendants and relatives of THOMAS DUTTON met at his residence in Aston township, to celebrate the completion of his 100th year of existence. For some time previous considerable anxiety was felt lest the weather should prove stormy, and thus mar, if not entirely prevent, the anticipated pleasures of the day; but it turned out quite as favorable as could be expected, considering the season of the year. The day was cloudy, and consequently somewhat cool and chilly, but this was compensated by the ground remaining dry and frozen. Those from West Chester and vicinity proceeded by rail to Rockdale, where they arrived a few minutes before 9 o'clock, and were soon met by those from Philadelphia, for whose accommodation a special car had been allowed. A few carriages had been provided for some of the more aged and frail; but the walking being good, the most of the company started off on foot, forming quite a procession. After passing down the picturesque valley of Chester creek about a mile, we turned to the right, and soon arrived at the old mansion, situated on the south side of a sloping hill. Here preparations had been made for the occasion on the day previous, by erecting a large tent adjoining the west end of the house, and in this a large stove and seats had been placed. Without this convenience, for which we were indebted to Dr. Rowland, of Media, there would have been much less comfort, as the house would not contain one half the assembled guests, although every room was thrown open for their accommodation. In addition to those who came by rail, a great many from the surrounding country soon after arrived in their own conveyances. It was pleasant to witness the many greetings amongst relatives and friends who had not met for years, but were now brought together on this unusual occasion. New acquaintances were also formed, while on the other hand a feeling of sadness could not but steal over the hearts of some, on recalling to mind the near and dear ones who had been removed by death, and whose absence at this time was realized afresh. At half-past 12 o'clock, dinner was announced, which was somewhat on the pic-nic order—many of the company having brought provisions with them. These being arranged on tables in house and tent, by the fair hands of granddaughters and great granddaughters, &c., presented a sight well calculated to make a hungry person feel happy. There were turkeys, chickens, cold tongue and other substantials, as well as a profusion of the more tempting, though less wholesome luxuries. Among the latter must be noticed several large and beautiful cakes, bearing inscriptions, or rather superscriptions, in raised letters on the white frosting; one of which read thus:—"Centennial Birth Day, Thomas Dutton, Feb. 2nd, 1869;" another, "To our Uncle, Feb. 2nd, Age 100." Dinner being disposed of, the descendants and near relatives of Thomas Dutton were collected in front of the dwelling for the purpose of having a photograph taken of the group by Alfred Hemple, an artist from Philadelphia. The roll was called, and the children with their consorts took their places on the porch, while below and in front were stationed in regular order, the grandchildren and great grandchildren. These being arranged, the venerable patriarch was brought out in his large arm chair, and placed in the midst of his children,

14

when in an instant, almost, the scene was photographed. Another
picture was taken of the old man alone, after which he was conveyed
again to his room, as it was feared that much exposure to the chilly
air might prove injurious to him.   A third picture was taken of all
the friends assembled, but I regret to say the second was accidentally spoiled.

After this a meeting was called in the tent, and on motion Samuel
Dutton, the oldest son living, took the chair, and Charles L. Cassin,
a grandson, was appointed Secretary.   An address was read, referring
to the great advances in civilization, science and agriculture, within
the century just closed ; also some portions of the genealogy of the
family.   By invitation, Samuel B. Thomas then delivered a short but
appropriate extempore address ; after which a song composed
by a granddaughter for the occasion, was sung and followed by
"Auld Lang Syne," when the meeting adjourned.   A book had been
provided for the purpose, in which those assembled were requested to
register their names and residences, and more than two hundred and
fifty did so.   The total number of Thomas Dutton's descendants, as
reported, is 70, of whom 56 are living and 44 were present.   Number
of descendants by marriage, 24—of whom 17 are living and 12 were
present.* Soon after 4 o'clock the company began to disperse to their
various homes, and many returned to Rockdale to meet the trains both
east and west ; those going to Philadelphia having a car for their own
use, as in the morning, through the kindness of Edward Hoopes,
one of the directors, who is also a nephew of Thomas Dutton.

Thus ended a day long to be remembered by all present, and every
one appeared to enjoy the occasion.

*Those of the lineal descendants who were present have been designated by an
asterisk (*) on pages 99 and 100.   The 12 descendants by marriage were the consorts of Nos. 331, 334, 335, 671, 674, 675, 676, 679, 680, 685, 688, 690.

THE DUTTONS OF CONNECTICUT.

Some of the Dutton family emigrated to New England more than fifty years prior to the settlement of Pennsylvania, and their descendants are now scattered all over the United States.

Savage, in his "Genealogical Dictionary of New England," states that John Dutton arrived in 1630, but he knew not where he seated himself. Thomas Dutton of Woburn, perhaps a son of John, was born about 1621 and lived for some time at Reading, where, by his wife Susan, it is thought he had

THOMAS, born 1648.
MARY, Nov. 14, 1651.
SUSANNA, Feb. 27, 1654.
JOHN, March 2, 1656.

but the following probably at Woburn:

ELIZABETH, Jan. 28, 1659.
JOSEPH, Jan. 25, 1661.
SARAH, Mar. 5, 1662.
JAMES, Aug. 22, 1665.
BENJAMIN, Feb. 19, 1669.

He removed to Billerica, and was there in 1675, with his sons Thomas and John. His son Thomas was wounded and had a remarkable escape in 1677, when Capt. Swett and many of his men were killed in the Indian war at the East.

His wife died May 27, 1684, aged 58, and he married 9, Nov. following to Ruth Hooper.

Chester Dutton of Lake Sibley, Kansas, has furnished an extended record of his ancestors and relatives, which is here given in an abridged form:

My family record goes back with certainty only to Thomas Dutton, of Wallingford, Conn., who, in the early part of the 18th century, was living there with three brothers—Samuel, Benjamin and David. These four brothers are understood to have been sons of David Dutton, who, at a still earlier date, was living, together with his brother Jonathan at Barnstable, Mass.; and these again may have been grandsons of Thomas Dutton of Woburn and Billerica.

Samuel Dutton of Wallingford, was born in 1700, and at an early age removed to East Haddam, Ct., where he married Sally Cone, a noted beauty, and from her his numerous descendants very generally inherit black eyes. The late George Dutton of Utica, N. Y., a great grandson of Samuel, devoted considerable attention to the family history, and left a record in manuscript which is still preserved. His son William Henry Dutton is an extensive dealer in pianos in Philadelphia, Pa.

Thomas Dutton of Wallingford removed about the year 1757 to Washington, Ct., and afterwards, in the decline of life, lived ten or twelve years with his son Thomas in Watertown, Ct. At the age of 85 or 86 he visited his younger sons in Vermont, and died there, at Royalton, in 1802, at the advanced age of 93 years. He was distinguished for his religion and personal piety, and of his sons all who lived to manhood were members of, and four of them officers in christian churches. His children were—

(SECOND GENERATION.)

1. **Abigail**, who married Thomas Parker of Washington, Ct., and had eight children. Judge Amasa J. Parker of Albany N. Y. a great grandson.

2. **Thomas**, b. Jan. 31, 1735; m. Mar. 1756 to Anna Rice (*Roys* in the old records,) of Wallingford, and removed to that part of Waterbury, New Haven Co., which is now Watertown, Litchfield Co., Ct., and settled upon a farm of 200 acres, which at the time was bounded on all sides by " the King's land." Besides his farm he carried on the business of a house joiner, and nearly all the churches and meeting houses standing in that part of the country as late as 1830, were built by him, and nearly all the joiners of middle age or older had learned the trade of him. He was captain of a company of militia in service at the defence of New York in 1776, but the title which he most affected, and by which he was generally known among his neighbors, was that of Deacon Thomas Dutton. He died Jan. 29, 1806.

3. **Lois**, m. a Mr. Mosely and settled at Poultney, Vt.; had several children.

4. **Samuel**, moved from Washington, Ct. to Woodstock and Hartford, Vt. ; had 12 children.

5. **Matthew**, died young and unmarried.

6. **Amasa**, moved to Royalton Vt.; had a large family.

7. **Asahel**, died young and unmarried.

8. **John**, moved from Washington Ct., to Hartford Vt.; died in middle life, leaving five children.

9. **Asenath**, m. to a Mr. Hopson; moved to Chatham, Ct. ; died young, leaving two children.

10. **Nathaniel**, moved from Washington to Hartford, Vermont; had several children.

THIRD GENERATION.

Children of Deacon Thomas (No. 2,) and Anna Rice Dutton.

11. **Reuben**, b. Feb. 18, 1757 ; d. May 23, 1757, in infancy.

12. **Reuben**, b. Mar. 21, 1758 ; d. June 11, 1759, in infancy.

13. **Thomas**, b. Mar. 21, 1760 ; d. Sept. 18, 1835 ; m. Sept. 15, 1782, Thankful Punderson of New Haven. He died at the old homestead in Watertown, where he spent his whole life, except a few years at one time when in the mercantile business in the neighboring town of Plymouth. He practiced his father's and grandfather's trade of house joiner, and some houses of his building are still standing in New Haven and Watertown, which are conspicuous for the elegance of their finish. His later years were devoted to his farm and the society of his numerous friends, who delighted to listen to his fascinating conversation. Although a member of an orthodox congregational church, he was decidedly independent and out-spoken in his opinions, on both political and religious subjects.

14. **Matthew**, b. May 14, 1702; d. June 18, 1788; m. Rachel Foote of Watertown.
15. **Anna**, b. May 31, 1764; d. Feb. 6, 1770, in infancy.
16. **Keziah**, b. Mar. 27, 1768; d. Nov. 20, 1773, in infancy.
17. **Roys** (Rice), b. April 24, 1770; d. Oct. 17, 1773.
18. **Anna**, b. Sept. 13, 1775; d. Sept. 15, 1847; m. Jan. 15, 1801 to Allyn Wells, of Plymouth, Ct.
19. **Aaron**, b. May 24, 1780; d. June 12, 1849; m. April 20, 1806 to Dorcas Southmayd of Watertown. He graduated at Yale College, Sept. 1803, and settled as pastor of the 1st Congregational Church in Guilford, Ct., 1806; where he remained 30 years, and for 24 years was a member of the Corporation of Yale College. The Rev. Dr. Leonard Bacon of New Haven, said of him—that during the whole period of his pastoral service the youth of Guilford were more indebted to him for the means of intellectual improvement than to any other person.

FOURTH GENERATION.

Children of Thomas (No. 13,) and Thankful Punderson Dutton.

20. **Matthew Roys**, (Rice), b. June 30, 1788; d. July 17, 1825; m. May 20, 1819 to Maria Hopkins. He graduated at Yale College in 1808, and was tutor in the same from 1810 to 1814, when he settled as pastor of the 1st Congregational Church in Stratford, Ct.: in 1821 was elected Professor of Mathematics and Natural Philosophy, and Astronomy in Yale College.
21. **Chester**, b. July 3, 1785; d. Dec. 24, 1797 in infancy.
22. **Anna**, b. Jan 2, 1788; m. April 24, 1810 to Benjamin Noble.
23. **Betsey**, b. Aug. 31, 1790; d. Jan. 6, 1862; m. Dec. 15, 1814 to Alpha Hart of Goshen, Ct.
24. **Daniel Punderson**, b. Jan. 30, 1793; d. July 31, 1801; m. Oct 10, 1812 to Nancy Matthews, of Watertown. He lived his entire life, with the exception of about three years, on the old homestead at Watertown. The old house in which six generations of the family have lived, and which all the descendants of Deacon Thomas Dutton have always regarded as *home*, is yet standing—the property of Mrs. Anna Dutton Noble.
25. **Henry**, b. Feb. 12, 1796; d. April 26, 1869; m. Sept. 8, 1823 to Eliza Elliott Joy of Fairfield Ct. He graduated at Yale College 1818;—tutor in same from 1821 to 1823;—attorney and counselor at law in Newtown, Bridgeport and New Haven;—author of Dutton's Conn. Digest;—commissioner for the revision of the State Statutes, and of Swift's Digest;—Prof. of Law in Yale College;—Member, Clerk and Speaker of Conn. House of Representatives;—State Senator and Governor of Conn., and Judge of the Supreme Court of Errors.
26. **Sally**, b. May 4, 1798; m. Sept. 4, 1822 to Jireh Platt of Plymouth, Ct. About the year 1834 or '5 they removed to Mendon, Adams Co. Illinois.
27. **Lucy**, b. Feb. 17, 1801: d. Sept. 27, 1839, at Auburn, N. Y.; m. June 1, 1820 to Horace Hotchkiss of Waterbury, Ct.
28. **Laura**, b. Mar. 18, 1803; d. May 8, 1829; m. Oct. 6, 1824 to Timothy Clark of Watertown.
29. **Alma**, b. Dec. 20, 1806; d. Sep. 24, 1850; m. Dec. 25, 1826 to Julius P. Baldwin of Watertown.

Child of Matthew (No. 14,) and Rachel Foote Dutton.

30. **Keziah**, b. 1783; d. July 28, 1865: m. June 1, 1800 to Allyn Merriam of Watertown, Ct. Second marriage May 8, 1814 to Daniel Hickox of Watertown. 3d husband Elam Beardslee of Watertown.

Children of Anna Dutton (No. 18,) and Allyn Wells.

31. **Joseph Allyn**, b. Nov. 16, 1805. 32. **Aaron Dutton**, b. June 14, 1808. 33. **James**, b. Oct. 8, 1811. 34. **Thomas Wright**, b. Aug. 9, 1815. All now living and have families,—Joseph in Waterbury, Ct., Aaron and James in Plymouth, Ct., and Thomas in Jefferson Co. N. Y.

Children of Aaron (No. 19,) and Dorcas Southmayd Dutton.

35. **Mary**, b. 1807; removed to Cincinnati about the year 1832 with the family of the Rev. Lyman Beecher, and in company with Catharine and Harriet Beecher, opened a young ladies' seminary in that city, which they conducted until the marriage of Harriet Beecher to Prof. Stowe. She then returned to Conn. and purchased the Grove Hall Female Seminary in New Haven; which institution she carried on with distinguished success for about 30 years. After the death of her sister Mrs. Gilbert and brother S. W. S. Dutton, she again went west.

36. **Dorcas Southmayd**, b. 1809; m. Rev. Mr. Gilbert, pastor of congregational church in Wallingford, and left two sons.

37. **Thomas**, b. 1811; graduated at Williams College, and now a congregational minister at Durant, Iowa: m. Maria Whiting of Reading, Ct., and has children.

38. **Samuel Wm. Southmayd**, b. Mar. 1814; graduated at Yale College with high honors in 1833 : was tutor from 1835 to 1838, when he accepted a call from the Old North Church of New Haven, of which he remained pastor until his death, or more than 30 years :— was married but left no children.

39. **Aaron Rice**, b. 1816; graduated at Yale in 1837; Attorney and Counselor at Law in Cincinnati, O.

40. **John Southmayd**, b. 1818 ; d. April 1834.

41. **Anna**, b. 1820; d. Nov. 1831.

42. **Matthew Henry**, b. 1823; d. Mar. 1841; member of the Junior Class at Yale College.

FIFTH GENERATION.

Children of Matthew Rice (No. 20,) and Maria Hopkins Dutton.

43. **Thomas**, b. May 4, 1817; d. July 15, 1866; graduated at Yale in 1837; circumnavigated the globe about the year 1840, and after his return explored the north shores of Lake Superior in the service of an English mining company. For many years before his death he was secretary and actuary of the Hartford Gas Co. In 1865 he married Miss Goodrich of Hartford, but left no children.

44. **Henry**, b. Mar. 20, 1819; d. Sep. 27, 1857, in Philadelphia, unm.

Children of Anna Dutton (No. 22,) and Benjamin Noble.

45. **Mary Ann**, b. Mar. 8, 1812; d. Feb. 25, 1838.

46. **Benjamin Rice**, b. June 23, 1814; d. Aug. 17, 1857, leaving two daughters, at Cuyahoga Falls, Ohio.

47. **Henry Dutton**, b. Feb. 8, 1818; d. 1860, leaving 5 children, at Brookfield, Ct. Rector of Episcopal Church.

48. **Charles Merriam**, b. June 4, 1823 ; lives on the old Dutton homestead at Watertown ; has children.

Children of Betsey Dutton (No. 23,) and Alpha Hart.

49. **Abraham P.**, b. April 23, 1816; m. Sept. 5, 1838 to Angeline Badger of Elmira, N. Y., where he is an artist.

50. **Harriet Newell**, b. Dec 14, 1818; d. Nov. 1838.

51. **Jane,** b. Oct. 11, 1821; m. to William Martin.
52. **Matthew Rice,** b. June 20, 1824; d. Feb. 26, 1855, at Goshen, Ct., leaving two children.

Children of Daniel Punderson (No. 24,) and Nancy Matthews Dutton.

53. **Chester,** b. Mar. 24, 1814; graduated at Yale College in 1838, and in 1842 settled on a farm at Wolcott, Wayne Co. N. Y., and married Mary Ann Mellen by whom he has had 9 children, —all born at Wolcott. He has furnished the information here given of the Duttons of Conn. In 1868 the family removed to Lake Sibley, Cloud Co. Kansas, then on the very frontier of the State.
54. **Julia Anna,** b. Mar. 11, 1816; m. Sept. 1, 1840 to David Kellogg Merriam, by whom she has had eight children.
55. **Maria,** b. July 29, 1818; living in Wolcott N. Y.
56. **Thomas,** b. Oct. 29, 1820; m. Dec. 1840 to Martha Ann Elizabeth Hatcher of Alabama, who died Nov. 1843, leaving one son. He married again Dec. 1845 to Adaline Elizabeth Brooks of Washington, D. C., by whom he has had eleven children.
57. **William,** b. Jan. 14, 1823; d. July 4, 1862; m. 1846 to Lucy Jane Matthews by whom he had four children. He was a member of N. Y. House of Representatives;—Col. 98th N. Y. S. V.;—graduated at West Point in 1846 and settled on a farm at Wolcott in 1848. He had charge of a brigade of N. Y. troops in the Peninsular campaign and was worn out with his arduous duties. The officers and men of his regiment erected a monument to his memory in the Wolcott cemetery.
58. **Mary,** b. Feb. 23, 1825; d. Oct. 10, 1860; m. George E. Chipman of Waterbury, Ct., and removed with him to Wolcott, N. Y.; had four children.
59. **John,** b. July 29, 1827; d. Nov. 21, 1830.
60. **Matthew Rice,** b. May 17, 1829; removed to Wolcott, N. Y., and married Maria Mellen, and in 1857 again removed to Oskaloosa, Kansas, where he has held the offices of County Clerk, Clerk of the District Court, and Probate Judge. In 1864 he was adjutant in a mounted regiment operating against Price in Missouri, and the same autumn was elected to the Kansas House of Reps., and removed to Grantville, near Topeka, where he now resides: has three children.
61. **Laura Jane,** b. July 3, 1831; d. Dec. 24, 1855; m. Oct. 23, 1851 to Elmer Hawley Northrop of Brookfield, Ct., by whom she had two children.
62. **John,** b. April 10, 1833; m. Henrietta M. Tuthill of Utica, N. Y., and lives at Waterbury, Ct., where he carries on upon a larger scale the ancestral trade of a builder.
63. **Henry Bryan,** b. Jan. 8, 1835, at Goshen, Ct.; removed from Watertown in 1855 to Germantown, Philadelphia, Penn., where he married Mary Isadore Rex and has children.

Children of Henry (No 25,) and Eliza E. Joy Dutton.

64. **Ann Eliza,** b. Oct. 15, 1824; m. 1845 to William Keeler of Bridgeport, Ct., and has three children. During the war he was paymaster in the Navy, and was on the Monitor at the time of her action in Hampton Roads, and also when she afterwards sunk off Cape Hatteras; on which latter occasion he was accompanied by his eldest son Henry Dutton. Both were saved.
65. **Mary Elliott,** b. Oct. 9, 1826; d. Feb. 5, 1865; m. H. B. Graves of Litchfield, Ct., and left two daughters.
66. **Harriet Joy,** b. Oct. 12, 1834; m. George H. Watrous, (her father's Law partner in New Haven,) and has several children.
67. **Henry Melzar,** b. Sept. 1838; killed Aug. 9, 1862 at the bat-

tle of Cedar Mountain, while charging a rebel battery. A colonel's commission was at the time of his death waiting for him in a newly raised Litchfield Co. regiment, which was afterwards called the Dutton Guards.

Children of Sally Dutton (No. 26,) and Jireh Platt.

68. **Henry Dutton**, b. July 13, 1823; congregational minister near Alton, Ill.; has a family.
69. **Enoch**, b. Feb. 9, 1825; is married and living at Wabaunsee, Kansas; has one daughter.
70. **Sarah Julia**, b. Dec. 4, 1826; d. Oct. 20, 1857.
71. **Mary**, b. Jan. 23, 1830; d. Dec. 11, 1850.
72. **Jeremiah Evarts**, b. May 28, 1833; is married and has four sons;—Prof. of Mathematics at Agricultural College, Manhattan, Kansas.
73. **Luther Hart**, b. Dec 10, 1836; minister in service of congregational Home Missionary Society;—now at Wichita, Kansas. He has a wife and two children.
74. **Martha**, b. May 7, 1839; m. A. A. Cottrell of Mendon, Ill:—has four children.

Children of Lucy Dutton (No. 27,) and Horace Hotchkiss.

75. **Mary Lucinda**, b. Feb. 24, 1833.
76. **Sarah Lucy**, b. July 15, 1835.

Children of Laura Dutton (No. 28,) and Timothy Clark.

77. **Eliza**, b. July 14, 1825; d. July, 1841.
78. **Henry Dutton**, b. May 8, 1829; living at Delphos, Ohio, with a wife and several children.

Children of Alma Dutton (No. 29,) and Julius P. Baldwin.

79. **George Dutton**, b. Feb. 24, 1828.   80. **Benjamin Joseph**, b. Aug. 13, 1830.   81. **Lucy Ann**, b. Aug. 1834. About the year 1840 the family removed to Mendon, Illinois.

Children of Keziah Dutton (No. 30,) and Allyn Merriam.

82. **Matthew Dutton**, b. Aug. 26, 1801; lives near Burton, O.
83. **George Allyn**, b. July 24, 1804; d. Feb. 15, 1831.
84. **Anna Kezia**, b. June 27, 1806; m. July 4, 1844 to Joseph Allyn Wells, of Waterbury, Ct.

By second husband, Daniel Hickox.

85. **Caleb Thompson**, b. Feb. 5, 1817.